THE WALTER SYNDROME

THE
WALTER
SYNDROME

Richard Neely

The McCall Publishing Company

NEW YORK

Published simultaneously in Canada
by Doubleday Canada Ltd., Toronto.

The McCall Publishing Company
230 Park Avenue
New York, New York 10017

PRINTED IN THE UNITED STATES OF AMERICA

To my wife

LAMBERT POST

I

I BEGAN TO THINK Charles Walter was a special breed of cat from the moment I heard his name in the summer of 1938. The name had a regal ring to it. Charles, Duke of Walter. Or Sir Charles Walter, Lord of the Manor. Or—maybe even better in that crazy era in New York—Charles Walter, Prince of Playboys. The name connoted not only authority but also urbanity, sophistication, and perhaps a touch of refined menace.

What a far cry it was from my own miserable name. Lambert Post. Jesus, the trouble I'd had with that one! Lam Post, the kids had called me. "Say, Lampost, what's this I hear about you supporting a bunch of drunks?" "Hi, Lampost, any dogs been pissin' on you lately?" Hilarious.

Charles Walter did a lot to change all that. He made me feel things I'd never felt in my whole life. Self-respect. Manliness. Confidence. Joy. He also made me feel anxiety and terror—but that came later.

I remember the first day he started on the job. Mouth curved into a mocking smile, deepset eyes twinkling with jesting pride as he announced to those around him, "I'm Charles Walter. Furnished Rooms." Then he sat down tall and straight, like an enthroned king, on the flat cushion of the funny little curve-backed chair that rolled on casters into the slot of the desk. Actually, it was a single long desk divided up by wood-framed glass partitions, to seat three people. There were ten rows of these desks on each side of the room. That meant sixty classified ad solicitors. Sometimes all of them were yammering into their phones at once, especially when the supervisor, Jean Hooper, was at her desk—perched on a raised platform in front of the room—and plugged into her switchboard. She could listen in to anyone without him or her knowing it, so the solicitors generally held on to a few of their best leads until Jean Hooper was seen monitoring the calls. Then they'd give it all they had, trying to look good just in case she was on the wire. The sound of their voices damned near drowned out the rumble of the presses below.

Charles Walter was in the last row, smack up against the flaking brown radiator pipes and next to one of the huge windows that you pulled slantingly open and secured with what looked like an old-fashioned toilet chain. Next to him, in the middle, sat Henrietta Boardman, who solicited Help Wanted ads. Henrietta was small, with black hair and glasses as thick as Coke bottles. You forgot about the glasses when you glanced at her full red mouth that looked like it could be lots of fun in all sorts of ways, and at her breasts stretching the pink sweater, and (when she pranced up the aisle to turn in ad copy) at the wiggle of her round, compact ass. Dottie Friedlander—she peddled Real Estate ads—had the aisle seat. She was a block of a girl, built like an icebox, with frizzy cinnamon hair, squinty eyes, and a lightly bearded face, bleached, that she plucked at constantly with tweezers while staring into a magnifying mirror.

It was shortly before nine on a warm Monday morning. Henrietta and Dottie and Charles Walter, like most of the others in that big oblong room, began checking their leads—want ads that had appeared in competing newspapers. These had been clipped early that morning by a crew of girls and were pasted on sheets of yellow paper, with phone numbers written beside them where necessary. Charles Walter knew the procedure even though it was his first day as a telephone solicitor. Before that, he had been an outside man, assigned to call personally on those furnished rooming houses that couldn't be reached by phone and were located between Fourteenth Street and Thirty-fourth Street on New York's West Side. It was a tough, brownstone section where most of the landladies would as soon sock a salesman with a wet mop as look at him, and Charles Walter had been spectacularly unsuccessful. Not because he couldn't sell, but because after a few tangles with those crones he refused to set foot in the territory. At ten dollars a week and five dollars drawing account (which he never exceeded) why the hell should he? Better to just take the dough as long as it lasted and meanwhile spend his days at the 11 A.M. salesmen's matinee at the Paramount or the Capitol when, for a quarter, he could catch Frank Sinatra or Tommy Dorsey in person along with a first-run movie; or at Minsky's, where he could enjoy the bumps and grinds of Ann Corio. He'd done that for two months, knowing he'd be carried for three before getting the pink dismissal slip. His only business gestures had consisted of early morning and late afternoon appearances in the office and the required report by telephone to a supervisor sometime during the day.

It was the daily telephone call that had got him the job inside. His voice, the supervisor kept telling him, was low and intimate —"real sexy, like Ronald Colman's without the accent"—perfect for phone solicitation. He had resisted the offer, unwilling to pen himself up in an oppressive cubicle under the watchful eyes of Jean Hooper, who everyone said was a genuine wall-to-wall bitch. Then he was told that the job paid twenty-two dollars a week. Twenty-two dollars! My God! He couldn't wait to clamp the headset on and strap the black mouthpiece to his chest.

Charles Walter recalled later how he felt on that Monday morning just before making his first phone call. He knew that Dottie Friedlander and Henrietta Boardman were watching him from the corners of their eyes. Glancing up to the front of the room, he saw Jean Hooper pulling a big comb through her fluffy, gray-flecked hair and had the impression she was looking straight at him. "I felt like I was naked in front of three women," he said, laughing in his outgoing, infectious way, "and they were betting I couldn't get it up." But when he put on his headset and looked down at the mouthpiece that curved up to his lips, he realized how protected he was. He, Charles Walter, was a disembodied voice, a voice that could be soft, persuasive, deeply personal, projecting an image of a handsome, masterful male. Nevertheless, as he tapped a pencil down the strip of pasted-down ads, he sought the additional security of an address that was at least vaguely familiar.

He decided on a rooming house on Twenty-third Street. He didn't know the house, but the address told him that it was west of the Chelsea Hotel. A poor neighborhood; maybe the landlady was more desperate than most.

He fumbled for a moment with the buttons set into the edge of the desk, then pushed the one for outgoing calls. Next to it was a small black lever, which he switched to the right. An outside operator came on and he gave her the number. He doodled on a lined pad while the phone rang and rang. He was about to give it up as a DA—Don't Answer—when:

"Hello!"

The shrill voice spat out the word like a curse.

"How do you do. This is Mr. Walter calling. Charles Walter." He let the grandness of it sink in. "I understand you have a room for rent."

The woman's voice immediately began to purr with avarice. "Why, yes-s-s, Mr.—"

"Walter. Charles Walter. Are you the manager?" Manager sounded much better than landlady.

"Yes, I *am-m-m.* I'm also the owner. Mrs. Sloat's the name. And it's really a *lovely* room. First floor on the front. It's—"

"Just a minute, Mrs. Sloat. Perhaps I owe you an apology."

"Apology?"

"Yes. It just occurs to me—the phone rang so long—maybe I caught you at an inconvenient time. I could call back."

"Oh, *no,* Mr. Walter. Well, I *was* upstairs on the third floor, just tidying up. The phone's here on the first floor. . . ."

"You're a very gracious woman, Mrs. Sloat." Charles Walter said it with deep sincerity.

"Thank you, Mr. Walter." Mrs. Sloat's voice melted almost into girlishness. "You sound like just the kind of gentleman I'd like for a tenant."

There was no question about it—Charles Walter's thrilling voice had traveled beyond Mrs. Sloat's ear right down to her groin.

"I saw your ad in this morning's *Times,* Mrs. Sloat. Talking to you now, I'd guess you're a lady of unusual taste."

Modestly: "Well, I like to think so."

"Then I'd say the room you're offering probably reflects that good taste. But your ad doesn't tell me so. It just says it's a large, airy front room, kitchen privileges, close to transportation, and the price is reasonable. Tell me, isn't there something particularly nice about the *furnishings?*"

"Well, yes, I'd say so. I made the drapes and slipcovers myself. Just put them in yesterday. And the mattress is brand new. And the carpet looks good, not a sign of wear." She spoke proudly, but a touch of wariness had begun to taint her voice.

Charles Walter became mildly remonstrative. "There you are, Mrs. Sloat. Just by adding one phrase you'd get a much better response from the ad. Here, I'm writing that phrase down: 'Newly furnished and decorated.' Now, don't you agree that has a lot of appeal, Mrs. Sloat?"

"Yes, I guess it does." Suspicion now dominated her tone. "Mr. Walter, are you interested in renting this room?"

It was the crucial moment. Charles Walter spoke with brisk authority. "That's *exactly* what I'm interested in. I'm a newspaperman, Mrs. Sloat. With the New York *Journal,* New York's largest evening newspaper. I specialize in renting rooms and—"

"Oh!" Her gasp implied disillusionment more than rejection. "Tell me, Mrs. Sloat, does your husband read the *Journal?*"

"I'm a widow." Then, stiffly: "And very busy, Mr. Walter."

"Now, that's odd."

"Odd? What's so odd about being busy?"

"No, about being a widow." His voice lowered. "I know something about that situation. You see, I lost my wife some time ago."

A whoop exploded from the front of the room. Raising his eyes from his doodling, Charles Walter could see Jean Hooper at her big raised desk laughing hilariously. Apparently she was plugged into his call. To be expected, considering he was a rookie. There was silence on the other end of the wire. Finally Mrs. Sloat said gently, "I'm very sorry, Mr. Walter." The pitch of her voice seemed to place her age in the mid-thirties. Charles Walter was twenty-two.

His voice became philosophical. "These things pass." He brightened. "Tell me, Mrs. Sloat, do you play any musical instruments?"

Again the whoop from the front of the room.

"What?"

"You know—piano, violin, harp, calliope?"

"Well, I used to play the piano a little."

"Great! I'm a clarinet man myself. The poor man's Woody Herman. We'll have to get together sometime for a jam session."

"Oh, Mr. Walter, aren't you the one!" He could almost see her pleased grin.

"But let's get that room rented first. I'll just rewrite this ad and we'll start it in tomorrow's paper. That'll put it in the hands of more than six hundred thousand people. Shall I schedule it T.F.?"

"T.F.?"

"Oh, excuse me. That's trade parlance, Mrs. Sloat. It means Till Forbid. In other words, we just let it run until you rent the room. Then you call in and cancel and we bill you only for the days it ran. Shouldn't take but a few days, really."

"Well, I don't know . . ."

"I'll be calling back to see how you're making out."

"Oh. Well . . ."

"Now, I'll need your first name. I have to write it on the order." He chuckled suggestively. "Of course, I'd like to know it anyway."

There was only a moment's hesitation before she said, "It's Eunice."

"Thank you. Now you just leave everything to me." His tone implied that he was willing and able to shoulder all of her burdens.

As he rang off and rewrote the ad on the insertion order form, he could feel Henrietta Boardman and Dottie Friedlander regarding him with smiling admiration. With a deft motion he tore off the ad copy, keeping the carbon, pulled the phone plug, pushed the headset back so that it circled his neck, and stood up, tall and commanding. He was coatless, and he unknotted the multicolored tie that splashed across his white shirt. He smiled down at Henrietta, who had licked her ripe lips to make them glisten.

"Is that the way it's done?" he said.

She laughed. "I'm glad it wasn't my mother. She'd be running out to buy black underwear."

Peering into her magnifying mirror, tweezers at the ready, Dottie Friedlander said, *"Chutzpah.* Mr. Walter, you got it." She yanked a black hair from beneath her chin and inspected it with a look of satisfaction.

Charles Walter strode up the aisle and dropped the ad copy into a wooden box set on a table near Jean Hooper's desk. It was the department's first ad of the day.

"Mr. *Walter*," Jean Hooper said from behind him.

He turned, dark eyebrows arched in surprise, as if he had been unaware of her presence. Jean Hooper was grinning, showing very white bucked teeth. There was a rumor that those teeth had been in certain male places that her husband, an insurance executive, would not have appreciated. Jean Hooper used her maiden name, a clue perhaps that she was not immune to extramarital diversion.

"Damned good," she said in her brisk voice. "You stopped just in time. A little longer and you'd have laid her on the phone and forgotten to get the ad."

Perhaps because she'd called him Mr. Walter, he felt a sense of power. Or maybe it was because she'd used the word "laid" and that made it sort of man-to-man. Anyway, he topped her with, "I'd never have settled for a one-time insertion."

Jean Hooper's grin widened. "I know. A T.F. I heard it all. It looks like you're a phone man, honey. The outside was never for you."

Reflecting on it later, Charles Walter recalled wanting to knock those white teeth down her crepey throat. But he managed a lop-sided smile.

"Miss Hooper—"

"Jean."

"Jean, anytime you're hard up for kicks, just tune in Charles Walter."

She frowned slightly. "What have *you* been smoking? That's only one call. And she was a pushover."

"I *made* her a pushover."

Jean Hooper's pink, sagging cheeks pouched as she set her small jaw. "Just don't get any ideas about personal follow-ups."

"Jean, you shock me."

Smiling, he turned away, twirling the corded phone plug, and sauntered back to his seat.

Now maybe you think Charles Walter hadn't done anything so great, sweet-talking a poor landlady into an ad and then patronizing his boss. But if you'd been me, Lambert Post, you'd have figured him for some sort of superman. God knows, I could never have acted that way. Just thinking about it made my stomach quake and my throat dry up as if I'd swallowed a sock. I was the plodding, introspective type—intellectual, some people said—and women scared the hell out of me. I'd have bet that the only way to sell ads was to make a zillion calls, give the canned sales talk, and rely on the law of averages. None of that for Charles Walter—he threw the book away. By ten o'clock that first morning he'd sold five ads, every one by sheer force of personality. He did it in only eight calls, and then quit. The rules said that every solicitor had to make between eighty and a hundred calls a day. You entered them on a long sheet of lined paper, which you turned in every night. The phone company also kept a record and submitted it to the newspaper with each monthly bill. Charles Walter covered himself on that. As soon as Jean Hooper was off the switchboard, he simply called one number over and over again—MEridian 7-1212, which was a recording of the correct time—and listed a fake number for each call. He'd learned right away that the actual phone numbers were never verified, only the total amount of calls. Now do you see why I began to admire him so much? A real slick character.

I learned more about Charles Walter at lunch. After chuckling over that first phone call to Eunice Sloat, he put me on to something I'd never thought of before. The way he saw it, life was just a big game of Bullshit. He said, "Take you, Lambert Post, for example. Where'd you go to school?" "East Orange High in New Jersey," I said. "I never got to college." "That starts you out as a nothing," he said. "But suppose you told people you graduated from Harvard. Presto. Right away you're a big man. You could back it up because you talk like you read Proust instead of comic books. Who'd call you a liar?" "People in East Orange, New Jersey," I said. "Sure," he said, "but nobody *here*. That's the trick. You tell people here you're a Harvard man. In East Orange, New Jersey, you tell the people you're an *editor* on the New York *Journal*. Both ways you're a hero. That's how you win at Bullshit."

Well, I couldn't play Bullshit, but Charles Walter sure could. He proved it right after lunch by going to a pawnbroker on the Bowery near Chinatown and paying six bucks for a watch chain and a Phi Beta Kappa key. When he got back to the office he put on his vest, leaving it unbuttoned, and let the chain and key dangle carelessly across it. Neither Henrietta nor Dottie seemed to notice it, but Jean Hooper did when he was turning in another ad.

"Don't tell me that's a Phi Beta key," she said as he turned toward her desk.

He smiled wryly, as if he'd had to put up with that observation a million times. "All right, I won't tell you," he said, but he moved closer.

She was too impressed to take offense. "Christ, that's what it *is*. Where'd you get it—from a Cracker Jack box?"

"They don't eat Cracker Jacks at Harvard."

"Harvard, he says." Her feather-duster hair danced as she shook her head in disbelief. "What's a brain like you doing soliciting want ads?"

"There's a Depression, remember? Recession I guess they're calling it this year. Stockbrokers are peddling magazines. Bankers are selling Fuller brushes. I'm selling want ads. And very successfully, too." He glanced at the box on the table. "That's my seventh ad today."

"I've been listening to you," she said. Then, sarcastically: "You might remember to mention the name of the paper at least once."

"What paper?" he said innocently and grinned his way back down the aisle.

That night after work Charles Walter was with me as I stood in a crowd of people outside the huge gray-stone building waiting for the rickety newspaper bus that ran continuously back and forth to Park Row, behind City Hall. I gazed across South Street—broad and cobbled and dirty—and beyond the East River piers, up to the dark girders of Brooklyn Bridge, now orange and purple in the evening sun. For the first time in my life I felt a sense of freedom, of hope, a belief that destiny could be managed, if not entirely mastered. Romantic, I guess, but at the same time cold and hard. I recognized it as a vicarious notion, inspired by the presence of Charles Walter. But it belonged to me nonetheless. Suddenly I wanted to be away from the crowd and alone with Charles Walter.

We didn't wait for the bus; instead walked up to Chatham Square and caught the Second Avenue El to Eighth Street. We strolled across on Eighth to Greenwich Village and stopped to enjoy silently a couple of drinks at the Jumble Shop bar. Then, feeling like splurging, I put out a dollar for a bottle of gin, and we went home to my basement apartment on West Twelfth Street. In the kitchenette off the single square room, I made drinks of gin and water and lemon peel, bringing them to the rust-colored studio couch where together we leaned back against the wall and stared at the fading light filtering through the barred, crescent-shaped window that opened on the sidewalk above.

I was gripped by a strange excitement. It took four drinks and an hour of conversation with Charles Walter before I understood the reason for it. For the first time in memory I was not lonely.

I didn't want Charles Walter ever to leave.

II

CHARLES WALTER FOUND IN ME the most fascinated and sympathetic audience anyone could have. So he stayed, and it was like suddenly being gifted with a brother. A much older brother (though actually we were the same age) who was big and strong and protective, yet who talked to me as an equal, exciting me with tales of exploits that no Lambert Post would ever have dared. Every evening I would lie on the studio couch, sipping gin, reliving with him the events of the day, relishing mental images of his past. And slowly I pieced together the whole man.

Charles was an only child, as I was. But beyond that his life had been all that mine had not. For one thing, his mother and father adored him. They lived in a big sprawling house in Maine, and Charles had been brought up surrounded by dogs and cats and horses, and he'd owned a boat, which he'd sailed along the rugged New England coast. His father was immensely rich and Charles didn't really have to work at all. But he was determined to make it on his own. (I often thought how proud his family must be.) It delighted me to learn that he actually *had* gone to Harvard, that he *was* a Phi Beta, so the pawnshop gag was nothing to be ashamed of. There had been a lot of girls in Charles's life, wealthy girls who had attended schools like Vassar and Wellesley and Smith. He'd slept with a number of them, but had never been seriously involved. He took women on his own terms, not theirs—theirs consisting of snaring a rich husband they could boss around and acquiring fat, pink babies they could publicly show off and privately ignore. Charles was sensitive and, when you got to know him as I did, kind, but he belonged to no one but himself. It's un-

derstandable that some people—those who were selfish or cruel
—thought him remote and arrogant.

Now maybe you think that Charles was simply conning me with
his game of Bullshit. Well, I know better. For one thing I'd seen
his strikingly handsome picture in the high-school yearbook and
under it the college he was going to, Harvard. Sure, I know that
plenty of kids had listed fancy colleges under their names, and
then, when their fathers went broke in the Depression, were lucky
if they could graduate from high school to grease monkey. But
you could tell that was not true with Charles. The authors he'd
read—Plato, Nietzsche, Schopenhauer, Racine, Dostoevski, Shaw
—demonstrated he'd had a higher education. And he spoke in the
cultured tones of a gentleman, pronouncing each word precisely
and with quiet authority. But the most convincing evidence of his
honesty was the way he took me into his confidence, telling me his
intimate thoughts and feelings: like the resentment he felt when he
had a wet dream, or his suppressed rage when in the company of
overbearing women, or the pledge to himself that he would never
be pushed around by anyone, especially a female. If you still don't
believe he was leveling, ask yourself why a man like Charles Walter would bother to pretend for anyone as unimportant as Lambert
Post.

Charles changed my way of living immediately and dramatically. The food became infinitely better. Where once there were
beans and spaghetti and the cheapest hamburger, there now were
fried chicken and lamb roasts and sirloin steaks. (If that seems un-
believable on a small salary, remember that sirloin steak was then
only twenty-nine cents a pound, on sale.) The apartment, rented
for thirty dollars a month, was transformed into a handsome room.
No more clothes strewn about the floor, no more dirty dishes left
in the sink. I turned the Axminster rug completely around, hiding
the threadbare section under the studio couch. I painted the walls
a deep green and hung them with van Gogh prints bought on
Fourth Avenue. I installed yellow draw drapes on the street-level
window (blocking out the legs of passersby). I bought soft-glowing
copper lamps at a rummage sale. The place became the kind that
anyone—even Charles Walter, with all his affluent upbringing—
could enter without feeling ashamed. I even changed the way I

dressed. Taking money from my small savings, I went to Browning King and splurged on two suits—English drape models with padded shoulders and pleated, peg-top trousers—and bought a pair of spade-toed cordovan shoes at Regal's. When I got all dressed up and sat, drink in hand, in that immaculate, tastefully decorated room, I felt like I belonged in Charles Walter's well-bred world.

Charles also changed my inner life, mostly by giving me a sense of security. It may sound strange, but as far back as I can remember—back to when I was a very small boy—I had lived with a feeling of dread, as though at any moment I would be crushed by some unknown disaster. And there *had* been disasters, enormous ones to a kid's mind. Once—it's all pretty vague—I broke my arm just by falling out of bed. Another time I was sleepwalking and plunged down the cellar stairs, suffering so many bruises and lacerations I had to be hospitalized. Then—it couldn't have been much later—I was boosting myself up on the stove reaching for something and I got this awful scalding from a pot of boiling water. God, it hurts just thinking about it. So I guess it's no wonder that I was always in fear of being struck by some physical misfortune, even though, after I grew up a bit, I never so much as turned an ankle.

But it was more than fear of broken bones and torn flesh that made me insecure. I was also emotionally apprehensive, afraid that someone or something would so depress me that I would be unable to function as a man. The problem must have started with my father and mother. Doesn't it always? I'm not trying to be a psychiatrist, but the fact is I always felt terribly lonely and unwanted. You see, this wasn't my real father (my real father was killed in a machine-shop accident when I was two) so you couldn't expect him to have any great love for me. And he sure didn't. He treated me like I was vermin. Jealous, I guess because I was a constant reminder of the man my mother used to sleep with. Sure as hell my mother gave him no reason to be jealous. Every time he picked on me—and he was *always* picking on me—my mother was on his side, shouting away right with him. I remember one time when mother and I were playing pool on the small, second-hand table my stepfather had bought for Christmas. A number of times when it was my mother's turn, I'd lean over behind her and pretend to show her how to hold the cue and line up the shot. Actually, after the first time, I was just doing it as an excuse to peek down the V of her dress and look at her white breasts. Well, without either of us hearing, my father had come into the house and had been standing in the doorway watching. I could feel the blood empty out of my face when I turned around and saw the rage in his eyes. He raised his big fist like a bludgeon and started for me. I was sure he was going to kill me, or at least somehow cripple me. But then my mother shouted, "The police! The police! Don't hit him!" His arm quivered down to his side and for a minute I was grateful to my mother, loving her. But after he told her what I'd been doing, she joined him in yelling at me, and they kept me locked up in my room for a week.

Then there was that time when she and I were alone in the house one day after school. I'd had a bad time on the way home, a bunch of kids taunting me, and I guess I wasn't ready for it when my mother bawled me out about leaving clothes on the floor. You'd think I'd crapped on the rug or something. Anyway, I broke down, crying and sobbing like I'd never stop. It was the first time that had ever happened over something so unimportant. I closed myself in my room and pushed my face in the pillow, trying to smother the tears. But they kept coming. After a while I got up and started for the hall bathroom, thinking that maybe it would help if I washed my face in cold water. My mother was just coming out of the bathroom as I got there. She was getting ready to go somewhere and all she had on was her underwear. A chemise, I think you called it. Purple. Well, just looking at her made me feel weak and helpless, and I ran to her and threw my arms around her, still sobbing. She went stiff as a door for a couple of seconds, then I heard her breath come out and felt her body soften, and she hugged me close to her. I pressed right into her, like I wanted to crawl inside, and I had the feeling she was pressing back. A strap of her chemise fell off her shoulder and part of one breast swelled out over the purple lace. I pushed my face against it, smelling the perfume, and my mouth opened and—well, suddenly she wrenched away as though I'd stuck a knife into her and she shrieked, "That ugly, filthy mouth, don't you dare touch me with it! You're a nasty, nasty boy!" I jumped back and stared at her, scared to death. She had her fingers clamped over her lips and her face was angry-red, but shocked too at what she'd said. I ran to my room and slammed the door, madder than I'd ever been in my life. But the crying stopped and I never cried again.

Those things stand out in my mind, but something like them seemed to be happening all the time. I never could make a connection with anybody. I was lousy at sports, but I went out for them anyway, and all I got was another name—Tanglefoot. When there was a game of stickball or ring-a-levio, I was always the last guy picked, that is if they *had* to have someone. Kids used to shove me around on the way home from school; it was kind of a tough neighborhood. I tried to stop that by buying a cheap peaked cap (I'd been saving money from deposit bottles) and I broke the cardboard-lined visor and purposely spilled ink on it and pulled it down on my forehead, making me look real tough. But that didn't work. A few days later a big tomboy girl—a *girl!*—yanked the cap off my head and flung it down a sewer. Oh, that bitch! I still shake inside when I think about it.

So what did I do? I did what a lot of left-outs do, I guess. I spent almost every dime I could get my hands on at the movies and for movie magazines. I was Douglas Fairbanks as The Black Pirate and Lupe Velez was my exotic slave girl. I was William Haines wisecracking my way into women's hearts. I was Ramon Novarro and Buddy Rogers and Rod La Rocque and Rudolph Valentino, and I made love to gorgeous creatures like Billie Dove and Mary Brian and Anita Page and Vilma Banky. And when I'd get home, I'd sneak back to my room and gaze longingly at the sepia portraits of the stars in *Photoplay, Modern Screen, Film Fun.*

Later, I became absorbed in books. I figured if I couldn't beat the bastards any other way, I'd do it by becoming a brain. After a while, I didn't care so much about becoming a brain, because the pleasure I got out of books seemed reward enough. God, I read everything, from *The Swiss Family Robinson* to *Das Kapital.* Of course, that just made my relations with the other kids worse, because now I was a greasy grind. Even the teachers seemed to resent it—imagine that!—although they had to give me straight A's.

All through high school I was a loner. I remember sitting by myself on the school steps and overhearing guys talk about girls and sports and what they were going to do over the weekend. Some would be driving dates down to the Jersey shore—Asbury Park or Sea Girt or Spring Lake—where they'd break into one of their family's summer cottages and drink in front of a roaring fire, then pair off to go upstairs and get laid. Some were going to The Meadowbrook on Pompton Turnpike to dance to Frank Dailey's band. Others—the richer seniors—were headed for the Yale Bowl to watch Albie Booth tear Princeton apart. Or to Glen Island Casino where they'd sway around the bandstand humming along with Ozzie Nelson and his blond singer, Harriet Hilliard. Or maybe to Manhattan to tea-dance to Paul Tremaine at Young's Chinese-American, then make the rounds on Fifty-second Street—Swing Lane—to hear hot jazz at The Famous Door, or see Sherry Britton do her erotic dance at Leon & Eddie's, or roar at the customers being insulted by Jack White at the Club 18. (I read all the Broadway columnists—Walter Winchell, Ed Sullivan, Louis Sobol, Lee Mortimer.) Me—I was going home and, when I wasn't doing chores, closing myself in my room to read something like Mencken's *Treatise on the Gods*.

When I graduated from high school, I got a job in New York. My so-called father arranged it. He was some sort of straw boss in the Newark distributing warehouse of a Manhattan film company, and I was hired as a messenger in their Twenty-third Street office, near Seventh Avenue. I knew my father wanted to get rid of me —my mother did, too—so I left home and rented an apartment the size of a broom closet in Greenwich Village. The job was boring as hell. All I did was carry film and messages from the Twenty-third Street branch to the main office at Forty-fifth and Madison, and vice versa. I'd ride the IRT subway to Forty-second Street, follow the lighted arrows to the shuttle train, take it to Grand Central, and go through the tunnel that came out on Madison Avenue. Back and forth, all day long. I had a lot of time to waste, so I'd bury a book in the big satchel I carried and sit in the Grand Central waiting room and read.

The only girl I knew was a skinny redhead who worked behind a cigar counter in the Grand Central tunnel. She'd see me go by at the same times every day, and pretty soon we began nodding and smiling at each other, just being friendly. Then I began to stop and talk, and finally asked her to a movie. We saw Myrna Loy and William Powell in a Thin Man movie at the Loew's on Lexington Avenue (Lowey's, she called it; she was from Brooklyn) and afterwards I took her home on the subway. She lived on the top floor of a four-story walk-up and when we reached the second landing—well, that's when I made my big mistake. I asked if she'd like to smoke a cigarette and she said yes, and we sat on the stairs while she lit up. I'd never even tried a cigarette, which I guess is understandable. I put my arm around her, sort of casually, and she didn't go stiff or pull away. Then, before I knew it, I was grabbing at her, trying to get at her breasts. She struggled to get away, and that just made me more excited. She managed to get half to her feet and kicked me in the jaw with her knee, slamming me back against the wall. I was dazed, but I heard her let out a huge gasp. I looked up and saw she was holding out the pleated skirt of her white dress. There was a big black hole in it. From the cigarette. The next day I changed my route through Grand Central. I never saw her again.

There was only one woman after that—a prostitute. A fellow in the stockroom got the address of this place on West Sixty-eighth Street and he said he'd fix me up. I said no at first, then he bought me a couple of drinks and I thought what the hell. He'd been told that only one guy at a time could go up to the apartment, and he went first. I walked up and down on the sidewalk, my heart hammering against my ribs, expecting that any minute a police squad car would come screaming up to the curb. When the fellow came down, I asked him how it was and he said the nuts.

Oh God, it was awful. I was limp as a baby. That's funny, because I was afraid I'd come before I even walked through the door. I figured if I was ever to get inside her, I'd have to use a spoon. She helped to solve that with her mouth but then, when I stuck it between her legs, I just shriveled up. Hell, being in her was like walking into a cold, empty room. Afterwards, while I was getting dressed, she went over to the corner and squatted down over a pan filled with some disinfectant that she dabbed into her crotch with a cloth. Boy, all we needed was chilled champagne and a violin trio. When I got back to my friend waiting downstairs, he asked how it was and I said the nuts.

Well, until I teamed up with Charles, that ended my career with women. Oh, occasionally I'd go rattling around the Village thinking I'd pick one up, but I never did. I'd sit at the bar at Julius's, nursing a beer and staring at the painted angels on the ceiling. Or stand at The Pepper Pot bar and watch the uptowners cutting up the dance floor. The Nut Club, Jack Delaney's, Nick's, Jimmy Kelly's—I visited them all. Always alone, making each beer last forever so I'd have money left if I met a girl. I got drunk only once, at the Stonewall Inn on Sheridan Square. It was New Year's Eve and I blew myself to a lot of rye-highs. Right after midnight, when they were playing "The Music Goes 'Round and Around," the place was in an uproar, everybody shouting and hugging and soul-kissing complete strangers. A girl in a red strapless came up to me at the bar and started to throw her arms around me, and when I swung around, she took one look and jumped back. "Oh, sweet Jesus," she said. I tied on a beaut after that, then lurched up to Twelfth Street and sat on a bench in tiny Abingdon Square and stared at the YWCA across the street, watching guys kiss their dates goodnight at the big institutional front door. I thought about all those girls lying in their antiseptic beds and suddenly hate burned through me so hot that I threw up all over the bench. I went out only a few times after that; once to the Pennsylvania Hotel, where I peeked into the Madhattan Room to see Hal Kemp and his band. Rudy Vallee was sitting at one of the tables with another man, both drinking coffee. But I found I was a lot less unhappy if I stayed home and read and, late at night, tuned in the big bands—Abe Lyman, Vincent Lopez, Peter Van Steeden, Shep Fields, Glen Gray, Isham Jones.

I quit my job in less than a year. That was a damfool thing to do, I guess, at a time when intelligent able-bodied men were selling apples and hot chestnuts on street corners. But I just couldn't stand it any longer. The monotony was bearable, but not the attitude of the people I worked with. You see, a lot of the men in the office knew my stepfather, and ever since I was a little kid, they'd been coming out to the house in East Orange. They called me Lammie then—the same as my mother did—and when I got the job as messenger, they continued to call me Lammie. So that meant everyone did. I couldn't go around asking everyone to please call me Lambert, so I just let it ride. But I hated them for it. I felt like they expected me to crawl up on their laps and show off how I could count. When the secretaries called me Lammie, I swear I felt like some five-year-old fruit. Anyway, I knew I could never be taken seriously until I got with people who'd never known me as a child. For the next few years I worked mostly at odd jobs—busboy at the Automat, delivery boy for a neighborhood liquor store, night clerk at a fleabag hotel—sometimes having a couple of part-time jobs at once.

Finally, one day I rented the basement apartment in the Village. That morning I'd been hired—along with about twenty other guys —to solicit classified ads for the *Journal*. I was the last one picked, the way it had always been. God, I practically had to get down on my knees and beg for a chance. Not that I wanted the job so much —it paid damned little—but it was the kind of reference that would impress a Village landlord. Lambert Post, newspaperman. That sounded good outside, but to the real newspapermen in the editorial department, a classified ad salesman had about as much prestige as a pimp.

I didn't make any friends on the paper, though I tried. (I'm not counting Henrietta Boardman; she was always nice to me in the office.) After work I used to go to The Rain House—a bar in the cobbled alley behind our building where *Journal* people hung out —and drink beer and try to strike up a conversation. But I didn't get any more attention than the bums who roamed the streets. Everyone, particularly the girls, seemed embarrassed to be seen talking to me. Screw them all, I finally thought, and stopped going.

So it was back to the apartment to read and listen to the bands on the radio. Saturday was the worst time, even though it was payday. We worked only half a day, and all the salesmen who worked out of town—the ones on Real Estate mostly—came in to write up their reports and just wander around the halls. There was almost a party feeling in the air. At noon the place cleared out like somebody'd yelled fire and I'd be alone in that big telephone room, accompanied only by the reverberation of the presses getting out the Sunday paper. I remember looking down through one of the huge windows at the cars parked facing the front of the building. A lot of the girls and guys I worked with would be piling into them to race uptown and get an early start on the weekend drinking. Some would begin at the Commodore bar where, for a quarter, you could get the biggest Tom Collins in town. Almost all of them would eventually hole up in apartments where, until late Sunday night, they'd get orry-eyed drunk, screw like mink, and sleep all over the place. When they'd all left the office, I'd go down to Friedman's—a hole-in-the-wall Jewish restaurant on the corner —and take out a chopped-chicken-liver sandwich and a container of coffee. I'd walk across South Street, dodging the heavy trucks, and walk out on one of the big piers, where I'd lean against a piling in the sun and eat my lunch. Occasionally I'd be distracted by the sight of cops grappling a stiff out of the river. Bums were always staggering out on the piers to sleep off the "smoke" they drank and would roll off and drown without ever coming to. Sometimes during the week we'd see a body, the face half eaten away by fish, hauled up to the pier, and someone, usually Sol Pincus, was sure to yell, "Don't eat at Friedman's today!" Real funny guys. Bastards. After I finished lunch, I'd go home and maybe listen to Ted Husing or Graham McNamee announce some sports event; if there was nothing on, I'd doze away the afternoon. Saturday night I might fight my way through the crowds on Fourteenth Street and see a movie and amateur vaudeville at the Academy of Music. Afterwards I'd usually sit for a while in Union Square and listen to the soapbox orators rant against everything from capitalism to monogamy. I often thought of bringing my own soapbox and blasting the shit out of the whole goddamned world.

On Sunday I'd sometimes wander through the Village's zigzag streets imagining stories about places made famous by the bohemians of the twenties: like the brownstone house on Waverly Place where Edna St. Vincent Millay burnt her candles at both ends; the Provincetown Playhouse on MacDougal Street, where Eugene O'Neill got his start; the rooming house on Washington Square South where John Reed had lived before joining the revolution in Russia and dying there. The only one left of that defiant, free-living crowd was Maxwell Bodenheim, a gaunt, tragic figure whom I once saw at the Waldorf cafeteria on Sixth Avenue selling for pennies a poem he'd written on a paper napkin.

Generally, though, I'd stay in the apartment, reading and thinking and just dreaming until it was time to go to work on Monday morning.

I guess it's pretty obvious that I didn't know who or what I was, or whether I was anything. I'd gotten so I didn't even realize that during every waking moment—and probably when I was asleep —my insides were one big raw ache. I'd never known anything else, so I accepted it without thinking too much about it, almost as a natural condition.

Charles Walter, as I said, made everything excitingly different. Because he was a somebody—self-assured, debonair, fearless—he made me feel like a somebody. He was interested in my views on books and people and the things I thought about. He felt sorry for me and spent hours sympathizing with me and telling me that nothing bad was going to happen to me as long as he was around. And he opened my eyes as to who my enemies were, despising them and encouraging me to despise them.

I never dreamed that he would need me every bit as much as I needed him. By the time I found that out, it was too late.

III

"CHARLES," I SAID TO HIM one night in the apartment, "Sol Pincus insulted me today."

Charles put down his drink, stood up, and stared out the window to the sidewalk. The yellow drapes were open, and he waited until a pair of legs went by before answering.

"Sol Pincus is a son of a bitch," he said, and I knew he hated him as much as I did. Pincus was the star telephone solicitor—Used Cars—a stocky guy with sleek black hair, a flat, doughy face, and a mouth like a knife cut. He strutted around the office as though he owned the place.

"Tell me exactly what happened, Lambert."

I went over it in detail. How I'd gone crosstown to the bar on Park Row for a couple of beers and the free lunch. How, walking back, I ran into Sol Pincus, who was taking a sport coat into a dry-cleaning shop. How Sol Pincus slid his oily eyes over me and said nastily, "Well, well, hotshot himself. You going back to see what ads you can steal?" I answered pleasantly, "No, I make out all right on my own." Sol Pincus sneered. "You make out because you're a shit artist," he said, "with an asshole for a mouth." He laughed and went into the cleaners.

Charles thought for a minute, frowning and gulping his gin. Finally his eyes lit up. "Lambert," he said, "what color was the sport coat he was having cleaned?"

"Cream-colored," I said. "And I think maybe it was cashmere. You know how Sol likes fancy clothes."

"Do you know the name of the dry cleaner?"

"Yes, the Jiffy Cleaners."

The next morning at his desk Charles got the number of Jiffy

Cleaners and called them. A man with an accent answered. Charles said he was Sol Pincus and asked if the sport coat was ready. No, the man said—five o'clock, that's the time it had been promised for.

"Forget it for today," Charles said. "I find I won't need it until day after tomorrow."

The dry cleaner thanked him; he had a lot of work backed up.

Thinking that Sol Pincus might take the jacket away uncleaned when he called at five, Charles said, "But there's something I'd like you to do today. Have you got any soldier buttons?"

"Soldier buttons? Sure, plenty soldier buttons."

"Good. What I want you to do is cut off the buttons that are on the jacket now and replace them with the soldier buttons. Understand?"

"You mean it? On a white cashmere coat? It'll look kinda funny."

"I mean it. It's the latest thing."

The next morning I passed Sol Pincus in the aisle. He glared at me from the corner of his eye as if I was a child murderer. But he didn't say anything; there was no way he could hang it on me.

Charles and I laughed about it at lunch. Then he sobered. He was thinking.

Before the lunch hour was over, Charles Walter was back in the office. He called Jiffy Cleaners again. The same man answered.

"This is Sol Pincus," Charles said. "About that sport coat—"

"Now look, Mr. Pincus, more swearing at me I don't need. The soldier buttons they're off. The old buttons they're back on. By five o'clock the coat'll be cleaned and ready to take out."

"Forgive me for getting sore yesterday," Charles said. "It was just some crazy mix-up, I guess. Tell me, do you dye clothes?"

"Dye? Sure we dye."

"On the premises, or do you send it out?"

"Right here. The premises."

"Good. Now about the sport coat—dye it black."

"Black! You said *black?*"

"Black."

"Such a beautiful white coat, you want it—"

"After what happened yesterday," Charles said, "you probably

want to verify this. So call me back. Sol Pincus at the *Journal*."
Charles gave him the number.

Hardly anyone, including Sol Pincus, was back from lunch, and
when Sol's phone buzzed, Charles was at Sol's desk and took the
call.

"That's right," he said. "Black."

Late that afternoon Sol Pincus himself called the dry cleaner to
make sure the coat would be ready to pick up at five. Over the
hubbub of voices, his came screeching out: *"Wha-a-t!* You can't
mean that! . . . Why, you crazy, stupid, kike *bastard!"*

After that, Sol Pincus spoke to me only once again, much later.

Charles Walter got even for me another time, with a solicitor
named Molly Hegeman. She'd been with the paper for years, calling furnished rooms in the best territory in Manhattan—Forty-
second Street to Fifty-ninth Street, East and West. Once I'd gotten
one of her leads by mistake, sold the ad and, without thinking, put
it through as my own. She caught it and set the record straight
with a few acid words. (That's what Sol Pincus had meant when
he asked if I was planning to steal some ads.) On this particular
day I sold an ad to the landlady of a rooming house in my territory, only to have Molly Hegeman point out later that the place
was actually owned by a real-estate firm in her territory, and
therefore the ad should be credited to her. This being the second
offense, she was convinced I was deliberately poaching. Boy, did
she give it to me! She was a big, dark, aggressive woman with a
foul mouth when she was mad, and she stood over my desk waving her arms and shouting every obscenity she could think of.

I didn't have to talk that one over with anyone. Everybody in
the place had heard her. After she'd finally gone away, it didn't
take more than five minutes for Charles Walter to decide what to
do. He knew that Molly had almost despaired of cracking The
Park East, a big apartment hotel that ran half-column ads in the
Times and *Trib* but had never given her so much as a line. Just
before five, Charles flipped to his outside line, called the *Journal*'s
number, and got Molly. Charles said he was the manager of The
Park East—he'd gotten the man's name—and he'd at last decided to
try a schedule in the *Journal*. He told her to insert the same *half-
column* ad that was in the *Times* and run it *for thirty days!* Well,

that was the biggest order Molly Hegeman, or anyone else on furnished rooms, had ever got, and she was so excited she nearly had a stroke. Ordinarily with an order like that, someone would call back and verify it, but Molly and Jean Hooper were so out of their minds with greed they didn't even think of that. The ad appeared in the paper the next day and the next, two days during which Molly got a twenty-five-dollar bonus and probably had visions of taking over Jean Hooper's job. Then, on the second day, the real manager of The Park East called in, so goddamned sore he was about to have a baby. He canceled the ad, said he wouldn't pay for the two times it had run, swore by God that so long as he was manager, the *Journal* would never get a line of advertising, and furthermore if anyone from the paper ever contacted him again, he'd call his lawyer. Molly sat there like she was in the electric chair just being hit by the juice. After that she gave me a lot of funny looks, but she never said anything. I guess she couldn't imagine that anyone like Lambert Post could pull such a thing. And, of course, Lambert Post hadn't—Charles Walter was the hero.

I guess those two successes convinced Charles that he had uncorked a genie; that a telephone and a persuasive voice and the power of the name New York *Journal* combined to make possible all sorts of marvelous happenings. Still, his first experiments were fairly modest. For example, he'd sit facing the window and call Dottie Friedlander on the outside line and pretend he was a secret admirer. Dottie, who was married, would get so thrilled she'd forget to pluck at her beard for all of ten minutes. Henrietta Boardman, sitting next to Charles, learned about it from Dottie and was afraid he might break up her marriage. She convinced him to make a confession. Dottie took it like a good sport.

Charles would also call press agents who represented shows and sports events, implying he was a big-shot newspaperman, and they'd send him free passes. After a while, he began to get bolder. One of his favorite pastimes was to pick a name at random from the telephone directory, call up, and announce: "Hel-*lo,* Mrs. Smith! This is Bat Guano of the K-R-A-P Lucky Bucks program. I want you to know you are the lucky winner of today's drawing for an all-expense trip for two to Atlantis. . . . That's right, Mrs. Smith, *Atlantis,* where you can frolic to your heart's content in the beautiful blue ocean. . . . Just one thing, Mrs. Smith. To qualify, you've got to prove you know the words and tune of 'Happy Birthday.' . . . What's that, you can't sing? . . . Try, Mrs. Smith, try. . . . Ah, that's better. A little louder please, Mrs. Smith. No, no, *much* louder." And Charles would sit back and listen to Mrs. Smith damn near snap her vocal cords.

Henrietta Boardman, who overheard a number of these antic calls, got a little worried. She mentioned it to me one day in the hall.

"They're funny, Lambert—but, well, sort of cruel too. Worse than that, if Jean Hooper ever hears of it, she'll get out her hatchet."

I tried lightly to dismiss it. "Oh, a man has to blow off a little steam now and then, Henrietta."

She gave me an anxious look. "I hate to say it, Lambert, but gosh, aren't you going overboard on this Charles Walter?"

"He's a terrific guy," I said and smiled.

"He's nothing like you."

"What's that mean?"

"You're a"—her face flushed—"a sensitive, sweet person, Lambert. You don't have to lean on any Charles Walter. You've got too much to offer in your own self."

Her tone was soft, almost tender. An emotion in me that I had thought forever frozen began to thaw. For once a girl had seen beneath the exterior and perceived something of value.

A catch came into my voice as I thanked her. "I'll try to do something about it," I said and hurried away.

But the only effect the warning had on Charles was to make him secretive. When he felt the need of a little frivolity, he would turn his back on Henrietta and speak in a low voice close to the mouthpiece. She never mentioned the subject again.

Soon Charles Walter cast about for more daring ways to amuse himself. That's when he started to read the death notices and the announcements of divorces.

For some reason Charles would turn to that page in the newspaper the first thing every morning. At first he protested that he did it only to see if some friend had died or had ended his or her marriage. But that didn't make sense because he knew almost no one in New York outside of the office. Abandoning that explanation, he then said jokingly about the death notices, "I just want to see if my name is there." The truth began to dawn on him when he realized that the dead people whose names he was looking for had to meet two conditions: They must be men, and they must be under twenty-five. (Of course, there were damned few in the death notices who were under twenty-five, but there were some—suicides or victims of accidents or some disease.) Charles would cut out these notices and paste them down on yellow sheets of paper, just as though they were leads. Between business calls he would ponder them, his imagination expanding as he wondered about the previous family life of "Alison, Thomas Anthony, beloved husband of Laura Alison; aged 24 years; after a long illness. . . ." or (under DIVORCES, COMPLAINTS FILED) exactly what had happened to provoke the terse announcement: "Bernard—Ruth vs. William."

Images of the bereaved widow or the disillusioned divorcée rose in his mind. He thought of their brooding loneliness, their boredom, their sexual frustration. God, how they must want a man in bed beside them, or soon would.

Why shouldn't he, thought Charles Walter, bring a little comfort and excitement to these young women in distress?

IV

CHARLES APPROACHED his new project cautiously. In the case of a death, he would wait a week or ten days after the notice had appeared before calling up the widow. He'd say that he had known her husband some years before (which always elicited useful facts about him) and wanted to express his condolences. He would have called sooner, he said, but he had just returned from a Mediterranean cruise and heard the terrible news only the day before.

Almost invariably the widow was so appreciative, and apparently so lonely, that she'd babble away as though confiding in her oldest friend. In a few minutes Charles could put together a picture of the kind of woman she was—approximate age, appearance, education, likes, and dislikes. If the picture was inviting, Charles would turn on the charm, speaking in a gentle, understanding voice, and in no time he'd gain an insight into her vulnerability. (Once he got a widow who cut him off as though he was a bill collector. A few days later an item in the paper reported that she was being held for her husband's murder.) Before ringing off, Charles would say that he was leaving shortly for an extended business trip to South America but would call again when he returned, in case he could be of any help. The magic of his voice, his sympathetic manner, and the allure of the Mediterranean—South America references had most of the women practically drooling into the phone and insisting that he drop in so they could talk about Johnny or Bill or Tom. If Charles felt that the invitation had interesting implications, if she was childless, and if she sounded particularly attractive, he'd draw a star next to her name and make a few notes. In a couple of weeks he had starred seven promising widows.

Divorcées were a more difficult problem. For one thing, they were often impossible to reach. Charles would look up the former husband's name in the phone book, make the call, and as often as not, get the *husband—he'd* kept the apartment or house. Or he might get a new tenant who'd never heard of the divorced couple. And sometimes he'd talk to a man who at that moment was living with the divorced woman. Nevertheless, Charles managed to contact a number of the divorcées listed.

The approach then became the challenge. To claim that he was an old pal of the former husband would probably make him poison. Charles solved this one pretty cleverly, I thought. Getting the woman on the line, he'd say he was representing a certain financial institution—he wasn't at liberty to divulge the name—and was seeking the former spouse in order to pay him a modest sum due from a legacy. Sometimes the divorcée didn't believe him, thinking the "financial institution" he represented was actually a collection agency. But that didn't stop her from doing her best to cooperate —why not shaft the guy who'd caused her so much misery? If they did believe Charles, they were even more cooperative, hoping to get their hands on a piece of the loot. Whichever their response, Charles, with his ingratiating voice and glamorous allusions, had most of them suggesting a personal interview to discuss the matter. Charles always said he would call back and—his voice mischievously suggestive—intimated that the visit need not necessarily be confined to business. In a few weeks he had starred five divorcées who had expressed pleasurable anticipation.

Seven young and lonely widows; five presumably young (at least they had no children) and eager divorcées—a dozen women apparently susceptible to the pleasure principle. It was, Charles thought amusedly, as though he owned the only key to a free whorehouse.

But *would* it be free? I put the question to Charles one night in the apartment.

"They'd expect you to take them to the fanciest places in town," I said. "Why not? After all that hooey about Mediterranean cruises and trips to Rio."

For the first time I experienced Charles's contempt. "You're afraid."

"Yes. It could lead to trouble."

"Trouble? Just from bouncing on a bed? Hell, they'd be over-whelmed with gratitude. It would be a genuine public service."

"Look, it was a *game*. You're ahead. Why not quit now?"

"It's only half time. I'm in the locker room. The coach is yelling pour it on, pile up the score, rush the balls through the center."

"But have you got what it takes?"

"Money?"

"Not just money."

That made him angry. Dark frown. Clenched jaw. Knuckles hammering against teeth. It was out of character for him to be so perturbed.

"Are you saying I'm not man enough?" he said.

"Oh no," I said miserably, "you're man enough. But women—they can tear you apart."

"Speak for yourself, Lambert," he said harshly. "But don't speak for Charles Walter."

The name, enunciated with pride, had the same effect on me as when I had first heard it. Charles Walter was of a special breed, I reminded myself. Above the crowd. Kingly. Seemingly possessed of divine rights.

"It's only the money," I said appeasingly. "Nothing else. One night on the town could cost you more than you make in a month. These girls must think you're Café Society. They'd expect El Morocco or the Stork Club."

There was no more conversation for a long while. I tried to efface myself completely while Charles silently groped for an answer. Finally his chin came up. He stroked his black, shining hair. Although I couldn't see his eyes, I knew they were glowing.

"The thing to do," he said, "is to know these women as they really are. That means staying out of the glamor spots, where they'd try to act up to the atmosphere. It means meeting them in their homes, maybe sitting on worn slipcovers and listening to drab stories of life with Willie. Pretty dull stuff. But right away you'd separate the bright-lights kids from the ones who'd settle for a nice warm feeling."

I laughed. "But Charles Walter—world traveler, intimate friend of Brenda Frazier and Lucius Beebe—he couldn't very well suggest a quiet evening at home."

"No, he couldn't," Charles said, smiling. "But Lambert Post *could*."

I felt my heart knock against my ribs. "I was afraid you were getting to that."

Charles rehearsed his plan, which was quite simple. He would telephone a name on the list and say how much he would like to see her but that, as he'd already mentioned, he had been called out of town for an indefinite period. Meanwhile he had this old friend on his hands, Lambert Post, a classmate at Harvard, who had just breezed in from Bar Harbor, Maine, and didn't know a soul in New York. Now if only . . .

"And of course," Charles said, grinning and slapping the arm of the chair, "the young lady will say, 'I'll be delighted to meet any friend of yours. Lambert Post—what a distinguished name!' Maybe *you'll* make out—sure as hell I'll have given you the credentials—Harvard, Bar Harbor, I'll think of some more. If you don't, well . . ."

I began to tremble inside, but more with excitement than fear.

"We'll start with a widow," Charles said. "Widows have no right to be out jazzing around anyway."

The next night I was no sooner home than I was in the shower preparing for my first date. Charles's exuberance overwhelmed any qualms I might have felt.

"Tonight, Jennifer Hartwick," he said, rolling the name over his tongue. "Gorgeous voice—soft, breathless. And ready. Man, is she *ready!* She salivated so much in the phone I thought I'd have to use a bath towel on my left ear. And her husband dead only two weeks! Pete was his name. Pete Hartwick. An auto accident cashed him in. Four in the morning. Jennifer wasn't with him, so maybe he'd been out playing around. Maybe she's not so bereaved as she pretends. Anyway, I knew him at a camp in Connecticut where we were counselors—*she* mentioned it, I didn't—that's the story. That's all you have to know, Lambert. Charles Walter and

Pete Hartwick. Great old buddies. Cocktails at six-thirty in her hotel room. *Hotel room!* God, she sounds like a pushover. Attaboy, soap those armpits."

I knew the Court Hotel from having passed by it often in my days as a messenger. It was on Forty-fourth Street just off Broadway, a location that suggested tourists and people in show business. A rounded chrome marquee featured the name in red neon tubing. I walked beneath it and through a revolving door into a small square lobby furnished with cracked leather chairs and tall lamps with pink shades. A fat, dark man with hair like a fright wig sat behind the desk peering at a folded copy of the *Racing Form*. I took a deep breath and it was like inhaling the dank, airless atmosphere of the subway.

To my right another neon sign, blue, announced BAR. I pushed through the plate-glass door and entered a long narrow room dimly aglow with pink back-bar lights that reflected against cellophane palms rising in the corners. Although I'd already had two gins at home, I ordered another, straight and with lots of ice. My parched Adam's apple gave a painful little jump as I downed the gin in one swallow. I waited for it to hit me, then strolled back into the lobby, found the house phone, and called Jennifer Hartwick.

Her voice came on breathless and friendly. "How do you do, Mr. Post. Please come right on up. Room 418."

A bent, bald-headed man with verminous eyes took me up in the creaking elevator. Getting off, I heard shrill voices, mostly women's, piping through the transoms. Naturally—it was cocktail time. I found Room 418 and paused to look at my watch. Exactly six-thirty. I wiped the palms of my hands on my jacket, held my breath, and knocked. In a moment the door was flung open by a woman in her early twenties wearing snug black hostess pajamas, taffy-blond bangs, and a wide Pepsodent smile. I heard a confusion of conversation behind her and saw people hoisting glasses. Oh God, a party!

Introducing myself, I held my face partially averted but with eyes cast on her.

"Welcome, Mr. Post. I'm Jennifer Hartwick. And do forgive

me. It seems some old friends of mine had the stupendous idea of dropping in on me. Please do come in." Her voice had the emphasis and affected English intonation of someone who has taken drama lessons; yet there was a slight residue of pure New York.

I turned my head to face her fully and something happened to her eyes and her smile. There was really no perceptible change, but I had the impression that a light had been snapped off from behind her pupils and that her curved lips had become fastened by invisible wires. It was an experience I'd never grown used to.

She blinked rapidly, turned, and I followed her into the living room, realizing that she must occupy a suite (there was a doorway off to the right leading down a short hall, presumably to the bedroom and bath). The room was cheaply furnished with angularly modern pieces; still-life prints decorated the pale-green walls. A touch of opulence was simulated by a curved bar of imitation black leather standing in a corner next to one of the draped windows. Two girls stood with feet perched on the thin brass rail facing a red-faced man in a houndstooth sport coat who was stirring martinis. Lounging on the orange sofa were two shirt-sleeved men flanking a slim, dark girl with upswept hair. Another girl, with long gold-blond hair like Ginger Rogers's, was stretched out at their feet resting on a hip and an elbow. Everyone was talking animatedly, no one listening to anyone else. It seemed obvious they had been there for a number of rounds.

Jennifer Hartwick swept to the bar, introducing me on the way with wiggles of her fingers. Her guests responded with quick glances and nods, one man on the sofa simply raising his hand as if asking permission to go to the bathroom. They had names like Lisa and Celia and Brian and Ronald. My arrival failed even to punctuate the flow of talk.

The houndstooth sport coat moved from behind the bar, saying to the two girls, "It's all a big poker game. Hitler's bluffing. But he doesn't have the cards."

"Hitler'th a thorehead," one of the girls lisped. "He can't thtand it that Joe Louith knocked out thuperman Max Thmeling in the firtht round."

They wandered off. Jennifer made me a martini, saying, "So

you're a friend of Charles Walter. I guess you know we've never even met. But he sounds like such a dear. Do tell me about him. I understand he's quite the world traveler."

That and the martini relaxed me a little. I told her that Charles was the finest man I'd ever known, a strong, dynamic personality, yet kind and gentle to those in need. I could say it very sincerely because it was what I believed. My eyes were on my drink and I felt them begin to water.

She said with a forced laugh, "He *does* like women, doesn't he?"

The implication made me mildly indignant. "Yes," I said evenly, "he likes women. Why else would he be interested in you?"

"Of course," she said soothingly. "A man so attractive must have scads of women."

I took the bait. "I guess so, but no one he really feels close to. I think he's looking for the particular girl, although he's never said so." I looked at her and saw that her big eyes had become wistful.

"Why must he travel so extensively?"

The question inspired me to answer as I thought Charles Walter would. I explained that he had inherited from his father substantial interests in many far-flung enterprises—copper mines in Chile, a shipping corporation in Italy, a textile mill in Scotland, a steel plant in France. On a hunch I added, "But he also spends a lot of time here in the States. He has to in order to keep an eye on his M-G-M holdings."

"M-G-M? You mean . . ."

"Metro-Goldwyn-Mayer. Charles's father provided part of the capital that started the studio."

Her body twitched as though she'd been goosed. She sucked in a breath, bit her lower lip, and rolled her eyes.

"But that's fabulous," she breathed.

"Are you interested in motion pictures? You know, you look a bit like Jean Arthur."

She swung around the bar and leaned back against the rim, swelling her breasts as she faced me. The light behind her eyes had snapped back on.

"I'm an actress," she said, smiling warmly. "I did six months with Katharine Cornell. Bit parts. I had a walk-on in *Page Miss*

Glory with Gladys George and another play with Ruth Chatterton that folded in Boston. Yes, I'm very interested in motion pictures." She affected a forlorn expression. "I'm just waiting to be discovered."

"Perhaps Charles can introduce you to some people who can help."

"Now, wouldn't that be nice."

I felt my face flush with guilt. But she seemed unaware of it as she pointed out that all her guests were in some way associated with show business. Lisa had just finished a month of summer stock with Maude Adams in Ogunquit, Maine. Celia was a dancer who had appeared in George White's *Scandals*. Ronnie was about to depart with a road company of *Babes in Arms*. Brian was an assistant stage manager with the Group Theatre. And so on.

"Right now," Jennifer said, "I'm at liberty, as the saying goes."

The remark struck me as grisly when I recalled that her husband had died only two weeks before. I waited a minute and then offered my condolences.

Her face hardened slightly. She said crisply, "Pete and I weren't working at it. He was supposed to be my agent, but most of his negotiations were with touts at the track or drunks at the bar. The only payoff that amounted to anything, he didn't get—his insurance, and that wasn't very much. Enough, though, to get me out of the foul dungeon we lived in and into this hotel suite. I've been here for a week."

She asked me more about Charles and I expanded fancifully on his life as an international glamor boy. But I began to tire of the game; in fact, felt a pang of resentment that Jennifer expressed not a word of interest in me, Lambert Post. After all, hadn't Charles suggested that I might be the one to enjoy her favors? On my third martini we were sitting on the sofa, the others having left to group noisily around the bar, when I said, "Charles has asked me to accept a position at M-G-M. In the talent department." I tried to throw it away, but it came out as the preamble to a proposition.

Her smile remained but turned counterfeit. "Ah. Then you'll have your very own casting couch."

The slight sting in her voice made me think of the time when I was a small boy and had bragged to some bigger kids that I'd been a bat boy with the Yankees. My mother and father heard about it and whaled hell out of me for lying.

"I probably won't accept it," I said, then got in deeper. "I'm too busy writing."

Her eyebrows arched skeptically. "Is that what you are, a writer?"

"Yes, a playwright. Fortunately, my parents—they're dead—left me plenty of money to live on."

"Have you ever had anything produced?" Her tone, edged with disbelief, cut like a knife.

"Well, not yet. But Guthrie McClintic is interested in a play I recently finished."

"Guthrie McClintic, the famous producer, no less. As you probably know, Guthrie McClintic is Katharine Cornell's husband. I'll speak to Kate about it. She has great influence with Guthrie."

Obviously she was baiting me. Perhaps my own masquerade was so transparent that she now doubted everything I had said about Charles.

"Please don't," I said wretchedly. "It's . . . uh . . . being handled by my agent and he might be embarrassed."

"As you like." She sprang to her feet. "I need a drink," she said and joined the others around the bar.

In a few minutes I got up and stood outside the circle of drinkers. It was, I thought, no different than when I stopped in at The Rain House behind the newspaper office, or when I had gone pub-crawling in the Village: I was totally ignored. Suddenly I wanted only to be back in the apartment talking to Charles. But I stayed on, my ears picking up scraps of conversation.

". . . and he just can't act. Christ, even Major Bowes would give him the gong."

". . . blind drunk when she auditioned. No wonder she got the part."

". . . so I said to Rose, 'Listen, Billy . . .'"

". . . and they call FDR a Communist. My God, he's trying to *save* the system."

". . . dialectical materialism . . ."

"Tallulah was a riot. And Dottie Parker, she said . . ."

"Woollcott should forget the theater and stick to those Seeing Eye dogs in Morristown."

"I may join the Abraham Lincoln Brigade . . ."

". . . a goddamned Trotskyite . . ."

And on and on and on.

Two more couples came in, not bothering to knock, and joined the drunken bedlam at the bar. I fidgeted with my empty glass, finally backing off and setting it on the coffee table. I wandered about the room, examined the framed prints, gazed down at the traffic choking Forty-fourth Street. No one noticed me. I made up my mind to disappear silently out the front door, but decided to visit the bathroom first. I went down the short hall and found the bedroom closed tight. I turned the knob slowly and found it unlocked. I opened the door and started to step inside. A man sat at the softly lit vanity table pulling a large comb through his stalks of yellow hair. He was stark naked.

Before I could turn away, he saw me in the mirror. "Hi," he said, unperturbed. "Did you come to see the family jewels?" He swayed around on the seat, cupped his hand under his genitals, and bounced them. "You're in luck. Usually they're kept under glass."

I grinned weakly and was about to turn back when the bathroom door burst open and a naked blond girl skipped out, dangling a bath towel. "Gil, who are you telephon—" She stopped, seeing me.

"My, my," she said pleasantly, "a voyeur. You're too late. The ship sailed. What a shame."

I felt myself being shoved aside, heard a voice shrill furiously, "*Gil! Janice!* Just *what* is going on in here?"

Gil and Janice looked perplexed. Gil said, "We were screwing. Isn't that what you expected we'd be doing?"

"I guess we should have locked the door," Janice said. She made no attempt to cover herself with the towel. I stared down at my feet.

Jennifer's eyes blazed with anger; not, I was sure, because of shocked surprise but because I, and therefore Charles, had been a witness. She grabbed my arm, pulled me outside, and shut the door. She fixed me with an aghast look.

"Never, never have I been so insulted," she said. "Why, I had no *idea* . . ."

I said nothing. I was still smarting from her previous skepticism and the way she had abandoned me.

"Please," she said pleadingly, "I'd be so grateful if you would keep this from Mr. Walter."

I looked at her for about five seconds, seeing not a vibrant, pretty young actress, but a slut of a woman who wanted only to use me.

Coldly I said, "I'll tell Charles Walter that you run a nice clean house."

She lurched back as though I'd slapped her. Then her jaw clenched, her eyes narrowed, and she hissed, "You dirty bastard. All that shit about a big job with M-G-M, about being a playwright. Mister, there's only one place for you in show business—and that's in a *sideshow!* Hurreee, hurreee, hurreee, step inside and see the Grinning Boy. My God, I think your mother took one look at you and then kept the afterbirth!"

I raised my hand in a trembling fist; then dropped it. I shouldered past her, rushed blindly through the living room, and plunged out the front door, rage scalding my whole body.

V

I LAY IN BED and went over it with Charles. When I had finished, bitterly emphasizing the hate and contempt poured on me by Jennifer Hartwick, I said, "I think we'd better give up this game."

Through a void of silence I tried to make my mind a blank, hoping even to erase Charles, who had unwittingly sponsored my humiliation. But in a few minutes I could sense him stirring.

"Lambert," he said sincerely, "you really deserve to be proud of yourself. You took a woman who posed as a sweet, kind person and you stripped off her mask. You showed her up for the bitch she is. If she'd been what she pretended, she'd have cared about your feelings. Now you *know*. That's one of the objects of the game—to expose women as they really are."

"But she didn't actually pretend anything. *I* did all that."

"She pretended to accept you, just so she could meet Charles Walter, get his money, crash the movies, cruise around the world. If it was only you, Lambert, she'd have spit in your face. In fact, that's about what she finally did."

Fury pounded through me like a giant pulse.

"She should be punished, Lambert."

I buried my face in the pillow, trying to smother my response. But a word sneaked out: "How?"

There was another long silence before Charles said, "I don't know. It has to be thought out. Now try to get some sleep. Just leave it all to me."

I spent a miserable night, not seeming to sleep at all but knowing I had because of the terrible dreams. I remember an enormous, disembodied hand pursuing me as I tried to run, run, run, but with leaden feet. I remember reaching a towering precipice, the hand striking me, the heart-gasping panic as I sailed through the air, the huge splash into a boiling inferno. I felt someone drag me out, but not to save me—to lock me in a tiny black box with a pair of glaring eyes and the shriek of drunken laughter.

I woke up in soaking wet pajamas, blinking at a shaft of sun slanting through a crack in the drawn drapes. I stumbled out of bed and into the shower, turning it on cold. I had finished shaving and was half-dressed before I was even aware of Charles. His presence again triggered the hate I had felt the night before, now aggravated by the clinging dreams.

I found myself disappointed that Charles had not yet thought of a punishment for Jennifer Hartwick. Instead, in a soft, musing voice, he suggested a phone call to another name on the list.

Standing at the bureau fastening my tie, I felt my insides writhe.

"Charles, I can't face that again. I tell you they ignored me, she insulted me. What's the sense in asking for it again?"

"Wouldn't you rather *know* who your enemies are?"

I didn't answer.

"Isn't that better than making believe people love you, then finding out they'd gladly cut you into little pieces?"

I felt a wave of self-pity. "I . . . wel-l-l . . . yes, I guess it is."

"But I agree, there's no sense in taking on so many people at once. I hadn't anticipated that. This time when I telephone, I'll make sure the young lady will be alone. Let's check the list."

A few minutes later he said, "Diane Summers. D for divorcée. Twenty-three—she even told me her age. Attitude E.E., for Extremely Eager. Yes, I remember her. She practically had her tongue in the phone."

I was like a drunkard with a huge, remorseful hangover who feels compelled to seek euphoria in more drink, knowing it will lead to an even more painful aftermath. I recalled the old joke and its truth: A drink makes a new man of you; then the new man wants a drink. Where would it stop? Charles seemed determined to avenge single-handedly all the world's cruelties. No, that was not true. Every reprisal he had undertaken was in defense of me. He was my friend, my protector—the first I'd ever had. What did it matter that he had come to dominate me almost to the point of possession? If this divorcée, Diane Summers, should hurt me, he

would impose a righteous penalty, just as I knew he would with
Jennifer Hartwick.

An astonishing question flared in the pit of my mind: Did I
want to be abused in order to provoke Charles to retaliate against
my tormentors? I refused to answer. But I felt like my guts were
sweating when I agreed to have him telephone Diane Summers.

He called from his desk late that morning. Diane was as friendly
as he remembered but said she had just stepped from the shower—
could she call him back? Charles hesitated, saw that Jean Hooper
was not at her desk, then gave her his inside private number, which
was different from the one you called if you wanted the newspaper
switchboard. Ten minutes later Diane called back, her manner
vivacious, her voice airy with expectancy. Oh, he was leaving the
country that afternoon? How tragic, she had hoped his trip had
been postponed. A Harvard classmate? A stranger in town? Why,
she'd be delighted to see him. Lambert Post, what a nice name.
Oh, he was shy, uncomfortable in a crowd? Well, then, she'd
meet him alone. Why not have him drop up to the apartment?
They'd have a few drinks and talk about Charles. Six o'clock?
Seven *would* be more convenient. Seven was fine.

When Charles rang off he swung around and saw that Henrietta
Boardman had been observing him curiously through the glass
partition separating their desks. He was sure she had not overheard him because his back had been toward her and he had spoken very softly, lips pressed to the mouthpiece. Her heavy-lidded
eyes, enormous behind the thick lenses, seemed to invite an explanation.

"A cancellation," he said. "And I thought that ad would run
forever."

Henrietta smiled, her lips like ripe red fruit with a sparkling
white center. "That wasn't business," she said. "It was your direct
line. I heard the buzzer."

Charles smiled back. "So I have a social life."

"Is she pretty?"

"Henrietta, she doesn't hold a candle to your magnificent
charms."

"Oh, Charles Walter, you *are* a card. Why don't you try being
more like Lambert Post?"

"Lambert Post is afraid of girls."

"I wish he wasn't."

After hearing that, I started to wonder about Henrietta Board-man. All it proved, I guess, was that not every girl was looking for a Charles Walter.

Diane Summers lived on East Sixty-second Street not far from Central Park, a neighborhood of fashionable and therefore expensive apartment houses. But hers wasn't one of them. It stood like a fat dwarf among giants, five stories graying with age, the iron grillwork on the heavy entrance doors beginning to shed its black-enamel skin. Inside the tiled vestibule I found her name on one of the brass mailboxes, pushed the button, and in a few moments shouldered through the buzzing inner door into a lobby furnished Spanish style with big carved chairs and tables and lots of shabby red velvet. I took the self-service elevator to the fourth floor, walked to the end of the dim corridor, and pressed the bell. It triggered the incongruous sound of chimes, disconcerting me as if someone had blown a trumpet in a museum. The door opened slowly and a tall, willowy girl with feathercut hair welcomed me with a dazzling smile.

"Lambert Post. I'm Diane Summers. How nice you could come."

I murmured a greeting and followed her inside, noticing that her hair was chestnut, and that her lime-colored dress packaged a beautifully erect body powered by a gently rotating stride. The room we entered looked like it had been done by a color-blind interior decorator. Everything was white—chairs, sofa, leather-topped tables, lamps, drapes, deep-piled carpeting. The only contrast, slight, was provided by paintings clustered on the white walls—all pale pastels. It was the kind of room I had seen only in the movies, in a Busby Berkeley musical or belonging to Mr. Big, played by Edward Arnold or Otto Kruger. A white tray containing bottles, glasses, and a white leatherette ice bucket sat on a long table in front of the curved sofa.

She waved me to be seated, slipped down beside me, and asked what I'd like to drink. She was having a martini and I said that would be fine.

I made them, fumbling with the ice, dithering with the bottles of gin and vermouth. As I stirred the mixture with nervous briskness, she said, "That looks perfect. I'm always partial to a man who makes a good martini."

I stopped, unable, I guess, to conceal my surprise. Her words, though innocent enough, conveyed an intimacy that seemed to say she found me attractive. It was the first time in my life I had drawn such an inference. A pocket of warmth formed inside me, and when I presented the drink, it was with a steady hand and a sudden feeling of command.

I lifted my glass and, testing her, said, "Here's to Charles Walter."

She clinked her glass against mine, gave her head a charming little shake, and answered, "Oh no. Here's to Lambert Post."

And damned if I didn't become the center of the conversation! Oh, we covered Charles, and she seemed interested enough in his comings and goings, mildly impressed by my description of him as a handsome man of the world. But he soon slipped away as she began to probe the life and times of Lambert Post. I felt like the one-eyed man who had always been shunned until one day he was miraculously transported to a world of the blind, and there he was king. Diane's attentiveness and the martinis (which she began to make) combined to release my inhibitions and I confided things to her that I had never told anyone except Charles. All my loneliness, all my frustrated yearnings came pouring out on a wave of gin and sympathy. In defense I can only say that I avoided any tone of self-pity, recounting everything with an air of wry humor.

"But that's all in the past," she said softly. "Now you're a mature and I'd guess a successful man. And you have a wonderful friend in Charles Walter."

The name abruptly reminded me that I was part of a hoax—a Harvard man, scion of wealthy though alienated parents, and (I was prepared with this) something of a financial prodigy.

"Yes," I said, reluctant now to play the role, "Charles has helped me in lots of ways." I was surprised to find that the mention of his name depressed me and I tried to change the subject. "Now let's talk about you. What do you do, Diane?"

She laughed and said candidly, "I'm a parasite. At the moment I'm living on alimony." She made another martini—she had been merely sipping hers—saying, "More important, what do *you* do, Lambert?"

So there was no escape. "I'm an investment analyst. I advise Charles on his holdings." Woodenly I gave my recitation on copper mines, shipping corporations, textile mills, and so on.

Oddly, she didn't seem overly impressed. I was relieved when, swaying closer to me, she said, "I gather you're not married, Lambert. But is there someone special?"

The way she looked at me with those appealing brown eyes gave me the courage to say, with ginned-up nonchalance, "Not until now, Diane."

I could feel her breath warm my left cheek as she gave a satisfied sigh. "You mean you find me attractive?" The question was asked very seriously.

I became equally serious. "More so, Diane, than anyone I've ever met."

"Ah, Lambert."

And suddenly she was wrapped in my arms. We didn't kiss, but what happened then was vastly better. She pressed her mouth against my throat, curved into me and gently stroked my thigh. I slid my hand down—it all seemed so natural—and cupped her breast, then caressed it with my open palm. Her hand lifted from my thigh and for a moment I thought I had gone too far too fast. I held my breath, feeling a paralysis in my chest. Then her hand reached up to the neck of her dress and unfastened the top two buttons. Exhaling slowly, I slipped my hand inside and grasped firm, rounded flesh. She gave a little squeak of pleasure. Then she drew away and looked mistily into my eyes.

"I think it's time you saw the bedroom," she said.

She lit a cigarette—"for my nerves"—and requested that I go on ahead. "I'll join you when you're . . . the way you should be." Her smile promised erotic adventures I had only dreamed about.

Just as the living room was all white, the bedroom was all black. In the feeble glow of a night-light dimmed by a black shade I sat on a black satin chair and fumbled mindlessly with my shoelaces, dragged my pants off inside-out, fretted my tie, finally managed to denude myself and stand raw and quaking beside the big bed, my back to the door. I heard a little click. I reached down to pull back the black satin spread. The blow that struck the back of my neck felt as if it had been fired from a howitzer.

I reeled forward but never landed. Arms with the bulk and strength of fire hoses locked inside my elbows, yanked them behind me. Pain shot through my head in all directions. My chin dropped to my chest, my body slumped, but the arms that ruled me staggered me around to face the door. It opened and Diane Summers strolled languidly in, still smoking the cigarette. My captor, whoever he was, had come from the bathroom.

His voice, just above my ear, was harsh and grating. "The dumb bastard is all ready to play house," he said.

From the feel, sound, and smell of him I had an image of a barrel-chested, jowly creature who smoked fat cigars.

Diane stood in front of me, feet wide apart, expression a mixture of triumph and contempt. She flashed back her arm and cracked me across the mouth.

"Maybe today you'll learn something, Lambert Post," she said viciously. "First, you ought to know how I found out about your evil little game. I'd suspected something funny when Charles Walter first called me, but I figured it was all just good, clean fun. Then when he called the second time, this morning, and tried to fob off Lambert Post on me, I got real suspicious. So I asked Charles Walter if I could call him back. He gave me the number and I called Information and got an emergency listing on it. The New York *Journal!* I called the *Journal*'s regular number, went through the switchboard, and got some dame who told me who Charles Walter really was, and who Lambert Post really was. Big mining operator, big in textiles and shipping, big financier. My ass, Lambert! A goddamned classified ad peddler! Thinking you could set me up for an easy lay. A girl who must be a roundheel, a pushover, simply because I'd gotten my divorce papers. Oh, Lambert Post, you are a poor, sad, stupid son of a bitch!"

"That's enough talk, baby," the man said. "Now start the lesson."

She stoked the cigarette, took a step forward, and ground it out slowly in my navel. I let out a shriek. The arms behind me jerked, nearly cracking my shoulder blades. I clamped my mouth shut.

Then Diane Summers thrust out ten long red nails and began me-thodically to rip my chest and belly to ribbons. I tried not to cry out but could not control the whimpering. Looking glassily down my body, I saw her fingers slice crimson rivers into my flesh, the rivers joining into a sea of rushing blood. I was about to faint and I sagged bonelessly forward.

"A towel," the man grunted.

She darted into the bathroom and brought back a huge maroon bath towel. The man relaxed his grip on my elbows enough to allow my hands to move forward, clutch the towel, and press it against my body. He turned me to face the black chair heaped with my clothing and said, "Now get dressed. But don't turn around."

I dropped the soaked towel and dressed silently, feeling the blood ooze through my shirt and shorts. I was too agonized, too bewildered, too frightened even to feel hate. My only thought was to get out of there. I was jamming my tie into my jacket pocket when something that felt like a knuckled club smashed into my kidney. I went down like a malleted animal. Big heavy shoes began to kick me—my back, my belly, my groin. *"Oh God, oh God. Charles, Charles, please help me."* I heard Diane Summers laugh. Then I blacked out.

I came to, body raging with pain, lying on a concrete walkway and wedged against the side of the building. Apparently I had been brought down to the basement in the elevator and hurled into the service alley. I groaned to a sitting position and sat there for a minute sucking in air. With each gasp I could feel the sticky blood on my shirt pull at my skin. I eased out my wallet and saw that the eight dollars I had brought were still there. So there had been no thought of robbery, only the infliction of pain.

I labored to my feet and, bent almost double, limped to the street and turned toward Central Park. Reaching Fifth Avenue, I managed to flag down a cab. As I flopped down on the seat, I had the strange feeling that I had relived a part of my life.

The bed creaked as I gingerly pulled my knees up into a fetal position, wishing I had never left the womb.

"Charles?"

"Yes, Lambert."

"Do you realize how horrible it was? Do you realize that they damned near killed me?"

"Yes, I realize it."

"But nothing can be done. They know our names, where we work, what we do. If we punished them, they'd tell the police where to go."

"I know. But they *must* be punished."

"Diane most of all. She led me on, humiliated me, then butchered me. Oh God, the blood."

"Steady, Lambert. It has to be thought out coldly, dispassionately. I got you into this. Let it be my problem."

"How can women be so cruel, so merciless?"

"Because they really hate men, Lambert. They want to destroy them. They'd castrate you if they thought they could get away with it."

"Even Henrietta Boardman?"

"I'm not sure. Maybe she's an exception."

"I know she couldn't be like Diane Summers. Charles, Charles, she's got to pay for this. She's got to suffer. Right now nothing else matters."

"You're forgetting something, Lambert. The girl at the hotel— Jennifer Hartwick."

"Yes, she's got to suffer too."

"Go ahead and hate, Lambert. You have every right to. Pretend you have Diane alone in this room, the door locked, the window closed and bolted. You rip her clothes off and knock her to her knees. She's begging for mercy, clutching at your ankles. But you kick her flat on her back. She lies there sobbing and . . ."

"Charles! Don't . . . please . . ."

". . . and you go into the kitchen and get that pointed sharp knife with the black handle. You look at her lying naked on the floor, her eyes terrified. You spit on her. Then you drop down on one knee and you flick her breasts with the knife. She cries out, but she's too frightened to move. She's afraid you'll stab her with the knife."

"Oh God. Look at me. It's like a knife. I can't stand it, Charles."

"Just let me handle it, Lambert. I'll do it. I'll do it all."

I knew then what I had scarcely suspected in the beginning. I wanted Charles Walter to possess me completely.

CHARLES WALTER

VI

FROM THE DAY I sat down at my desk and announced that I was Charles Walter, I think I was fated to become Lambert Post's supreme alter ego. He needed me the way a stray wretch of a dog needs a firm, protective master. And that's what he got. I was the only one in Lambert Post's whole miserable life who ever felt true pity for him, who sympathized with his grievances and acted to redress them. He, in turn, offered me a slavish adulation that strengthened my righteousness. In a world that needs both the heart to discern evil and the fist to smash it, we were the perfect pair: Lambert the outraged voice of torment, and I the militant instrument of vengeance.

Considering my miscalculations with Jennifer Hartwick and Diane Summers, you may think that instead of exalting me, Lambert should have held me in contempt. If so, you would be overlooking what Lambert knew to be my true purpose: to expose their callous greed and later to humble them. Both had exceeded my worst expectations, Jennifer with her foul abusiveness, Diane with her bestial brutality.

Their punishment, I decided, must be far more severe than anything I had anticipated. I would start with the first offender, Jennifer Hartwick.

Three days later the plan was set. In preparation, I had read a number of issues of *Variety,* perused the business notes in the *Times,* called a West Side Hotel, and poured about a hundred nickels into a gray wool sock. Then I telephoned Jennifer Hartwick, raising the pitch of my voice and giving it a mushy English accent. I introduced myself as Winston Robey, chief assistant to the well-known theatrical producer Lawrence Langley.

"Perhaps you have heard, Miss Hartwick, that Mr. Langley is casting a new play scheduled for late fall opening."

"Why, yes-s-s, Mr. Robey. I read about it in the trades."

"Perhaps you also know that the ingenue lead has yet to be selected."

"Well, no. But—"

"Mr. Langley has seen you in several performances, Miss Hartwick. Something you did with Katharine Cornell particularly impressed him. He has instructed me to ask if you would be interested in auditioning for the role."

"Why, Mr. Robey, how flattering. I'd be—"

"Perhaps you would like to think about it."

"No. No. Oh, ordinarily I'd ask you to speak to my agent. But unfortunately he died just recently. So I'll just have to make my own decisions. And the decision is yes, I'll be delighted."

"Very good. Now, a point you may not be aware of: For all his successes, Mr. Langley is having some difficulty raising the necessary production money. The play involves a large cast and a number of expensive sets. Therefore—really, I *detest* having to make this request—it will be necessary for you to audition before some gentlemen who are potential financial backers."

"Ah yes, the angels. That really isn't too unusual."

"It is for a man of Mr. Langley's reputation. But, as I say, it will be an extremely costly production."

As Winston Robey, I then made an appointment to meet Jennifer Hartwick at the Park Central Hotel at nine o'clock that evening. I regretted that it must be so late but it was the only time convenient for everyone. I suggested meeting her in the lobby as the suite to be used had not been decided on. Now, how would I recognize her, knowing, of course, that she was very beautiful? She gave a pleased laugh, mentioned her taffy-blond bangs and, after a moment's thought, said she would be wearing a green silk mandarin coat and matching pillbox hat. Excellent.

Shortly before six that evening I entered the Park Central Hotel and went immediately to a mezzanine ballroom packed to overflowing with members of the American Association of Garment Manufacturers. Before speaking to Jennifer Hartwick, I had telephoned the program chairman and learned that the meeting, the first in a three-day convention, would adjourn promptly at six. It went on until six-fifteen, and by then I had overheard the numbers of five suites that were set up for post-meeting conviviality. Surrounded by weary, thirsty members, I filed out of the ballroom and went downstairs to the bar. I nursed a drink until seven, then left to make a tour of the convention cocktail circuit. Each of the suites I visited was thronged with euphoric drinkers who accepted me as a fellow garment executive seeking diversion. By the time I had inspected all five gatherings, I had mentally graded them on the basis of hilarity and probable longevity. One in particular stood out as being both the most raucously gay and the most likely to survive well into the night. The lobby of Room 617 opened on a huge living room with two portable bars and was flanked by hallways leading to bedrooms. In the corridor, I checked the number of the bedroom immediately off to the left. Room 615. I tried the doorknob: It was unlocked. Entering, I found the room empty, lamps lit. I snapped the switch on the wall, throwing the room into darkness. I switched the lamps back on and left. Luck was blessing me.

At a few minutes to nine I was downstairs leaning against a side wall of the lobby, face half-hidden behind the *World-Telegram,* when Jennifer Hartwick whirled through the revolving door. She paused for a moment to smooth her green mandarin coat, adjust her pillbox hat, and fluff her bangs. Then she walked to a lounge chair facing the entrance and sat down, crossing her legs. I sauntered across the crowded lobby behind her, closeted myself in a pay telephone booth, dialed the Park Central Hotel, and asked to have Jennifer Hartwick paged.

"Ah, Miss Hartwick. This is Winston Robey. I do apologize most humbly, but I have been unavoidably detained. I should be along in about twenty minutes."

"Don't give it a thought, Mr. Robey. I'm quite comfortable."

"How good of you. But, Miss Hartwick, there is really no reason to wait in that stuffy lobby. I have a vision of hordes of people milling about."

"Yes, it *is* crowded. But—"

"I suggest you go on up to the suite. I now have the number. Let me see. Yes. Room 615. You will probably find it unoccu-

pied, but it adjoins the room—a large living room—where the audition will be held. The gentlemen we are interested in, and whom
we hope to interest, should be congregated there now. Mr. Langley has arranged to relax them with proper libations." I gave a
little chuckle.

Jennifer Hartwick laughed understandingly. "I may need one or
two myself. I must admit I'm a little nervous. I forgot even to ask
you what you want me to do. Is it a scene from the new play? I'd
have liked to have been a bit more prepared."

"I will have the play manuscript with me. You may either do a
scene from it or anything else you choose. The main thing is for
these gentlemen to see you, experience the charm that Mr. Langley says you so radiantly project. We'll have a chance to discuss it
before joining the others."

"Fine, Mr. Robey. I believe I *will* go up. Room 615. Oh, I
don't have a key."

"Stupid of me. You wait there for a few minutes, then go up. I
will call one of the gentlemen in the adjoining room and see that
Room 615 is unlocked."

I stayed in the phone booth, door half-closed, until I saw Jennifer Hartwick leave the house phone across the lobby and hurry
into the bar. I guessed that the drink she would order would be
stiff and straight. So much the better. Alcohol on her breath would
fit the situation neatly. I strode to the elevator. Going up, I had to
admit to a small surge of panic, like a cold breath blowing inside
me. But I controlled it with the reminder of the venom spewed on
Lambert Post by Jennifer Hartwick at her drunken party.

By the time I reached Room 615, I was icily calm. I opened the
door, stepped inside, and closed it quietly. Moving briskly down
the short hall to my right, I turned the lock on the connecting door,
pausing briefly to listen to the confusion of happy voices on the
other side. I returned to the entrance door and snapped out the
lights. Pasted against the wall in the darkness, I waited.

Five minutes passed. Ten. Then there was a timid knock on the
door. I gripped the warm material in my right hand. The door
swung slowly open, admitting a wedge of light. Jennifer Hartwick
stepped into it, hesitated, turned, raised her hand to search for the
light switch. Coming silently from behind the door, arm fully ex-

tended, I cracked her below the right ear with the bunched weight of a hundred nickels knotted into the toe of the gray wool sock. She went down as if she'd been chopped off at the knees. She made no sound and she did not stir.

I closed the door, locked it, and switched on the lamps. For almost a minute I stood looking down at Jennifer Hartwick's prone figure, legs splayed, thighs exposed, pillbox hat dangling from a lock of taffy hair. I knelt down and examined the skin beneath her ear. A lump resembling a cracked lavender Easter egg had risen just below the mastoid area. There was no sound of breathing. I rolled her on her back, listened to her heart, felt the pulse in her neck. She was alive.

I dragged her to the bed, stretched her across it and, working quickly, stripped her of everything except her sheer silk stockings. My eyes toured her limp, rounded flesh and I found I was breathing shallowly. Propping her up, I yanked off the bedspread, turned back the blankets, and dropped her on the sheet. Then I did the thing that from the beginning had teased at my mind but had not been consciously planned. I raped her.

It took only a few minutes. And less than that to rearrange myself, unlock both doors, slip out to the corridor, and catch a descending elevator.

In the lobby I went to one of the house phones and called Room 617, scene of the revelers. A slurred voice answered. I said, "I don't know whether or not you know it, but there's a prostitute passed out in one of your bedrooms—Room 615." I hung up, flashed the operator, asked for the desk, and said to the clerk, "Something wild is happening in Room 615. There's a drunken whore up there and she sounds like she's giving the boys a bad time."

Then I threaded my way through the lobby, pushed through the revolving door, and headed for the subway.

"Charles, I'm scared."
"There's nothing to be scared about."
"But what if she *dies?*"
"She won't die."
"But what if she does?"

"She *won't*."

"But . . ."

"She'll have deserved it. Think what she did to you."

"Yes, I'm thinking."

"Now go to sleep."

"I'll try. . . . Charles?"

"Yes?"

"She *did* deserve it."

VII

Shouted the *Daily News:* ACTRESS FOUND NUDE, UNCONSCIOUS, IN HOTEL PARTY ROOM.

Leered the *Mirror:* PARTY GIRL IN COMA, SANS GARMENTS AT GARMENT SPREE.

Sitting at my desk, I compared the two stories, stretched across the bottom of page three in both newspapers. The photo of Jennifer Hartwick in the *News* was an ethereal-looking studio portrait, no doubt swiped from her hotel room. The *Mirror* featured a publicity shot of her in white tights.

The reports were identical in substance. Jennifer Hartwick, an unemployed minor actress, had been found lying naked and unconscious in a bedroom of a lavish suite at the Park Central Hotel. A house detective, summoned by a tip from an anonymous caller, had burst into the room to find the inert body surrounded by stunned members of the American Association of Garment Manufacturers who had been enjoying a cocktail party in the adjoining living room. The victim, recently widowed, had sustained a murderous blow to the head by an unknown instrument and, still unconscious, had been rushed to the emergency ward of Bellevue Hospital, where her condition was listed as serious. Preliminary examination established that either immediately before or immediately after the attack she had engaged in sexual intercourse. (*She* had engaged? Ha!) Three men representing a leading Seventh Avenue garment house had reserved the suite for the entertainment of prospective buyers. They, too, had allegedly been alerted to investigate the bedroom by a phone call from an unidentified man. Their names were being withheld pending further inquiry and interrogation of the victim when she regained consciousness.

Police speculated that the "tipoff man" might have been a convention delegate who had arranged an assignation with the girl, argued with her to the point of physical violence, perhaps over money, and then, fearing she was dying, had placed the warning calls.

To any reader the inference would be clear: Jennifer Hartwick was a hooker who preyed on convivial conventioneers. That should keep her from appearing on any legitimate stage for a long, long time.

There was only one danger. She was bound to remember Lambert Post by name and recall how her insults had driven him from her suite. Would she put the finger on him to the police, leading to an investigation that would also include the name Charles Walter? It seemed unlikely for a number of reasons. One, Lambert Post was too obviously a timid soul to be considered a candidate for mayhem. Two, it should strike her as absurd that her brief verbal attack could incite such calculated and Draconian retribution. Three, an admission that she had encouraged the advances of a man she had never met (Charles Walter) and had invited to her home another who was even more of a stranger would simply reinforce the suspicion that she was a prostitute. Finally, a girl who traveled in such fast company as Jennifer Hartwick did was almost certain to have provoked many men with much more logical motives for revenge. It seemed a safe bet that Jennifer Hartwick would not even think twice about Lambert Post.

My buzzer rang. I flipped the lever and Jean Hooper's voice rasped, "Look, glamor voice, we pay you to solicit ads, not read the newspapers. It's ten minutes to ten and you haven't even cleared your throat."

"Just checking my leads, Jean."

"In the *News* and the *Mirror?* Need I tell you they don't carry furnished room ads? No, you've been drooling over that naked call girl story. I stood behind you and saw it." Her tone became heavily sarcastic. "One of your more respectable friends, I imagine."

My stomach twitched. "I just wanted to see if you two were related."

I heard her breath suck in. "Why you insolent—"

"Easy, boss. I'll start my motor running."

"You *do* that. And *keep* it running!"

Henrietta Boardman shot me a sidelong glance. "Jean bawling you out?"

"It seems I should start talking to little old landladies."

"She's got a nerve. You've been selling more ads than anyone in the place."

"That, Miss Boardman, is appreciated. Tell it to Jean Hooper."

"Oh, she knows. That's the only reason she lets you get away with being so fresh."

"Me fresh? I'm really very gentle, a softie. You know that."

She considered me with lidded eyes, big and unblinking behind the thick lenses. Her tongue circled her full lips, leaving them glistening. "Yes, that could be true," she said with sudden gravity and turned away.

For a minute I stared at the high color of her skin, the moist confection of her lips, the tautly profiled breasts under the pink rayon blouse. She was really a damned desirable woman.

She looked straight ahead and said, "Now, Mr. Walter, you'd better get your mind on business."

It amazed me to think that perhaps Lambert Post was more her type.

At noon I went up to the city room and got an early edition of the *Journal*. The story I wanted was where I might have expected it, below the fold on page one. (The city editor, Sam Stein, was famous for his alliteratively stated editorial policy: "People are interested in just three things—crime, cash, and cunt. That's what I want on the front page every day.") The headline read, HOTEL PARTY GIRL TALKS.

I didn't read it until I was seated in Friedman's having a hot pastrami on rye and a bottle of beer. Until then I could feel Lambert Post's fears building up inside me, hear his voice sawing away at my guts: "I'm scared, Charles, scared." The fears receded as I read. Jennifer Hartwick had regained consciousness early that morning and had been interrogated by police at Bellevue. She had babbled out as much as she knew of the circumstances: the phone call from a Winston Robey, alleged emissary of Lawrence Langley (Langley said he had never heard of Robey or of the girl); the second call, at the Park Central, suggesting she go upstairs; the ambush in Room 615, with no opportunity even to glimpse her assailant. Did she know anyone who would wish to harm her? No. Did she know or meet anyone attending the garment convention? She bristled; certainly not. Why hadn't she checked back to verify Winston Robey's credentials? She was too excited to think about it. Had she been robbed? No. Didn't she think it incredible that anyone would go to such elaborate lengths to commit rape? She supposed so; she didn't know she'd been raped. Where was her husband? Dead. How was she able to support a suite at the Court Hotel? With her husband's insurance. Five thousand dollars (they'd checked it)—was that enough to warrant a *suite,* particularly when she was unemployed? Please, she wanted to be left alone; the concussion had left her with a blinding headache. A doctor intervened and the police left in a cloud of skepticism. They would, I was sure, make a few more routine inquiries and then quit. Why break your ass over someone who was apparently just another cheap hustler? The reports would be filed away in a folder stamped UNSOLVED.

Now for Diane Summers.

She was obviously a lot tougher assignment than Jennifer Hartwick. So brutally had Diane Summers and her anonymous goon companion abused Lambert Post, he would inevitably be the chief suspect should she be harmed. Moreover, she had already traced both Lambert Post and Charles Walter to the *Journal,* assuring that reprisal by her or the authorities would be a speedy certainty. The man who had pinioned and then beaten Lambert was doubtless her lover. That made two to contend with. It was the biggest challenge I had yet faced. That intrigued me—the greater the odds, the more exhilarating the triumph.

In searching for a solution I tried to keep Lambert Post out of it. I could not permit his fear of consequences to curtail what should be a terrible vengeance. Only once did he get through to me: late at night, in a voice that whimpered, "Give it up, Charles. It's too tough, too risky." I was annoyed at his weakness; then indignant as I evoked images of long fingernails ribboning his flesh; finally righteous as I sentenced her explicitly to cringing abasement. Lambert's fears were overwhelmed. From that moment on, I alone controlled the plan.

VIII

DESPITE THE SULLIVAN LAW, it was easy for anyone to get a gun in the thirties. You simply strolled the Lower West Side, looked overhead for three brass balls, handed the pawnbroker your money, and walked out with a nice shiny weapon. Mine was a .25-caliber Colt, small enough to drop into my jacket pocket without my looking like a bodyguard for Lucky Luciano.

A knife, of course, could be picked up at any hardware store. I chose one with a six-inch pointed blade, sharp enough to shave with. I slipped that under my belt.

By then—four days after the Jennifer Hartwick settlement—I had learned what I needed to know about Diane Summers and her boyfriend. For two days I had played sick and tailed them. She was not, as she had told Lambert Post, living on alimony alone, but was a manicurist in a subway-arcade barbershop beneath Chambers Street, working from 10:00 A.M. to 6:00 P.M. He was a nine-to-five typesetter in a big printing plant on Third Avenue near Eighty-first. Apparently they weren't married—only her name, by her former husband, was on the mailbox—but they seemed to be living together full-time.

While they were at work, I made a spot inspection of the premises—lobby, elevator, hallway, stairs, basement. The basement, lit by a few bare, low-watt bulbs, opened on a narrow concrete service walk running out to the front sidewalk. That meant, of course, that deliveries were made by way of the basement. And that could mean dumbwaiters; lots of apartments had them.

Sure enough. They were spaced along the basement walls, the same drab green paint flaking from the doors. (I had thought they were lockers.) I found the one that connected with 4C, Diane

Summers's apartment, opened the door, and stared into a black void. Ducking my head into the shaft, I looked up and saw the bottom of the cage a couple of floors above. I straightened, tugged at one of the thick ropes, and lowered the dumbwaiter until it rested in front of me on the shaft's cement floor. It was the usual three-sided boxlike cubicle, solidly built of thick wood, varnish worn off the inner surface. Big enough, I wondered, for a man to squat down inside, reach out to the rope, and hoist himself to the floors above? I got in and tested it for a few feet. Yes.

After that, the plan seemed a cinch.

I was standing in a doorway across the street when he got home at five-thirty. He looked something like Alan Hale, the movie heavy—big shoulders and belly, ruddy face, thick brown wavy hair. The humidity had wilted his striped seersucker suit, and as he trudged through the door and checked the mailbox, he whipped out a handkerchief and mopped sweat from under his tieless open collar. I guessed he wanted nothing more than to get into a cool shower and a cold drink. He disappeared inside the dark lobby. I waited. He should be alone up there in 4C until at least six-thirty. An hour. Then Diane Summers would arrive.

Just before six I figured he had got himself comfortable. I crossed the street, sauntered down the service walk, squeaked open the door to the basement, and sidled through. I paced around in the yellowish light and made sure I was alone. Reaching the dumbwaiter door, I grasped the cold handle and eased it open. The wooden cage stood inside, as I had left it. I hiked myself up backwards and squeezed myself into a bent sitting position, my chin almost between my knees. The knife under my belt pricked my groin, so I switched it to my left jacket pocket. From the other I slid out the gun and tucked it where my right thigh met my abdomen. Anchoring my heels, I reached out and to the side, grabbed the jittering rope as high up as possible, and pulled down with all my strength. The cage began to ascend. Hand over hand, groaning and leaking sweat, I tugged myself up that black shaft until I reached the door, framed by cracks of light, that should open on Diane Summers's kitchen. I stopped and listened. No sound came from the other side. I wound the rope around my left wrist and pushed my other hand silently and steadily against the door. It did not budge. Locked.

I was disappointed but not surprised. Lots of people left their dumbwaiter doors unlocked, but more didn't. I would just have to do it the hard way.

I descended slowly, feeling the prickly rope burn my palms. Getting out, I stretched until I creaked, then looked at my watch. Ten past six. I would have to hurry to beat Diane Summers. I examined the panel of buzzers next to the door and pressed 4C. In about ten seconds a door above rasped open and a deep voice called down, "Yeah?"

I cupped my hand to my mouth and shouted in a train announcer's voice, *"Groceries!"*

"Groceries? I didn't— Oh. Okay. Send 'em up."

This time I had guessed right. He thought Diane Summers had called in the order.

I crawled back into the wooden cage.

Going up took longer this time because the rope kept slipping through my damp palms. Halfway there I heard a door in the shaft above make a sticking sound. Apparently he had closed it after speaking and had opened it again. I stopped, hands knuckled on the rope. Hopefully, the man would get bored with waiting and turn away into the kitchen. When I thought I heard the sound of shuffling feet, I resumed pulling on the rope. Suddenly a slice of light cut across my face. I was hanging suspended in front of Diane Summers's dumbwaiter door, open about three inches. I gripped the gun, pointing it straight ahead at chest level, as I twisted the rope around my left hand. Slowly I placed the muzzle of the gun against the door and gave it a little push. The door swung half-open. There was no one in sight. I hiked myself forward, suppressing a grunt, and saw the man standing at the sink. He was plucking ice cubes out of a tray. Throwing out my feet and snapping my back into an arch, I leaped to the floor, releasing the rope, hearing it slap back against the shaft. The man whirled around.

He was a ludicrous sight. Color drained from his beefy cheeks. His eyes bulged, like Stepin Fetchit's in a midnight graveyard. His mouth gaped as if the hinged bones of his jaw had snapped. He

stood like a cardboard cutout in his light, blue-checked robe, bare-
footed, one ham hand curled around two dripping ice cubes.

His eyes searched my face and all his features began to congeal.
He said, "Well, I'll be—"

His eyes dropped to the gun.

"—goddamned," he finished in a thin whisper.

The ice cubes clattered to the floor.

"Finish making your drink," I said.

He cocked his big, wavy-haired head as though he had not quite
caught the words. But he turned—slowly, like a man under water
—and picked up two more ice cubes and dropped them into a glass
slugged with gin. He faced around, again eyeing the gun, expression bemused.

I jerked the gun toward a big bottle of mixer standing beside
the sink. "You haven't finished."

He glanced at the bottle, then down at the straight gin. "I've finished," he said, letting out a breath.

"Fine. Then we'll go into the bedroom."

The same black bedroom where Lambert Post had been shred-
ded and beaten senseless. I sat him on a black chair, backed away,
and dropped down on the black bedspread. Only the dim light of
the summer evening lit the room. He gulped half the drink, squeez-
ing his eyelids shut and clenching his lips to keep it down. He
looked up with darting eyes.

"Money," he croaked. "If it's money . . ."

"It's not money."

"You'll never get away with this," he said hopefully.

"You sound like a Monogram movie. You're the one who's not
getting away with half-killing Lambert Post."

He massaged his heavy cheeks, stretched his jaws, combed his
hair with his fingers. He started to speak again, but the words stuck.

I reached to the night table and switched on a small radio.

The clipped accents of H. V. Kaltenborn rushed out: ". . . in-
cidents in the Sudetenland increasing in both frequency and
violence. Herr Hitler has served notice on both Prime Minister
Chamberlain and Premier Daladier that he will no longer tolerate
. . ." I flipped to another station and got a recording of Russ
Columbo singing "Prisoner of Love."

My watch said almost six-thirty. I twirled the radio knob, turning up the volume full blast. I roved my eyes over the three windows. They were all shut tight, probably to keep in the cool air of the morning. I got up, swerved around him, and closed the bedroom door. He downed the rest of his drink and set the glass shakily on the carpet. The glass toppled over. He ignored it, placing his hands flat on the chair arms and following my movements with a peripheral, terrified stare.

Some deep-throated girl singer was now rendering—shouting—"Old Man Mose." The huge, strident sound vibrated the radio, shattered off the walls. I stepped up close to the man's right side and pushed the muzzle of the nickel-plated gun against his porcine cheek. He blinked but looked straight ahead.

"What's your name?" I asked.

"Jesus Christ, fella—"

"You're lying. You can't be Jesus Christ. Unless you've shaved. Unless you've taken on a lot of lard."

"Ed Cranston," he said. And again, in a treble voice: "Jesus . . . *Christ!*"

His eyes rolled toward me, seeming to circle around me as if he was commanding his sight to pierce the bedroom door, travel the hall, penetrate the front door, in a desperate hope that Diane Summers would be standing there, key about to enter the lock. I could smell animal fear seeping through his perfumed lotion.

"Old Man Mose kicked the bucket . . ."

"We'll miss you, Ed," I said.

". . . buck, buck, BUCKET!"

His head turned half around. His lips hung open like a wound. He just couldn't believe it.

I squeezed the trigger and blew half his head off.

"Old Man Mose is dead!"

I crossed to the radio, turned it off, and wiped the knob with my handkerchief. I went to the bedroom door, opened it, and strode through the apartment, inspecting the kitchen, living room, and closets. A precaution—Diane Summers might have entered while the radio was blaring. I returned to the bedroom and gazed at what was left of Ed Cranston.

His position was pretty much as it had been when I first pressed
the gun to his cheek. Sagging a bit, perhaps, and his blue-checkered
robe was open to expose a meaty chest matted with hair. His left
hand was still on the chair arm, the other hung limply at his side.
His head was thrown back and from the line of his sideburn forward there was no face, only a thick current of scarlet pulp. I
walked around him to glance at the side of the bureau and at the
carpet. They looked like they had been splattered with hog en-
trails.

I came back and stood in front of Ed Cranston. I wiped the gun
clean with my handkerchief, kneeled down, and placed it gently in
the hand, still warm, that drooped at his side. I worked his fingers
around the grip, then released them. The gun lurched away but the
grip still touched his fingertips. I stood up.

The metallic sound of a key fitting a lock spun me around. I
skipped across the room and into the bathroom, leaving the door
slightly ajar.

The front door slammed shut. One, two, three seconds of silence. Then: "Ed?" No concern in her voice. High heels tapping
in the kitchen. The rattle of the ice tray. "Ed, you left the ice out.
It's half-melted." Silence. "Ed, are you back there?" Slight annoy-
ance. Feet slapping down hard on the hall carpet. "Ed, why don't
you answer? . . . *Ed! Oh my God. Ed!*"

An enormous wail, rising to a prolonged, climactic caw. Snap of
light switch. Trembling moans, as if muted by her hand. Frantic
whisper: "Oh God, Ed, why, *why!*" She had seen the gun. Then a
silence so tangible it seemed like the air had jelled. She was looking for a note. Five seconds. Feet slithered toward the bathroom
door.

I grabbed her by the left elbow as she came in. She gasped and
her right hand shot up in reflex and formed a fist. It froze there as
she caught the glint of metal and felt the blade crease her throat.

"One little sound, Diane Summers, and I slice it."

Her brown eyes turned chocolate, the pupils expanding as
though struck by darkness. Her body suddenly seemed starched.
Slowly the raised fist opened to reveal the long, lethal fingernails,
red as the blood of Lambert Post. She brought the hand carefully
down to her side. She didn't even try to speak. I yanked her

around and with the point of the knife prodded her into the bedroom.

She moved her tall body as if balancing a book on her head, chin high, gaze avoiding the mess in the chair. I pushed her to a seat on the bed and stood over her, the knife about a foot from her white throat. Under the shaded overhead light and against the background of black bedspread, her face was as pale and listless as an undernourished child's. Apparently she was in shock. But her eyes never left the knife.

"Charles Walter," I said quietly. "Obedient servant of Lambert Post."

She seemed not to hear.

"You do *remember* that beautiful evening?"

Her head nodded woodenly. Then she gave it a shake, bouncing the chestnut hair. "You murdered Ed. Isn't that enough?" Her tone neither accused nor pleaded.

"You've got it wrong. Ed killed himself."

Her eyes came up to mine and I saw a glimmer of comprehension.

"You're crazy," she said.

I flicked the knife just below her throat and severed the silk ribbons clasping the oval collar of her yellow manicurist's blouse. The collar parted and dropped, exposing the upper roundness of her breasts.

She recoiled. "Don't, don't . . . *please, please, please* . . ."

I flicked the knife again and slashed her cheek.

She opened her mouth to scream. But it never got out of her lungs. It was canceled by the six-inch blade plunging into the hollow of her throat between the collar bones.

I stripped her. Then, as methodically as she had employed her fingernails on Lambert Post, I went to work with the knife.

When I finished, I wiped the handle clean and pressed it into the stiffening hand of Ed Cranston, disturbing the gun only slightly. I withdrew the knife and dropped it on the floor between Ed Cranston and the thing on the bed that had been Diane Summers. I went into the kitchen, did some more wiping, and lowered the dumbwaiter.

I left by the front door.

IX

EVEN *The New York Times* front-paged the story:

TWO DEAD IN SUSPECTED MURDER-SUICIDE

The bodies of a man and a woman, his face shot away, she mutilated almost beyond recognition, were found in the bedroom of an East 62nd Street apartment early last night, victims of what police believe was a murder and suicide.

The man was Edward Cranston, 43, a widower, employed as a printer. The woman was Diane Summers, 28, a manicurist recently divorced. Both resided at the same address.

In reconstructing the tragedy, police said the two apparently had engaged in a violent argument, terminated when Cranston seized a six-inch kitchen knife and stabbed the Summers woman to death, inflicting multiple wounds. He then, it is surmised, sat down in a chair, pressed a .25-caliber Colt revolver to his cheek, and shot himself. Cranston's fingerprints were found on both weapons.

Police were summoned to the scene by a telephone call from a neighbor reporting that he had been alarmed by the blasting of a radio, punctuated, he thought, by the crack of a gun. The neighbor said that on two previous occasions he had been disturbed by the sound of bitter argument and had called once to protest.

The condition of the corpses and the bedroom was described by police with horror. Homicide officer George Pittman stated, "I've never seen anything like it. I thought I was in a slaughterhouse."

The rest of the story failed to become more specific.

The tabloid *Mirror* headlined the story with less restraint. Black type jammed the entire front page: MAN BUTCHERS GIRL, KILLS SELF. The basic facts, however, were the same as in the *Times,* though more luridly expressed.

I felt like I was holding a pat poker hand, each card supporting the other: the fifteen-year difference in their ages, implying middle-aged jealousy; their illicit relationship; Cranston's finger-prints on the weapons; the testimony of the provoked neighbor, indicating a history of fierce quarrels.

There was only one jarring note. Both stories ended by saying that the police were checking out the gun. But I was certain they would never trace it to me. The pawnbroker had neither asked any questions nor required my signature. This time, I thought, the po-lice had a case they could close out as solved.

When I had returned to the apartment the previous night, I had suppressed any comments from Lambert Post. My mood had been exultant and I refused to risk having it spoiled by sniveling fears. I put him off with, "You've been avenged, Lambert. Avenged. Be satisfied with that for now." Soon he withdrew into a sort of wait-ing silence and I was alone with my thoughts, replaying again and again the scene in Diane Summers's apartment.

However, with the story blasting from the press, and the pass-ing of the day, there was no restraining Lambert. Surprisingly his attitude, though negative, was calm, almost judicial. Perhaps the experience with Jennifer Hartwick had convinced him that ene-mies must be disposed of with overwhelming force. It was a truth that had been demonstrated admirably by Adolf Hitler.

Still, he felt the need to challenge: "Was it necessary to *kill* them, Charles?"

I was stretched out on the studio couch, sipping a gin. "Abso-lutely. They knew who you were, knew about Charles Walter, knew where to find you. If I'd settled for merely injuring them, I'd be sitting in a jail right now. Would you want that, Lambert?"

"No! But you had provocation—you were defending me. If it had been only assault, a good lawyer could have gotten you off."

"Not after the way it was set up. No, I'd be thrown behind bars and kept there for years. Unless . . ."

"Unless what?"

I felt myself smiling. "Unless the lawyer could convince a jury I was crazy."

"Charles!"

"Diane Summers said I was crazy."

"Diane Summers was a vile, stupid woman."

"Do *you* think I'm crazy?"

"Don't talk like that. You're the only really sane person I've ever known. Look how you've outwitted everyone who's tormented me. Look how clever you are in your job. It's the others who are crazy. You see things clearly, realistically."

Later, there were misgivings.

"The gun, Charles. The police are investigating it."

"Let them investigate. They can't hang it on me."

"But it was probably registered to someone."

"So what?"

"They'll find out who that someone was."

"So?"

"They'll find out *he* was the one who hocked it."

"Sure, but it wouldn't be me."

"And it wouldn't be Ed Cranston either."

"Christ, forget it!"

"But they'll question the person it *was* registered to. He'll tell them the name of the pawnbroker. They'll question the pawnbroker."

"All *right!* They'll think Ed Cranston bought it there."

"But they'll show him Ed Cranston's picture. The pawnbroker won't recognize him. But he may remember what *you* looked like."

"Cut it out, Lambert!"

"So if the police know Ed Cranston didn't buy the gun, they'll have to suspect there was a third person in Diane Summers's bedroom last night."

"That's enough. You're borrowing trouble. I don't want to think about it."

I'd had about all I could stand of Lambert Post.

Throughout that night and all the next day I could not stifle his nagging voice. It whined through my sleep, pestered me all the way to the office, and interrupted my solicitations, costing me sale after sale. When the third landlady had banged down the phone, Jean Hooper called me to her desk and asked just what in the hell was the matter with me. She knew I had been absent those two days, ostensibly sick, but she wasn't the kind who would volunteer that as an explanation. She'd rather it came directly from me, an admission of weakness that would make her feel superior. Damned if I'd give her the satisfaction. "Hell," I said, "even Joe DiMaggio doesn't get a hit every time up." "No," she said acidly, "and he doesn't strike out every time either." I wanted to knock out her big white teeth. Instead, I turned on my heel and stalked back to my desk.

Henrietta Boardman looked at me curiously. I told her about it.

"The bitch," she said. "What does she expect when you've been so sick."

"I'm not sick now," I said defensively.

Her voice softened. "You've just got too much pride to admit it."

That calmed me down. With Lambert Post's pessimism bleating away inside me, it was at least comforting to know I had pride.

Henrietta said, "How'd you like to show Jean how hot a solicitor Charles Walter can be?"

"Sure. But today I haven't got what it takes."

She smiled like a conspirator. "Maybe not. But I have. There's a little trick I've used a few times when I've had a blank day. Look behind Jean Hooper—through the glass."

I shrugged, rose half out of my chair, and looked toward the oblong of plate glass stretching across the wall behind Jean Hooper's desk. In a room on the other side were banks of switchboards attended by girls wearing headsets and mouthpieces, the same as ours. They staffed the department called Voluntary, meaning they took ads from people who called in perhaps for the first time and had never been solicited.

"I've got a few girl friends in there," Henrietta said. "They'll be happy to cooperate. Wait until Jean takes a break. Then we'll see."

I made a few desultory calls, and in about ten minutes Jean Hooper left the room. Henrietta immediately got up, wiggled her lovely rear up the aisle, and disappeared behind the corner door that opened on Voluntary. She was back in five minutes, one arm hugging her stomach, a satisfied smile hooking the corners of her mouth. She slipped a hand under her blouse, withdrew three ad order forms, and handed them to me. I looked at them. Three furnished room ads, all filled out—advertiser's name, address, phone number, dates of insertions, and the copy itself written by obviously feminine hands.

"All you have to do," Henrietta said, pleased with herself, "is write them up on your own order form and put them through. Who's to know?"

I couldn't help grinning. "Now you know why I'm so crazy about you."

She pretended to be taken aback, saying, "Don't try that old smoothie line on me, Charles Walter."

I gave her cheek a couple of quick pats. Not only had she magically made me a star again, she had also silenced that inner doomsday voice.

"There's one other trick," she said. "You're so brilliant I'd 've thought you'd figured it out when you were selling on the outside."

I was rewriting one of the ads. "Go ahead, corrupt me some more."

"Well, you know about all the classified advertising agencies in town. The biggest is Diner and Drosking on Forty-second Street. They get ads from people we never even heard about, just like our Voluntary girls do. They send them down every afternoon by messenger—straight to the production department. Now, why shouldn't they give the furnished room ads in your territory directly to you? All you have to do is call—about three o'clock, say— and take them over the phone."

I stopped writing. "And why should they give them to me?"

She smiled, arching her black penciled eyebrows. "Because I'll ask them to. I know some of the agency girls who collect the ads. I'll introduce you over the phone."

By three o'clock she had introduced me to four agency girls, each time ringing off to let me give them some sweet talk. By four o'clock I had written up nine ads, including the ones from Voluntary. Yet I had made only about a dozen legitimate calls. It was like everything else—you had to know how to beat the system.

"Number nine," I said blithely to Jean Hooper as I dropped the order into the box.

She fluffed her hair, grimacing disdainfully. "I didn't know your relatives rented out rooms."

"Sure. Any time you and a *friend* want one for overnight, let me know."

Her eyes were flaring as I turned away. I had the old confidence back again.

A little later I knocked off and went upstairs to the city room. Apparently the last edition had been put to bed. The rewrite men had removed their headsets and were leaning back, feet on desks, thumbing through the paper or working the crossword. Only two men sat at the copy desk, one on the rim reading a book, one in the slot nodding in half-sleep. A five-man poker game was going on quietly in the far corner. Only the city editor, Sam Stein, and the assistant city editor, Paul McCarthy, seemed to be working; they sat at Stein's littered desk in the center of the room talking animatedly. A copy boy swung out of the composing room carrying a stack of newspapers. Stein stopped talking and looked up. "That the replate?" The boy nodded, placed a copy on the desk, and handed one to McCarthy.

A replate, I knew, meant the front page had been hurriedly revised in order to accommodate an important late-breaking story. "Can you spare one?" I asked the copy boy as he passed. "Sure" —and he handed me one, the ink still wet.

The reason for the replate was screamingly apparent. An eight-column banner proclaimed, MURDER SUSPECTED IN DOUBLE DEATH!

And of course the story made a prophet out of Lambert Post. The .25-caliber Colt had been registered to a traveling salesman named Donald Sternlove, who had bought it for protection during night driving. He had lost his job, needed immediate cash, and had hocked the gun a month ago to a pawnbroker on Vesey Street. The police had found and questioned the pawnbroker, confronted him with the gun, and showed him pictures of both Ed Cranston and Sternlove. The pawnbroker recalled Sternlove as the original owner, said he had never appeared to redeem it, and was adamant in asserting that he had never laid eyes on Cranston. He attempted

a description of the man who *had* purchased the gun—me—but
was hampered by not having been able to see him full face: "He
was turned away, like he was looking at something in back of the
shop. Just his left side, that's all I saw. In his early twenties, I
think. Good-looking. White skin, like maybe he lived on nothing
but chicken broth. Tall, six feet anyway, black hair, kind of
slicked down. All he did was point to the gun in the case and say,
'I'll take that.' Ten dollars. No haggling." Then, to avoid charges
of illegal sale: "I remember him good because he grabbed the gun,
threw down a sawbuck, and was out of there before I could ask
for a permit."

Quote from Detective Lieutenant Angelo Rubino: "That man
either sold or gave the gun to Edward Cranston; or he was in the
bedroom that night and used it himself. The only answer that
makes sense is the second one, based on evidence we have." Fingerprints? asked a reporter. "Just the opposite—no fingerprints.
The neighbor said he heard the radio turned up full blast. Well, to
do that, someone would have to touch the knob. Wiped clean. Another thing. Right after the shot was heard, the radio was turned
off. I ask you, how could a man who just killed himself get up and
turn off the radio?" How did he account for Cranston's finger-
prints on both the gun and the knife? "An old trick. The murderer
could have pressed the weapons into Cranston's hands." How
could such a vicious character have gained entry? "I think we've
got the answer to that. We inspected the dumbwaiter that opens
into the kitchen. A man could get inside that and pull himself up.
We tested it. And we found something. Not much, but something.
A few gray threads, the kind that belong in a man's suit. They
were snagged on some splinters in the dumbwaiter. Now why
would there be *suit threads* in a thing that's used to haul up paper
cartons and packages? The threads are in the lab. We may be able
to trace them, but that's a real long shot." Had he checked on
Diane Summers's ex-husband? "Yes, he was in Buffalo."

Another question: If it was murder, what kind of man would
the police be looking for? "We've talked to a couple of psychiatrists about that. A psychopath. A compulsive killer. No remorse
whatsoever. Clever. Outwardly he might seem perfectly normal,

even likable. But inside he wants to kill. Generally he thinks he has a real good reason. Revenge usually."

Did Edward Cranston and Diane Summers have any known enemies? "None we've been able to turn up yet. It could have been a completely senseless thing. People chosen at random, as sacrifices. But I don't think so. It was too carefully planned."

Finally: Would Lieutenant Rubino care to speculate on whether this mystery man might have been responsible for any previous unsolved murders? "Could be. We've got our files out, primarily checking on the method used to kill. I doubt if we'll find much there. We're also investigating known muggers. Routine. You newsmen may be able to help. Publish the description given by the pawnbroker, skimpy as it is. I'll give you a flyer if you want to print that. Ask anyone who has been attacked by an unknown assailant to contact me personally at Homicide if the description in any way fits."

One name leaped into my mind: Jennifer Hartwick.

I finished Rubino's quote: "It's a good bet this guy has struck before. Unless we nab him, I say he'll sure as hell strike again."

X

IT WAS OBVIOUS what had to be done, and done fast. Even though Jennifer Hartwick had not seen who hit her, it seemed a sure thing she would yield to Lieutenant Rubino's invitation. This time she would have a sympathetic listener, and somewhere along the line the names Lambert Post and Charles Walter would surface. The end.

Of course, Lambert Post moaned and jittered, but eventually calmed down with gin, and I was able to stretch out on the couch and think without interference.

Jennifer Hartwick. It had been five days since I had greeted her with a sockful of nickels at the Park Central Hotel; four since she had come out of the coma. Was she still in the hospital? I got the phone number of Bellevue, called and asked for her. She had been discharged the morning before. I then called the Court Hotel, thinking that after her experience she might have decided to get lost.

"Mrs. Hartwick?" a female voice tinkled. "One moment and I'll ring her."

"No, no, please don't disturb her. I just wanted to be sure she still lived there. I'm sending her a get-well gift, so don't mention I called."

So she was recuperating at home. Probably bolted in and still too terrified to poke her nose out the door. Probably taking her meals in her room and not receiving anyone. I wondered if she had seen the evening paper. It was a quarter to six. I could make it to the Court Hotel in less than twenty minutes.

I didn't really think too much about Lieutenant Rubino's other remarks to the press until I was jammed in with sweating rush-hour commuters on the IRT heading for Times Square. How could I have been such a stupid son of a bitch about that radio—wiping off the knob (I could have pressed his fingertips on it), turning it off after he was beyond all movement. The suit threads weren't so bad; at least they weren't a brainless oversight. Still, those weren't the worst things bothering me.

A psychopath, Rubino had said, a compulsive killer. God, wasn't that just like a thick-headed cop. He comes up against something his one-watt mind can't grasp, so he starts yelling maniac. And he gets a couple of psychs who live off criminal cases to back him up. That way he won't look so bad—after all, who would expect a normal, family-man policeman to catch anyone as strange and complicated as a psycho? Even if the cop strikes out, he gets nothing but sympathy. Rubino was probably a damned thorough investigator—he had indicated that—but he wouldn't know a psycho if it was his mother-in-law. Any more than he would understand a Charles Walter. He couldn't even begin to comprehend that for some people the laws written into the books by dried-up old men just don't apply. Some people are constituted by superior intellect and personal dynamism to make and enforce their own laws. Hitler, Mussolini, and Franco are good examples. Mussolini didn't get that bunch of organ-grinders and grape-stompers into line by appealing to the courts. He did it with bayonets and castor oil. Hitler didn't achieve military might and economic prosperity by petitioning the League of Nations. He did it by defying the confused, legalistic democracies and by turning his storm troopers loose on the Jews. And Franco—he didn't shirk his duty because the Spanish government was legally elected. He saw it was evil and decided to destroy it.

These may seem like absurd parallels to the action I had taken against Jennifer Hartwick, Ed Cranston, and Diane Summers, but the principle was the same. If their crimes had been left to legally appointed judges and democratically selected juries, they would have walked away scot-free.

It was six-thirty when I reached the Court Hotel. I entered the bar from the street, ordered a drink and, before it arrived, strolled to the men's room, glancing into the lobby on the way. It was nothing but wall-to-wall people; there was little chance that even a hunchbacked midget would be particularly noticed. I downed my drink, pushed through to the lobby, went to a house phone, and called Jennifer Hartwick. The phone rang eight times before it was picked up and a small voice said, "Yes?"

"Mrs. Hartwick?" I made my voice come out deep, with a rasping edge.

"Ye-*e-s*."

"This is Detective Lieutenant Angelo Rubino. Homicide."

She repeated the name wonderingly. "Rubino. Why . . . just one minute."

If I had guessed right, the name had rung a bell; she had seen it in the evening paper and was now checking it.

I had guessed right. She came back on the phone and said, as though out of breath, "Excuse me. Lieutenant Rubino—yes, I just read your name in tonight's *Journal*. Those horrible murders."

"I'd like to ask you a few questions, Mrs. Hartwick."

"You mean about the terrible thing that happened to me? I've already talked to the police."

"No, it concerns those two deaths you referred to—Edward Cranston and Diane Summers. We're interviewing everyone who recently has been the victim of an attack. You can see how your name would come up. It should take only a few minutes."

"To tell you the truth, I've been sitting here thinking about whether to call *you*. The paper says you suggested that. But I don't think I can be of any help. I never even saw the man."

"Mrs. Hartwick, you may know things you don't know you know. What happened to you may throw some light on this latest crime."

It took her a few moments of thinking to make the decision. "Can you wait about fifteen minutes? I have to get dressed."

I said fine and hung up. So it was going to be that easy. I felt a sagging disappointment. Staring down at the house phone, I tapped it impatiently with my knuckles. I thought for a while. *Too* easy. My heart surged. I grabbed up the phone and again asked the operator for Jennifer Hartwick.

"I'm sorry, that line is busy. Will you wait?"

I slammed down the receiver, every sense now alert. Jennifer Hartwick *could* have received a call from a friend right after mine.

But she also could have phoned outside; an odd thing to do if she was hurrying to get dressed. After the Park Central episode she was bound to be scared, jumpy, suspicious of any caller no matter how plausible his explanation. She would want to check him out. In the case of someone claiming to be Lieutenant Rubino, there was only one way she could do that.

Ten minutes had passed. Now I couldn't go up. Not unless I was willing to risk being caught in the act. I braced against the phone counter, stood on my toes, and gazed over the heads of the crowd at the revolving entrance door. One minute. Two minutes. My legs began to cramp. Then I forgot them as two heavyset men wearing dark suits and low-set, wide-brimmed hats whirled from the door and began to barrel through the thronged lobby.

They were halfway across when a thought struck me. Once more I called Jennifer Hartwick, resting my chin on the heel of my hand, pinching my nose, and affecting a nasal voice.

"House Detective Burns," I said.

"Thank God. Please hurry."

"You the lady called the police?"

"Yes. *Yes!*"

"They're just pulling up outside. But chances are the man they want is on his way up there right now."

"Oh God."

"Is your room near the door to the stairs?"

"Yes, just down the hall."

"Get out of that room this minute and go to the stairs. Stand on the landing behind the door. And leave *your* door unlocked for the police. Got it?"

"Yes, yes, I'm going!"

As I cradled the phone, I saw the backs of the two plainclothes cops' heads bobbing among a dozen others at the elevators. All three cars were on the upper floors. I skinned through the crowd and pulled up behind the cops. In a few seconds an elevator banged open, disgorging a full load. One of the cops bellied forward and flashed his badge at the operator. Before the message penetrated, the car had filled up. The cop waved a hand in disgust, pocketed his badge and, with his partner, backed inside. I was in the rear, wedged into a corner.

We sped to the fourth floor without stopping. The door slammed open and the cops burst out and legged it down the corridor. I squirmed out just as the operator, obviously instructed, shut in the other passengers. Nearing the end of the corridor, the cops skidded to a stop and veered through the door to Jennifer Hartwick's suite. The stairs were less than half that distance. I was there when the cops disappeared.

I faced a big brown-painted steel door. Grasping the cold brass knob, I gave it a silent wrench and pushed it forward about six inches. One flashing glance took in the rough cement walls, the concrete landing, the pebbled-steel stairs. I darted my hand to my belt, shoved hard on the door, swung around it, and pointed the rust-spotted carving knife straight down at the cringing, white-robed figure of Jennifer Hartwick. She had time only for her face to fall apart, her taffy-blond hair to give a jump, her larynx to squeak, before I slit her throat.

I had her spun around, white robe peeled off, pink silk pajamas slashed from neck to rump, before the blood puddled the floor. Half a minute later I had made Jennifer Hartwick pay her final, post-mortem penance.

I wiped the knife clean on the chaste hem of her robe, tucked the blade in my belt, and bounded down the stairs. I came out through a door in a corner opposite the elevators and jostled through the lobby crowd. Outside, two squad cars stood at the curb, lights blinking, radios crackling, motors running. I turned left toward Times Square.

Later that night I got my gray suit from the closet, wrapped the knife in it, added two bronze-lead bookends and a heavy lamp base, and locked them in a cheap black suitcase. I took the subway to South Ferry, caught the Staten Island ferry, and dropped the suitcase in the middle of New York Harbor.

XI

THE NEXT MORNING the furor was as great as if it had been the Lindbergh kidnapping. "Sex fiend strikes again," shouted the newsies on every other corner. Subway straphangers skipped the sports pages to pore over the fascinating details under headlines like NEW BUTCHER KILLING LINKED TO DOUBLE MURDER; MANIAC MURDERS, MUTILATES ACTRESS; PSYCHOSLAYER OUTWITS COPS, KILLS AGAIN!

The stories revealed that the two cops who had plunged into the hotel room thought at first they had arrived too late; that Jennifer Hartwick had already been killed and her body concealed somewhere in the suite. They had searched the premises from closets to bathtub to steamer trunk, then tracked the corridor peering into maintenance rooms. Finally they pushed open the big steel door to the staircase and almost slipped to their knees in what the inspired *Mirror* described as "a lake of blood islanded by an extinct female body, throat slit, torso carved in such a way as to mortify the woman's sex."

Apparently even the *Mirror* thought its readers too squeamish to tolerate a more explicit description.

The police of course had no doubt that the deaths of Jennifer Hartwick and Ed Cranston and Diane Summers were executed by the same person. This belief was based initially on my masquerade as Lieutenant Rubino, ostensibly come to make inquiries regarding the earlier double homicide. Rubino had been at police headquarters when Jennifer Hartwick called in to check. He had immediately ordered police in the Times Square area to the hotel, and had rushed up from Centre Street, arriving when the medical examiner had completed his business. The police could only surmise how the victim was lured from her suite to the stairs, but their guess was almost one hundred percent accurate. They had no description of the suspect—the elevator operator had been so upset he had scarcely noticed the third man who got off on the fourth floor.

Further evidence linking me to all three slayings came when the police reviewed the previous assault on Jennifer Hartwick at the Park Central Hotel. Considering subsequent events, they were now convinced she had been enticed to the convention bedroom by "the same psychopathic killer who last evening took her life." They deduced that the previous attack had been motivated by a compulsion for revenge and therefore she must have known her unseen assailant. Yet, it was pointed out, she had been unable at that time to name anyone she thought might wish her bodily harm. This suggested someone who had suffered a minor slight, or an imagined one, and had mentally blown it up to preposterous proportions—in itself "a symptom of a deranged mind." The motive for the second, mortal attack, police theorized, seemed clear: "He feared that Jennifer Hartwick would respond to Lieutenant Rubino's public plea for cooperation and that during the course of the inquiry she would mention his name and recall an instance that might have provoked his resentment" (quoth the chief of police). Everyone who had known Jennifer Hartwick was now being sought for questioning.

Well, even though they were unaware that the case involved both Charles Walter and Lambert Post, they sure as hell had it all figured out. Nevertheless, they had come to a dead end. They had merely the pawnbroker's sketchy description of the man they were seeking—useless, perhaps even misleading. As for Lambert Post's name, it was a sure bet that no one at Jennifer Hartwick's drunken gathering had even listened to it, let alone paid attention to the man himself. Except perhaps that naked stud and his girl who had been surprised in the bedroom. But the hall outside the bedroom had been dark, the man and girl somewhat oblivious, and Jennifer Hartwick had burst in to overpower the scene. No, the police should get nothing there.

Of course the most obvious argument for the single-murderer belief was the almost identical condition of the female corpses.

But all that bought the police was a chance to look mystically wise, to utter high-sounding statements of outrage, and to proceed with the wearisome task of searching for the knife, which would frustrate even a deep-sea diver. Hastily improvised as my tactics were, I was certain I had not left a single clue. This time there had been no printless radio knob, no post-mortem impossibility, no threads from a gray suit. In a city of seven million souls I was as immune to identification as though I didn't exist.

The story was the talk of the telephone room. Solicitors put aside their leads and, ignoring the glowering presence of Jean Hooper, discussed the case and conjectured about it in hoarse whispers. The girls, naturally, shivered with excitement and a number of them planned to spend the lunch hour buying sturdier locks as well as chains for their doors. Most of the men affected a breezy attitude, Sol Pincus saying airily, "I'll be forever grateful to my parents for not giving me big tits." All of them agreed that the wanted man, despite his mistakes, must be devilishly clever. God, how I wanted to stand up and proclaim that I, Charles Walter, was the mastermind who had so intrigued them.

Only Henrietta Boardman remained calm and strangely silent. When I waved the morning paper at her and asked, "What do you think of this?" her lensed eyes brooded and she said quietly, "I think he ought to be pitied." That ended *that* conversation, and I was left with a strange unsettled feeling.

After lunch I went up to the city room and filched an early edition. The size of the double banner headline would have done justice to a declaration of war: CITY MOBILIZES AGAINST MAD MURDERER! The chief of police had formed a special detail, headed by Lieutenant Angelo Rubino, to concentrate exclusively on the case—"one of the most horrible in the recent annals of crime." Mayor Fiorello La Guardia had gone on the radio that morning and in his high-pitched, lisping voice warned every citizen to exercize extreme vigilance coupled with caution. District Attorney Thomas Dewey promised speedy prosecution as soon as the killer was apprehended. Newbold Morris, president of the City Council, had called that body into special session in order to unify the efforts of the five boroughs. Psychiatrists were quoted. University professors. Judges. Lawyers. Priests. Ministers. Rabbis. Seers.

Astrologists. Bachelor girls. There was no question about it—everyone was having the time of his life.

Reproduced on page two was the police bulletin that had been distributed to all law enforcement agencies. It included an artist's rendering of what the fugitive might look like, based on the pawnbroker's meager description. I stared at it, and although it approximated my features, anyone comparing it with the actual subject would consider the drawing a bizarre joke. I swear, it made me look like a matinee idol—a young John Barrymore before he grew the mustache. Wouldn't that palpitate the hearts of the girls in the phone room!

The description, as far as it went, was exact: "Six feet tall, slender build, sleek black hair, straight features, pale complexion." That, I thought, should fit at least half a million males in the New York metropolitan area.

There were almost three pages of photographs—Jennifer Hartwick (a repeat), the actress's suite, the staircase murder site, the Park Central bedroom; Cranston, Summers, the bedroom murder site, the gun, the knife; Rubino, the two outwitted cops (looking faintly embarrassed); the pawnbroker.

Leaning against the railing that set off the city room, I sensed a lull as I turned a page. Looking up I saw a big, square, rumpled man with a broad red face amble through the gate toward the city editor. I turned as Sam Stein stared over his horn-rimmed glasses, jabbed a finger at the front page, and said, "Great stuff, Maury."

Maury. That rang a bell. I glanced back at the lead story and saw the by-line—Maury Ryan. The guy was famous as the paper's expert on exposés. The tea pads in harlem, the numbers racket, organized prostitution, labor union kickbacks, Murder Incorporated—Maury Ryan had investigated and sensationalized them all. Damned if I didn't feel flattered that he had been assigned to this story.

Maury Ryan rested a thick haunch on the corner of Stein's desk and ran a freckled hand through his sandy hair. "You'll get the recap for the final, Sam," he said. "I just came from the medical examiner's. Forget the rape angle. Jesus Christ, the way she was slashed up, who could tell?"

Sam Stein frowned. He was a short, chunky, dark man with

blue-black jaws and chin. "Suggest it, Maury. *Suggest* it, that's all. Remember, at the Park Central she *was* raped."

"But in this case there wouldn't have been time. He must have done the whole job in four or five minutes."

Less than that, I thought, offended.

"Some guys," Sam Stein said, "are quicker than bunnies." He grinned and jerked a thumb toward the assistant city editor sitting next to him. "Just ask Paul here."

Paul McCarthy dropped his face into the crook of his arm, as though embarrassed.

"Just suggest it, Maury. You can't deprive our six hundred thousand readers of at least hoping she was raped."

Maury Ryan was right. There had not been enough time. I remembered looking down at her for an instant and wishing I could risk a few more minutes.

Maury Ryan shrugged, got up, and passed me as he lumbered down the aisle. I caught up with him and said, "Mr. Ryan, your story was terrific."

He gave me a pleased glance. "Thanks. You don't get 'em like this very often."

"You think the police are holding back anything?"

"Not a damned thing. Everything they've got is in that paper under your arm."

I was in my shirtsleeves and I guess he thought I was a copy boy hoping to make reporter. "Think he'll get away with it?"

"Possible. You put a cop's two-plus-two mind up against a character like this and the cop's got the short end. The guy's too damned unpredictable. If the police could pinpoint a motive, maybe they'd start getting someplace."

"I thought I read they'd found a motive."

"That the guy's got a beef? Christ, who hasn't."

He gave his hand a quick wave and turned into the cubicle that was his office.

When I got back to the phone room, Jean Hooper stopped me with: "Where the hell have *you* been?"

"Just a normal human function, Jean. Golly, I forgot to raise my hand!"

"Oh, you are *such* a comedian. Here!" She yanked a slip of

paper from a pad and thrust it at me. "A Mrs. Sloat has been trying to get hold of you. By the neck, I hope. She's burned up about something. Call her."

Mrs. Sloat—the first landlady I had solicited on the day I started on the phone. A T.F. order. And I had never called her again.

As soon as I got the number, I heard a little click and knew Jean Hooper was plugged in.

"Hel-*lo,* Eunice Sloat. This is Charles Walter."

"Don't you Eunice Sloat me! You were supposed to call me back ages ago. About the ad. Now I've got a bill here that says the ad has run for *thirty-two days!* I rented that room two weeks ago. I'm not going to pay."

"Didn't you call in to cancel it?"

"Yes, today, when I called earlier. I'd forgotten it until I got the bill. Mr. Walter, it's your fault. You promised to call me back."

"I tried you a few times but you weren't there."

"I'm here all day, every day."

"Each time I got some man."

"Oh." Her voice became uncertain. "Maybe it was the new roomer. The phone's just outside his door. I guess he forgot to give me the message."

"You see? And here you are blaming it all on good, kindly, thoughtful Charles Walter. Shame."

I heard a soft snicker. "Oh you. You could charm the birds from the trees."

"No, only someone I *want* to charm. Tell me, Eunice, have you any more rooms for rent?" That was for Jean Hooper. I didn't give a damn if Eunice Sloat had a houseful of vacancies. It was too easy getting all the ads I wanted from Voluntary and the agencies.

"Not right now. But I'm expecting one next week. Now about the bill . . ."

"Tell you what I'm going to do. I'll get you a write-off for all the insertions since you rented the room. So tear up that bill and wait for a new one. How's that?"

"Why, that's fine, Mr. Walter."

"To you—Charles."

"Thank you . . . Charles."

"And call me when you have that vacancy."

"Oh, I will. Perhaps you'd like to come up and see it."

"I may try to do that."

I got the date of the room rental and rang off. Jean Hooper buzzed me. "Well, *Charles,* aren't you the generous one. I might have to dock that write-off from your pay."

But I knew she wouldn't. After all, I'd smoothed down a customer who was due for another ad.

On the way home from work I stopped at different newsstands and invested nine cents in the rest of the evening papers—*Sun, World-Telegram, Post.* I also had the final edition of the *Journal.* I spread out the four front pages and lined them up on the floor, pacing around them as I sipped a gin. I felt like God, all-seeing but invisible, defender of the maligned, relentless in the pursuit of evil.

The key word in many of its forms leaped blackly from the newsprint and I murmured aloud to Lambert Post: "Kill, murder, slay, butcher, slaughter, stab . . . death . . ."

He didn't cringe, seemed not even to hear.

"Death," I said again. "Why are people so afraid of it? If they really believed in a glorious hereafter, as they claim, they'd *celebrate* death. Hypocrites! They say things like 'gone to his *reward'* but they don't believe it. I'm not like that. I *know* there's a hereafter—not a hell, but a heaven where all who have sinned are instantly rehabilitated. Ed Cranston, Diane Summers, Jennifer Hartwick—they're in a state of grace now. Killing released them to the ultimate truth. I was their savior." I thought about that for a minute. "No, God is their savior. But I was his instrument—his temporal representative. You see that, don't you, Lambert?"

He said nothing, didn't even stir. I sat down on the couch.

"You asleep, Lambert?" I wished he were. One word of criticism from him—the man I had so spectacularly avenged—and I'd be afraid of what I would do.

"I feel funny, Charles."

"Funny?"

"Like I was being suffocated to death. All the excitement . . ."

"Aren't you enjoying it?"

"I don't know. I'm numb. I don't feel much of anything. I guess everybody else is enjoying it, though."

"You're damned right. Sure, everyone sounds shocked and scared. But they're really delighted this happened. They'd like to do it to somebody themselves, but they're cowards. So they do it vicariously—through me. They can't admit it but they see me as their leader. Remember your Nietzsche, Lambert. Superman—beyond good and evil."

There was a long silence.

"You're right, Charles. Oh God, you're so right!"

I could go to bed then. All night long I thought only of Diane Summers and Jennifer Hartwick. I couldn't sleep. I didn't want to sleep.

XII

FOR A WHILE after that, Lambert Post didn't speak to me. I don't think it was fear alone that caused the dissociation. Nor was it censure for what I had done. I think it was more a desire to avoid anything that might bring me down from the heights or shake my confidence.

Of course anyone who had lived as intensely with me as Lambert Post could not abruptly stop all communication. He found an easy solution: He left me notes. Not a day passed but that I'd find carefully worded missives taped to the bathroom mirror or the refrigerator or tucked under the phone.

Some read like horoscopes:

> A good day if you attend strictly to business.
> Talk to one who has inside knowledge.
> Think before you speak.

Others were encouraging:

> Yours is the real reality.
> Every genius has been thought mad.
> Might is the law of the enlightened.

And, once, wistful:

> Must heroes remain unsung?

Sometimes I would scrawl a reply below the message. On one that expressed admiration, I wrote boldly, *I'd like to relive it.* On another, sympathizing with my anonymity, I penned savagely, TELL THEM! TELL THEM! TELL THEM! but immediately slashed lines through it and added, *Forget it!*

As days passed without concrete developments, the story lost its prominence on page one. To keep it alive editors had to be content with reporting the side effects of the deaths. The police were so swamped with phone calls that they tripled their staff of switchboard operators. Everyone in New York seemed to have a clue or a suspect, usually a neighbor, an ex-mate, or a business associate. ("We have no bona fide leads," said Lieutenant Angelo Rubino.) Applications for gun registrations soared. Locksmiths prospered. Hotels reported a slump. A man in Queens called police headquarters incessantly to announce that he was the slayer. (Finally traced, he turned out to be the same man who for two years running had gleefully confessed to every homicide committed in New York. He was hauled away to Bellevue for observation.) A woman on a packed BMT train made a citizen's arrest, aided by a hefty guard, accusing a short fat man of being the suspect because he had his thumb up her ass. (The man said he was trying to steady himself.) Thirty-eight detectives from seven police agencies held an extraordinary meeting at City Hall to coordinate their efforts. ("We can't say we're any closer to catching the suspect," reported the chief of police.) Prominent officials issued daily appeals for citizens to be on the alert. Psychiatrists continued to add their two cents' worth: "A man of superior intelligence but too emotionally ill to realize he needs help" . . . "A frustrated genius" . . . "A drifter, too far gone to hold a steady, regular job."

The news coverage continued to shrink, yielding to the absence of substantial clues and overshadowed by the mounting Czech crisis. I became depressed, irritable, restless. Soon, I feared, the story that had electrified the nation's largest city would be pushed back with the obits.

Ironically it was the *Journal* that gave the faltering case a massive shot in the arm. In eight black-bordered columns stretching across the top of the front page it made a dramatic appeal to the killer to turn himself in: GIVE YOURSELF UP. WE WILL HELP YOU. It was written by Maury Ryan:

Three people—Diane Summers, Edward Cranston, and Jennifer Hartwick—lie dead at your hands, their bodies butchered and mutilated.

You are being pursued relentlessly everywhere in the city, the state, and the nation.

No place you can hide is safe. No one you know can help you. You are alone.

You must walk the streets, not as a free man, but as a hunted, tormented animal. And, like such an animal, you will eventually be destroyed.

Unless, willingly, you give yourself up.

We ask you to turn yourself in to this newspaper—to this reporter, if you wish.

We offer you something in return. Not protection, not sympathy—but something of far more practical value: the best medical help and the best legal counsel available.

More, we offer you the pages of this great newspaper to tell your story.

Why have you killed? What are your grievances? What kind of person are you?

We can only surmise that you are highly intelligent. We can only guess that you think your motives are just.

Don't you want the world to *know* why you killed?

We offer you hope.

Call the City Editor of the *Journal*—or me, Maury Ryan —anytime, day or night. The telephone number is DRydock 4-8900. Call collect. Your call will not be traced.

Call now!

I read that in the first edition at 10:30 A.M. while sitting in the men's room—and damned near fell off the throne. The city's largest evening newspaper and its star reporter were offering me, Charles Walter, the chance to be a public advocate of my actions, unrestrained by legal authority. The form and substance of such an article, probably a series, began immediately to form in my mind. Like Zola defending Dreyfus, I could inveigh against the evil of those I had executed (*J'Accuse! J'Accuse! J'Accuse!*). I could reveal the abuses suffered by Lambert Post, proving I had been motivated by a militantly Christian desire to defend the weak. I could tear to shreds the decadent society whose courts and churches and corporations and clubs favored the rich and well-born, solacing the meek with the promise of a hereafter which they themselves secretly scorned. Like Zarathustra, I could expound on the theme that "the great despisers are the great reverers" and thus are ordained to defy the petty laws of petty men. I could . . .

But of course I would be permitted none of this. Once I had surrendered, I would be clapped into jail, hauled before a judge, saddled by a shyster, harassed by a prosecutor, vilified before a jury, and deprived of eloquence. Maury Ryan's offer, sincere as it sounded, was no more than a cheap, venal trick that might well have been thought up by the circulation department. They cared not a damn about enlightenment; they cared only about selling papers. Yes, they would print my story, but they would so edit it and so prejudice it with surrounding editorial comment, that I would come across like the raving maniac they already were convinced I was.

Still, I felt no disappointment; in fact, was fired by a racing excitement. My exploits had been dramatically revived. Hundreds of thousands of people who had let the story fade from their minds were at that moment reprising it in all its exquisite detail, real and imagined. Women were testing their door locks. Men were checking their guns. The authorities, feeling themselves upstaged, were hastily calling meetings.

But obviously this appeal to surrender would be no more than a one-day sensation if there was no response. I thought about that, sitting at my desk and pretending to contemplate my pasted-up leads. Henrietta must have sensed my preoccupation because she said, "Anything wrong? You look like you're on another planet." Her perception triggered a warning inner quiver and I answered that I was simply bored. A few minutes later she left to take a break and by that time I had made up my mind. I looked to see that Jean Hooper was not at her desk, then, turning my back to Dottie Friedlander and holding my lips close to the mouthpiece, I called DRydock 4-8900.

Maury Ryan was in his office and took the call. I affected a deep, rumbling voice that seemed to start low in my chest. "You asked me to turn myself in."

I heard a sharp intake of breath. "Is this the kill—"

"Executioner," I said.

There was a brief pause. Even the case-hardened Maury Ryan had not expected this, not when the first edition was only then hitting the streets.

"Is there some way you can identify yourself?" he said.

"You think I'm a crackpot?"

"Sorry, but this town's full of 'em. They're always trying to screw me up." His voice had smoothed to a pleasantly conversational tone. Just a couple of pals talking things over.

"All right," I said, "identification. If you'll check with the medical examiner, you'll find that the bodies of both Jennifer Hartwick and Diane Summers were slit from rectum to navel. In both cases the breasts were severed and lay at their sides. That information was not published in any newspaper."

"No, not explicitly. I've seen the medical examiner. What you've just said is true."

"And if you check with those two detectives who stormed the hotel, you'll find that Jennifer Hartwick's door was unlocked. That wasn't mentioned either."

"Okay, you're the man. Do you want to come in here or would you prefer to meet someplace else?"

A small click made me start half out of my chair. I saw Jean Hooper plugged into the board and just starting to raise her headset to put it on.

"Not today," I said, and flicked the lever and yanked the plug.

Headset around my neck, mouthpiece still in place, I got up and started up the aisle. Jean Hooper would think I was going out to check an ad in production. As I reached her desk, she swung around and fixed me with a puzzled frown.

"What was *that* all about?"

I gave her an innocent look. "What was *what* all about?"

"That guy on the phone. You must have insulted him."

"Now, Jean, would I ever insult *anybody?*"

"He said, 'hello, hello'—then, 'son of a bitch.' And he slammed down the phone."

"Oh, *him*. He was just sore because his ad didn't deliver. I think he was drunk."

That sometimes happened. Jean Hooper had to shrug it off. Strangely, I felt no panic, no fright. Instead, like a kid at a camp-out, I felt an irresistible urge to move closer to the fire.

At noon I rode the bus to Park Row and picked up a news-paper at the stand under the El. The plea to surrender was still boxed across the top of the front page but beneath it, next to the word EXTRA, a huge banner headline screamed, TRIPLE KILLER TALKS TO JOURNAL! I had pushed Czechoslovakia below the fold.

Tucking the paper under my arm, I hurried to the free-lunch bar down the street. I ordered a beer, made myself three small ham-on-ryes garnished with mustard pickles, propped up on a bar stool, and read Maury Ryan's latest beat. He reported my conver-sation with him as faithfully as if it had been recorded, editing only my description of the two girls' wounds. He described my voice: "deep and vibrant, the words spoken slowly, enunciated clearly, the tone sincere—in my opinion, the voice of an educated man." My manner: "cool and confident, neither belligerent nor self-pitying. He might have been a successful businessman discussing a deal with his banker." Ryan emphasized that when he had started to ask if the caller was the killer, he had been instantly corrected: " 'Executioner,' the voice replied with just a touch of asperity. From this I could not escape the impression that he considers him-self the agent of some supernatural morality." Henceforth, Ryan referred to me as The Executioner, doubtless shrewdly believing that he had preempted for the *Journal* a label that would stick. For me, he had but one item of news: "A check of newspaper deliveries revealed that at the time The Executioner telephoned—10:45 A.M.—no *Journal* truck had made a drop above 42nd Street or be-yond Brooklyn Heights. Therefore, the call had to have originated from within this area."

Ryan concluded with an explanation and a personal appeal, set in bold type:

To The Executioner:
Immediately before you declined my invitation to meet and

rang off, I thought I heard a click on the wire. Perhaps you heard it too and believed you were being traced.

This is not true. You can trust me and this newspaper to make no attempt to trace your whereabouts.

I appeal to you to call me again—or the City Editor—at DRydock 4-8900. Your wishes as to the time and place of meeting will be respected and kept secret.

Call now before it is too late!

Passing the newsstand on my way back to the bus, I saw that two other afternoon papers had caught up with the news: SLAYER TALKS . . . KILLER ANSWERS SURRENDER APPEAL. How they must have hated themselves for having to tag along after the *Journal*. But the story was too big to bury.

I knew I had to do something or in a few days the whole thing would collapse.

I decided to have a talk with Maury Ryan.

XIII

I WENT UP TO THE city room in midafternoon and walked into turmoil. They were getting out the five-star final. I stood in the aisle at the end of the railing and took it all in.

Rewrite men, headsets on, eyes alert as they listened to reporters calling in, clattered their typewriters. On the rim of the horseshoe copy desk, editors, some with green eyeshades, worked stubby blue pencils over typewritten news stories handed them by the man in the slot. A skinny makeup man was reviewing a page layout with Sam Stein. Next to him, Paul McCarthy yammered into one of the desk phones, while a picture editor with a sheaf of glossy photos stood tensely by. Teletype machines chattered in a small room behind me and two copy boys sped past to strip them. There was a constant rushing in and out of the big green door to the composing room. The smell of ink, paste, sweat, and tobacco smoke hung in the air. Dominating everything, vibrating the railing where my hand rested, was the monotone thunder of the presses.

All this activity, I thought, all this dedication—repeated in similar rooms throughout the whole nation—all of it was at my disposal, to turn on and off as I wished. Ridiculously, I felt a lump swell in my throat.

"Boy!"

I turned, startled, and saw a shirtsleeved rewrite man waving a take of yellow copy paper at me. I smiled weakly and said, "Sorry, I'm in the . . . the business department." He swung away impatiently and I quickly withdrew. I sauntered down the corridor, past the long, narrow art department, past hole-in-the-wall offices of columnists, department editors, feature writers, until I came to Maury Ryan's cubicle. He was there, tilted back in his slat-backed chair, big feet piled on a scarred desk, staring out the huge window at a lone tugboat chugging down the East River.

His phone rang and he scrambled for it like he'd been jolted with electricity. God, I thought, feeling significant again, he must think it's me.

"Oh—you, Sam. No, not a goddamned word. I don't think he trusts us. Go ahead and put it to bed."

He dropped the phone, swung around, frowning, and saw me as I pretended to be passing by.

"Goddamn it," he said.

I paused in the door. "Excuse me, Mr. Ryan. I thought maybe that was The Executioner calling."

Ryan's lips fastened against his teeth. He pushed big fingers through his thick, sandy hair. "No, goddamn it. I think he's been scared off."

"You mean that click you said you heard on the phone? When he called this morning?"

His great head jerked in a nod. He stretched out his heavy arms, arched his broad back, then slumped in the chair. He plucked a crumpled pack of Camels from the pocket of his blue shirt and offered me one. I thanked him but said I didn't smoke. I moved a step inside. The offer of the cigarette made me think he wanted to talk.

"I guess it gets tiresome," I said, "just sitting there waiting."

He fired a wooden match with his thumbnail, lit up, and took a vast drag. "Christ, yes. I should be at police headquarters. I should be buttonholing Rubino. I should be *investigating*. But what am I doing? I'm sitting here on my big fat rosy waiting for some people-hater to call up and say hello." He stared gloomily into space. "Click or no click, I don't think the guy had any intention of turning himself in."

"What makes you think that?"

He seemed to measure me for a minute, then heaved a sigh as if to say, I've got to talk to *somebody*. Obviously he still thought that I, in my shirtsleeves, was a copy boy awesomely collecting pearls of wisdom from the great man.

"Something in his voice," he said, blowing a plume of smoke. "As though he was calling just for kicks. My imagination, maybe. But why the hell else would he have answered that bush-league appeal—Sam Stein's idea? Christ, so far he's as safe as if he was on Mars. The cops haven't got a thing. They're turning themselves inside out trying to get the egg off their face."

"Maybe he, The Executioner—that's a great name—maybe he just wanted to keep the story alive."

Ryan squinted an eye at me. "Yeah, sure, we thought of that."

He reached to the desk and picked up the edition headlined TRIPLE KILLER TALKS TO JOURNAL! "And he succeeded. But what if this is *all* he does? Telephone, hang up. Telephone, hang up. In that case, after a few days we'll say screw it and give him about a column inch back with the truss ads. He may be a nut but he's smart enough to know that."

"Then you think he might do something else?"

Ryan tugged at a lock of hair. "If he doesn't, pretty soon we'll let the police worry about it all by themselves. So will the other blats. And the way New York's finest are striking out, they'll be delighted to drop the whole subject as far as the press is concerned. Believe me, if this guy decides to clam up and get lost, a week from now nobody'll even remember what happened. They'll be too busy moaning about Europe, and licking their lips about new murders, and about society dolls getting messy divorces, and about virgins getting raped." He banged his fist on the wooden chair arm in frustration.

I felt sort of sorry for him. Here he had hooked one of the most sensational stories of the year and he saw it wriggling away. I backed out the door, excusing myself for disturbing him.

"Forget it. You did me a favor. I was about to climb the wall."

Back at my desk I brooded about what Maury Ryan had said. I was sure he wasn't being overly pessimistic in his belief that the story, lacking new material, would soon be overwhelmed by other events. I had felt the same way; that's why I had called him in the first place. The police—and Maury Ryan—needed something tangible. Depression made me wince.

I took from my drawer the list of widows and divorcées I had prepared and read the notes next to the names. Bitches, I thought, every damned one of them. Whoring their way through life. Paying for a man's devotion with currency counterfeited in that factory between their legs and advertised on their chests. They deserved to join Diane Summers and Jennifer Hartwick. But I had traveled that route enough. It was no longer merely Charles Walter vs. The Women. Now I was entered in a much more dangerous contest—Charles Walter vs. The Police. That would take all my wits. I couldn't waste them on clever, elaborate setups, especially one that might involve Lambert Post. No, it had to be something simple. Something direct. But dramatic. It would come. I began to feel better. Meanwhile, why not keep the pot bubbling.

It was four o'clock when I again called Maury Ryan.

When I said, "This is The Executioner," I could imagine his mouth falling open, cigarette dangling from his lower lip.

He breathed heavily and said, "I've been waiting for your call."

I said, "There will be another . . . incident." The sound of a footstep turned me around and I saw Henrietta about to sit down.

"When?" said Maury Ryan. "Look, you've got to—"

I flicked the lever, breaking the connection. But I pretended to be still on the phone. I was in no mood to speak to Henrietta or anyone else. I looked down at the small white pad I was doodling on and suddenly had to smile. Three times I had drawn the symbol for the male organ: ♂ .

I didn't know why, but I ripped off the sheet of paper and slipped it into my pocket.

A few minutes after five I stood on the crowded sidewalk waiting for the bus and gazing at the delivery trucks backed up at the long loading dock near the end of the building. Breaking away, I strolled down and stared at the top paper in a bundle that had just landed on a truck floor. KILLER CALLS AGAIN, VOWS NEW "INCIDENT"!

When I got to the apartment, I found myself alone; in fact, as alone as I had ever been in my life. I made a gin, sat with it on the couch, and looked at the other evening papers. They were all final editions, their stories dwelling heavily on the police "dragnet" concentrated between Brooklyn Heights and Times Square. None had the item that blackened the front page of the *Journal*'s replated five-star. Maury Ryan had a sensational beat that would sell thousands of extra papers.

I was glad about that. Maury Ryan had been decent to me.

By the third gin I was squirming in sweat. It was one of those hot August nights when you could smell the gutters and the garbage in the sidewalk cans—and yourself. I emptied my pockets, stripped off my clothes, hung them up, and went into the bathroom and took a long cool shower. I dressed very carefully—fresh underwear and socks, powder-blue slacks, clean white shirt, dark, lightweight jacket.

Not a word from Lambert Post. I decided to go out; it should be cooler on the streets. I walked over to Greenwich Avenue and down to the Sheridan Theatre where I stood under the blinking marquee and looked in the glass cases at the slick photographs of the stars: Charles Boyer and Hedy Lamarr in *Algiers*. I moved away, crossed over Greenwich Avenue, leaned my back against a brick wall, and stared up at the big, dark, narrow-windowed building to the south that resembled an armory. It was the women's prison. I thought about the inmates in their hot, cramped cells. All the while there was this mounting excitement.

A *Journal* delivery truck rumbled by, heading uptown. On the side panel was an all-type poster—black on yellow—that read: GET THE INSIDE—STRAIGHT! READ MAURY RYAN. The alert promotion department had acted fast. But they couldn't be specific about what they really meant; for all they knew, The Executioner might not give them another morsel to chew on.

I stayed perhaps twenty minutes, then returned to the apartment. I walked into the bathroom. A scrawled message was taped to the mirror: Call Eunice Sloat. It was written on the back of the notepad paper I had taken from my pocket—the one with my doodles of that symbol of the male organ.

That struck me as amusing and I laughed to myself.

But I stopped laughing when I thought about Eunice Sloat. Damn her, the last time she had called the office it was to make a complaint. She had bitched to Jean Hooper, trying to louse me up in my job. Then she had given me that "don't you Eunice Sloat me!" line. Real snotty. Then whiny: "Mr. Walter, it's *your* fault." Oh, but wasn't everything just fine and dandy when I gave her the write-off. Something for nothing. The bitch. Just another whore widow looking for a free ride.

A free ride. That was pretty amusing too.

My hand was trembling when I burned the message in the sink.

But my rage was steady and cold by the time I walked to Seventh Avenue and caught the IRT subway to Twenty-third Street.

XIV

WIDOW SLASHED TO DEATH!

Evidence Points to Mad Slayer of 3

A 40-year-old widow was knifed to ribbons last night in a killing so hideously bizarre that police immediately attributed it to the self-styled "Executioner" now being sought for the mutilation murders of Jennifer Hartwick, Diane Summers, and Edward Cranston.

The latest victim was identified as Eunice Sloat, owner of a rooming house on West 23rd Street, where the murder occurred. There was no sign of struggle, leading police to believe she had either been taken unaware or had known her assailant.

Reinforcing the belief that it was the work of the triple killer was a telephone call made late yesterday afternoon to an evening newspaper, during which the caller announced himself as "The Executioner" and stated, "There will be another incident."

Four hours later—at approximately 8 P.M. according to the medical examiner—the appalling "incident" happened.

MUTILATED

The body bore the same evidence of furious slashing that had brutally marked the previously murdered women. Her throat was slit and her chest and pelvic region were knifed repeatedly.

The body was found on the bed in Mrs. Sloat's third-floor

room by a tenant who had knocked on her door to report a
suspected gas leak in the downstairs kitchen. Having heard
someone enter a short time before and then leave, and getting
no response, he became alarmed and broke in. He was held
for questioning by the police but later released.

RAPE SUSPECTED

Although the condition of the body precluded scientific
certainty, the medical examiner believes he may have discovered evidence of sexual intercourse. A policeman who was
present was less circumspect: "Rape," he said. "No question
about it."

It was recalled that Jennifer Hartwick, in the first attack at
the Park Central Hotel, which she survived, had definitely been
raped. In the second, and fatal attack, apparently she had
not. Rape was also ruled out in the case of Diane Summers.
Police pointed out that in both instances the killer had been
pressed for time, which seemed not to be so last night.

CLUE

Detective Lieutenant Angelo Rubino, who heads a special
detail assigned to the apprehension of The Executioner, was
among the first on the scene. He took from the hand of the
murdered woman a small slip of paper on which was simulated, in heavy grease pencil, the graphic symbol of the male
sex organism, which looks like this:

$$\male$$

Rubino theorized that the symbol was deliberately left by
the murderer as a grisly joke to advertise his sexual potency
and dominance over women.

No other clues were found.

PSYCHIATRISTS

Psychiatrists, when questioned, spoke of the murderer's
need for "compensation," his obvious hatred of women, and
his total lack of conscience—decisive evidence of "a psychopathic personality."

Harking back to the Summers-Cranston case, one psychiatrist stated, "Edward Cranston was not a death object. He just happened to be there and had to be removed. The murderer's obsession concerns only women."

Other psychiatrists agreed, indicating that . . .

She had answered the bell by coming down from her third-floor room.

She peered through the door window at me standing atop the brownstone steps.

She frowned, cupped her ear and held it to the door and finally got the name.

Her face, thin and unlined, lit up. Her finger-waved hair, the color of ripe wheat, jiggled with her eager nod.

She opened the door.

It was dark where I stood. And it was dark on the carpeted stairs as she fluttered up ahead of me.

Only one small lamp was lit in her room. But when she turned, smiling, she could see all that she needed to see.

When the blade dented the skin of her throat she didn't even try to cry out.

She undressed as though she was just terribly tired and wanted only to lie down.

When I was on top of her I gripped the knife in my right hand.

As I approached the moment of climax I pushed up on the heels of my hands and looked down at her.

Her eyes were closed tight and she was holding a deep breath.

Her face seemed to have turned very old. Like Margo's when she left Shangri-La and perished in the mountain snow.

She seemed to have no sex.

In a minute I got up and made sure she had no sex.

She was no longer sinful.

Now I could take care of her.

I tried to tell her that when I pried open the knuckled hand at her side and put the slip of paper in it.

When I got home and slipped into bed I was pleasantly aware that Lambert Post was asleep.

XV

IT WAS TOO BAD the incident had to be timed so that the morning papers, particularly the tabloids, got all the benefit. Maury Ryan, who had been good enough to confide in me, would be left with nothing but a rehash. Even the name he had established for me— The Executioner—would cease to be credited to him as the other papers picked it up.

I decided to help him.

This time I called from the pay booth beside the elevators on my floor. It was 9:30 A.M. I knew that the presses for the first edition were about to roll.

He barked "yeah!" into the phone as if he were in pain.

"This is The Executioner."

"What! Wait. One second." I heard his voice, away from the phone, "Tell Stein to hold up for a new lead." Then, back to me, "Yes. I hoped you'd call."

"I guess you read about last night."

"Hell, yes. The morning blats got it all."

"And you have nothing new?"

"Only I-told-you-so. That's something, I guess. Tell me, did you know the woman?"

"I know *all* women."

"Why did you do it?"

"Mr. Ryan, I'm going to help you."

"You mean you'll meet me, turn yourself in?"

"Oh, no. But I'll tell you why the Sloat woman, and the others, had to be taken away."

"*Yes?*" He sounded as if he had crawled into the phone.

"They were evil. The Sloat woman was a widow. So was Jennifer Hartwick. They were abusing their husbands, defiling them, torturing them."

"But—you said it yourself—their husbands were dead."

"No one's *soul* is dead, Mr. Ryan. Remember your scripture—'world without end.'"

"How were they torturing them?"

"By whoring after other men."

"How about Diane Summers? She was divorced."

"She was worse. She tortured her husband while he was still on this earth. She left him, bled him, and whored with another man."

"But to kill . . . to *eliminate* them . . . *why?*"

"To save them. Now they are cleansed. Now I can watch over them. Now I'm their only true husband."

"You mean . . . you mean like nuns feel about Christ?"

"Something like that. Yes."

"What about the symbol? What's that mean?"

"That they have a man—a *total* man—to lean on. A man so strong they would never want to leave his protection."

"I understand. I *think* I understand. Hold it. The city editor—Sam Stein—just walked in. Will you speak to him?"

"Put him on."

"Hello. This is Sam Stein."

"Knock, knock," I said.

An instant's hesitation. Then, self-consciously, "Who's there?"

"Howard."

"Howard who?"

"Howard you like to kiss my ass."

I hung up. Maybe that would teach Sam Stein to let Maury Ryan handle this alone.

I had told Ryan what I had finally come to know was the truth. At first, my actions against Diane Summers and Jennifer Hartwick (I didn't count Ed Cranston) had seemed necessary only to avenge Lambert Post. Then I had begun to realize that my function was that of a purifier, surgically removing sin as a doctor would remove a cancer, enabling the subject to rise to a virginal state of grace. Now, with the purification of Eunice Sloat, I knew that all three women had become mine in an eternal union that no one could weaken or destroy.

God had imparted this knowledge step by step so that I would see it clearly and with utter conviction.

Perhaps Maury Ryan, with his superior intelligence and deep experience, had understood me. I doubted that many others would. The vast majority would judge me on the basis of all their simplistic beliefs about right and wrong—hypocritical folklore contrived by their masters to render them obedient eunuchs—and say I was crazy.

An hour later, when I heard the presses start to roll, I went up to the city room. The scene was as frantic as the one I had entered the day before. The edition was late, held up by my phone call, and about thirty men were racing furiously to receive, write, edit, and assemble the backlog of news. I stood at my usual place at the railing and waited for a copy boy to come by with an armload of papers. None came. Apparently the first edition had already been distributed. I looked past a rewrite man's head to Sam Stein's desk, about twenty-five feet away. A paper was spread atop the litter, the headline, though reversed to my eyes, obviously a screamer. I squinted, tried optically to turn it around, but was unable to read it.

A voice behind me called, *"Sam!"* It was Maury Ryan, now standing hugely beside me but seemingly unaware of me.

Sam Stein's dark head jerked up from the phone. He spotted Ryan and held up a hand. Ryan walked down a few paces and stepped through the gate. In a moment Stein yanked the phone away from his ear.

"Sam," Ryan said, "I'm going up to see Rubino."

"The hell you are," Stein said. "Sit your ass down at the desk over there and pick this up on number five. It's Hollister. He's got something." He shot a glance at his watch. "Make it fast."

Maury Ryan's bearlike figure seemed to become thinner and tautly agile as he strode to a desk by the window, threw on a headset and mouthpiece, spun a sheet of copy paper into the typewriter, and said, "Ryan, go ahead." Almost immediately he began to bang the keys. His face was expressionless.

I was distracted by a passing copy boy gripping an open paper. Turning, I glanced over his shoulder and caught a glimpse of the headline: EXECUTIONER SAYS: "I KILLED TO SAVE THEM." There

was a bold subhead that I couldn't make out. But I knew it must
state that I had called Maury Ryan just minutes before press time.

At noon I brown-bagged a chopped-chicken-liver sandwich and
a container of milk at Friedman's and took them on the bus to Park
Row. The newsstand beneath the El was doing a thriving business
in *Journals,* while the other papers, with their warmed-over reports, were being ignored. I bought a *Journal* from the few that
were left and walked across Chambers Street, passing under the
great gingerbread municipal arch, to City Hall Park. Sitting on a
bench facing the *Sun* building across the street, I thought happily
of how *their* newsmen were now sweating to catch up with my
paper. Looking back to the ancient, domed City Hall, I thought of
Mayor La Guardia, the Little Flower, wilting under the heat gen-
erated by aroused citizens. I opened the *Journal* and read Maury
Ryan's story. It had necessarily been written hurriedly, yet it reported our conversation almost verbatim, omitting, of course, his
initial chagrin and the intrusion of Sam Stein. Unless Ryan took
shorthand, which I doubted, he had a remarkably retentive mind.

Returning to the bus, I again passed the newsstand and saw its
proprietor standing outside personally hawking *Journals,* plucking
change from his apron as fast as his hand could move. It was too
early for the second edition and I assumed he had received a fresh
supply of the first. He was shouting something almost unintelligible
about The Executioner but I didn't bother to unscramble it. All I
cared about was that my phone call to Maury Ryan was selling
papers like they were printed on gold.

Not until I was back in the office and riding up in the elevator
did I learn what the newsy must have been shouting. It was ban-
nered across the front page of a *Journal* gripped by a man in front
of me. I caught my breath as I read, POLICE GET NAME OF EXECU-
TIONER!

The elevator door slammed open and I was squeezed out into
the musty lobby, staring stupidly at the old, Gandhi-like man behind the battered reception desk. He laid down the paper he had
been reading and glanced dimly at me over his steel-rimmed
glasses. He recognized me and nodded somberly.

"Mind if I have a look, Pop?" I said, indicating the paper.

He handed it to me, saying dolefully, "They better catch that loony quick before every woman in town's stacked up in Campbell's funeral parlors."

I knew before reading a word that it was the reason Sam Stein had sent Maury Ryan rushing to a desk to take the call from Hollister. They had then replated the front page.

The story was brief, set in bold type, and inserted above the one reporting my phone call:

Bulletin: The first name of The Executioner has been learned by the police! In announcing this to the press this morning, Detective Lieutenant Angelo Rubino refused to divulge it pending further investigation.

The name was revealed to police by a tenant residing in a ground-floor room of the 23rd Street rooming house owned by Mrs. Eunice Sloat, in which she was savagely slain last night.

The tenant, whose identity was not disclosed, reported hearing through his open window the voice of a man standing outside the main entrance door immediately prior to the time it is believed the murder occurred. The tenant was unable to catch the last name, and is uncertain whether or not it was mentioned, but said that the man repeated his first name several times before Mrs. Sloat opened the door and admitted him.

The bulletin had certainly not fulfilled the promise of the headline. Suddenly, walking down the corridor to the phone room, I found myself shaking with suppressed laughter. Above everything else was the irony of it: The informer, who lived on the ground floor, was probably the same man who had rented the room as a result of the ad I had written up for Eunice Sloat! Hoist with my own petard. But not really. He had heard and given to the police only the first name, Charles. And don't tell me, Lieutenant Rubino, you're going to track down and interview everyone named Charles residing in the city of New York. Nobody could live that long.

My mind took a small spin, and instead of entering the phone room, I walked on and stood in front of a window opposite a little-used freight elevator at the end of the building. Charles, I thought, was that the name the roomer had reported—*Charles?* I recalled with complete aural accuracy the interlude when I had stood outside the entrance door announcing my name to the wary Eunice Sloat. Pointing to my chest, I had twice said, "Charles *Walter.* Charles *Walter,*" emphasizing the last name, the way anyone would. Still getting no recognition, I had raised my voice slightly and said it again, bearing down even harder on *Walter.*

I was satisfied that the name the police were now working on was not Charles, but Walter, also naturally construable as a first name. So the police would be doubly confounded—they were seeking a suspect with the common first name of Walter, which in fact was the *last* name. I could not help but feel that I was being watched over by a higher being.

Jean Hooper seemed to be waiting for me as I breezed into the phone room. She motioned me to her desk. Her mouth was drawn back from her piano-key teeth, reminding me of a dog grinning in the heat.

"That woman who was murdered last night"—she made a face —"horrible. Her rooming house was in your territory. And her name sounded familiar—Sloat. Did you ever solicit her?"

I made a quick calculation. It had been at least a week since she had taken Eunice Sloat's irate phone call and written down her last name for me to call. Too many problems had intervened for her to remember it now.

"Yes, I phoned her a couple of times. In fact she'd run an ad with us. I remember—she sounded like a nice woman."

"Eunice Sloat," she said, knitting her plucked eyebrows and wrinkling her nose.

A light blinked in my head. Jean Hooper had been plugged in throughout every second of my last phone conversation with Eunice Sloat. Eunice had called me Charles, at my request. Almost flirtatiously, she had suggested I come up to inspect the room. I had given her a write-off. Eventually Jean Hooper would probably recall some of that. I had to make it appear I had nothing to hide.

"I have her down for a call-back," I said. "She was expecting a vacancy. This week, I think."

Her eyes opened wide. "Oh?"

I couldn't resist: "Well, she's got the vacancy. No question about it."

She gave me a nasty look. "Ver*eee* funny."

Sitting down at my desk, I seethed with conjecture. When the police decided to reveal the name Walter, as they were certain to, would Jean Hooper associate it with me, then with the phone call, and begin to wonder? If so, would she consider it her duty to contact the police, perhaps anonymously? After all, she despised me.

Vaguely I heard Henrietta Boardman and Dottie Friedlander discussing the case, Dottie quoting from the latest edition of the *Post* that she had bought at lunch. The police were being overwhelmed with calls from widows and divorcées demanding protection. A woman beaten up in Brownsville had called the local station house and accused her boy friend of being The Executioner. The male sex symbol was beginning to show up on sidewalks, walls, school blackboards, and the post office reported its appearance on the flaps of envelopes. The police chief had canceled all days off. Lieutenant Rubino's special detail was working round the clock.

The city was gripped by terror.

Sure as I was alive, Jean Hooper would be opening her big mouth to the police.

That night in the apartment Lambert Post finally broke his silence and began sniveling and wailing until I thought I'd lose my mind. *You've got to stop, Charles! They'll catch you, Charles! They'll nail you to a cross, Charles! They'll crucify you, Charles! No, Charles, no!* Over and over again. God, I'd like to have killed him.

Later, I snapped on the radio for the Boake Carter news.

That shut Lambert up in a hurry.

The police had arrested a man who lived in Eunice Sloat's rooming house.

His name was Walter Onderdonk.

MAURY RYAN

XVI

AN INVESTIGATIVE REPORTER—as I'm perfectly willing to have the *Journal* promotion ads call me—has a special advantage over a police detective. The reporter can get lost in blind alleys, run into dead ends, without having to answer to the public. Not so the police detective, especially the guy in charge. If he comes up with zero in a case that's got the taxpayers scared, they're apt to go after his badge.

I wondered if that wasn't the biggest thing worrying Lieutenant Angelo Rubino when he hauled in Walter Onderdonk for the murder of Eunice Sloat. Not that Rubino didn't have enough to convince the average citizen, if not a court, that the guy ought to burn. Onderdonk was a pretty sorry character. He'd once been nabbed as a junkie, but claimed he kicked the habit at the government hospital in Lexington, Kentucky. Twice he'd been convicted of armed robbery, once for knocking over a mommy-and-poppy delicatessen, once for sticking up an old man. He did six years at Sing Sing. Then he got closer to the sort of thing that made him a pigeon for Rubino. Pimp—suspended sentence. (Maybe the judge didn't want to make him a three-time loser.) Indecent exposure— thrown out of court for lack of evidence. Finally, sexual assault— dismissed when his lawyer produced witnesses who swore the girl was a whore. Now add that he was one of Eunice Sloat's fifteen roomers, that he had no alibi except that he was in his room alone, and that, God help him, he had been christened Walter, and it's easy to see why Rubino jumped him.

It made one hell of a headline and, considering the guy's record, a juicy story. But writing it, I got that hollow feeling in my belly that signaled Rubino had the wrong man. I used to get the same feeling just before I was faked out of a play when I was a second-string lineman at Notre Dame under Rockne. I got it sometimes when I was quizzing an on-the-make cop. Or listening to some silver-tongued politician. Once, God forgive me if I'm wrong, I got it interviewing a highly publicized Catholic bishop. And I got it, like no man should ever have to get it, three months before I found out that my wife—*former* wife—was parting the percales with an old pal who wrote fiction for the slicks. Suspicion—gut-killing suspicion. But I suppose it was an occupational asset.

I brought that suspicion along after Rubino called and invited me into headquarters for a talk. He had grilled Sam Stein after our surrender appeal and after each of the phone calls from the killer. But he had left me alone. Probably because I'd given him some grief in the past. I seemed to have a knack for making cops uncomfortable.

Of course there were practical reasons for questioning Walter Onderdonk's guilt, and I hit Rubino with them as soon as I crunched down on a slat-backed chair in his fumed-oak office.

"Angelo, if you believe this Onderdonk murdered the Sloat woman, then naturally you have to believe he was the same guy who murdered Jennifer Hartwick, Diane Summers, and Ed Cranston. Same M.O., excepting Cranston. And the crazy who phoned me late yesterday to call the shot on Eunice Sloat admitted to those three murders."

Rubino looked at me guardedly. He was a tall, trim man, with shoulders so square it looked as if the wire hanger was still in his dark, immaculately tailored jacket. He had black crisp hair and luminous brown eyes set deeply in a gaunt, sallow face, which showed no more expression than a movie gambler's. He was about my age—thirty-four—and was aching to make captain. I'd known him for about five years.

"So?" he said.

"So he's got to be smart enough to have thought up that first caper at the Park Central. Brave enough to have entered the Summers apartment via the dumbwaiter. Adroit enough to have outsmarted your boys at the Court Hotel and sent the Hartwick girl racing for the stairs. Last—and not at all least—he's got to be a psycho with a messiah complex. Now, does that fit your Walter Onderdonk?"

Rubino picked up a thick pencil and tapped it on his tattered green blotter. "You gonna print my answer?" His face was upper-crust Naples but his accent was lower Manhattan, with a bronchial rasp.

"Not if you tell me not to."

"Onderdonk couldn't find the cheeks of his behind with both hands in broad daylight. And unless maybe he's doped up—which he wasn't last night—he'd be scared to death to look in the mirror. For that I wouldn't blame him. He looks like a yellow-toothed rat. And he wouldn't know a messiah from a matzoh ball."

"Yet you're holding him for murder."

"For *suspicion* of murder. For *interrogation*. Why not? He's got a slimy record, including sex offenses. He's got no real alibi. He had opportunity. His name is Walter."

"Why would he ring for this Sloat woman, have her come downstairs, when he *lived* there?"

"He could have forgot his key, or pretended to. It was dark outside on the steps and she couldn't make out who was there. So he calls out his name a few times. He sees she's alone and everything's quiet. So he says he has something to talk to her about, maybe a complaint. She lets him into her room and he rapes her and stabs her to pieces. Or maybe the other way around. Anyway —you've got to admit it, Maury—he's a made-to-order suspect."

"But he's not your man."

Rubino shook his head slowly and solemnly. "No, he's not our man." He threw the pencil on the desk. "Earlier this morning we had a lineup. We had the pawnbroker there—the guy who sold the gun that blew off Cranston's face. The pawnbroker was positive—*absolutely* positive—that Onderdonk wasn't the guy who bought it. He laughed at us like we were working for Mack Sennett. Maybe we should be."

"So you've released Onderdonk?"

"Not yet. We're still holding him on suspicion. Without bail. We've got enough on him to do that without worrying about false arrest. But we can't hold him long. Two, maybe three days."

"Any shyster could get a habeas and wrap it around your ears. There goes captain."

"No lawyer outside the Legal Aid would have this creep. Too much stacked against him. And he's flat broke. A part-time car jockey for a midtown garage."

I stood up. "So you're going to hang on to an innocent man just to get the heat off you. Angelo, I can't go along. I may not have a conscience but I do have an editor."

"You've got a conscience, Maury. Maybe too much. As for the editor, I called Sam Stein while you were on your way up here. I leveled with him. I told him if he'd cooperate, chances are he'll get an exclusive when we bring in the guilty man."

"Cooperate how?"

"Do me a favor, Maury. Please sit down."

I sat down.

Rubino hunched his shoulders, folded his hands under his chin, and gazed at me earnestly. "Look, Maury. You *Journal* guys pulled a real grandstand play with that high-and-mighty appeal to the killer. Kid stuff, I thought when I read it. But it worked, *partly* worked. The man called three times. And he didn't call the city editor like most people would do—and he was listed first. He called *you*—Maury Ryan. Ask me *why*. I've got a theory." He leaned back and hooked a thumb in the top pocket of his jacket.

I lit a cigarette. "Okay, Angelo—why?"

"Because, I think, The Executioner, as he calls himself, believes he's got a lot in common with you. It's all in that last phone conversation you had with him—the one late yesterday. I read every word. I *thought* about every word. Maury, you got a big reputation in this town for crusading against the bad guys. He thinks he's a crusader, too—against dames. He said he wanted to help you, then proves it by spilling why he knocked them off—because they were whoring on their husbands and he had to save them. And why he left the sex symbol in the Sloat woman's hand—because she and the others too were now pure and had become his heavenly brides. Now why would he big-mouth all that unless he thought you'd *understand?* Unless he thought you were his *equal?*"

I grunted. "You mean unless he thought I was as nutty as he?"

"Have your joke. The thing is, the guy doesn't *think* he's nutty.

He thinks he's one of the few sane people walking the earth. He seems to think you may be another. A superior man who's also a crusader against evil. Isn't that what they call that sheet of yours —a crusading newspaper?"

"Yeah. Maury Ryan—Jesus of the Fourth Estate."

"The way The Executioner sees it, you may not be far off."

"You've been talking to the psychs."

"Sure. Part of my job in a case like this. Delusional is one of the words they use. And paranoidal. And schizo. I've heard 'em all. The thing is, the guy's off his rocker. Everything's out of proportion. He's the kind who pays back a slap on the wrist—and maybe it's only imagined—by yanking off an arm. After that, he maybe feels gentle. But no remorse, none. In fact, he thinks he's done the wrist-slapper a favor by straightening him out. There's your savior complex. He's shrewd, though, shrewd as they come, but he doesn't live in the real world. That's the nutshell of it. I don't say I understand it. But I believe it."

I ground out the cigarette. "Careful. You're talking about my buddy."

"A guy who may *imagine* you're his buddy. You played up The Executioner handle. He probably liked that. You didn't lecture him. You just asked the kind of questions he was aching to answer. And you said you understood him."

"I also wrote—in the appeal—that the *Journal* would provide him with medical help. That doesn't sound as if I thought he was qualified to run the asylum."

"I think he'd figure that was the publisher talking. The humanitarian angle. Remember, he called *you* with the tipoff on the Sloat woman's murder. Not anyone else. That's friendship, Maury."

I got up and circled to the bulletin board, examining the staring, unshaven faces of hoodlums on police flyers. I had an apprehension that I was about to be framed by Angelo Rubino with the gleeful assistance of my charming city editor, Sam Stein. I turned and faced Rubino.

"All right, goddamn it, you've made your case for me and this fruitcake practically going steady. I shouldn't ask, but what's that going to buy you?"

Rubino smiled like some gypsy playing schmaltz on a violin.

"You should know the answer, Maury. You're our best bet to bring him in."

"That I get. But how? Three times he called me. Three times he hung up." I was beginning to talk like Rubino.

Rubino's smile stretched. He rubbed his hands as though washing them. "Now a plan we've got."

I had noticed in the past that when Rubino got excited, he often lapsed into the inverted speech of his Mulberry Street boyhood. It must have made his law professors at Columbia night school wonder if it was all really worth it.

"This Executioner," he said, "he must have an ego big as a house. Do you think any guy who goes to such trouble to kill people, who brags he's a savior, who plants his trademark on a murder victim—do you think he's happy to sit back and let somebody else—a pimp and a junkie yet—take the credit?"

I said cautiously, "You've got a point, Angelo."

"To get back in the act, what would he do? One of two things." Rubino patted his crisp, glossy black hair and leaned forward. "He calls you again to set the record straight. He could then, of course, go out and butcher another dame, like with the Sloat woman. But this time not right away, I don't think. For a while anyway, he should get kicks enough out of being reinstated and seeing Onderdonk shown up for a phony. Maury, I'm giving odds he'll call you within the next twelve hours. *Less.*"

I had been thinking the same thing. I looked at the phone on Rubino's desk.

"Don't worry, Maury. Sam Stein says if he calls while you're here, he'll give us a quick blast. If the nut doesn't hang up, Stein can even transfer the call. I fixed that."

"So you tapped my phone."

"Not really a tap. I wouldn't do that to the press. Just a temporary tie-in between your phone and mine. Like an extension. In case you need me in a hurry." He made a palms-up, spread-fingered gesture. "I'm a cop, Maury."

I had to grin at him. Angelo Rubino was so much cop, I think he had N.Y.P.D. monogrammed on his shorts.

"All right," I said. "Let's assume he calls me. Let's say he denounces Onderdonk as an impostor, however unwilling, and demands recognition as The Executioner. I've got a story, a beat, a big, one-day sensation. But what have *you* got? My story would prove you'd collared the wrong man. You'd look like you shouldn't even be pounding a beat in Canarsie."

Rubino looked unruffled. "That's if you *printed* the story."

"*If* we printed it! What the hell do you think we're trying to do, fold the paper?"

"Maury, do me another favor."

"What?"

"Calm down. Please."

"Okay, I'm calm."

"Thank you. Now, suppose you sat on the story. Suppose you told the guy you thought he was a dirty liar; naturally, in a nice way. Suppose you said you thought that Walter Onderdonk was the guilty party. Suppose—"

"He'd hang up and go out and kill another woman, to prove I was wrong. Do you want that on your conscience?"

Rubino blew out air, as if trying to control his patience. "I think you can head him off on that, Maury. If he says there'll be another incident—or even if he doesn't—you tell him this: You tell him that another killing won't prove a thing because now everyone knows how this Walter Onderdonk operates and it would be easy to imitate his style. Leaving that male sex symbol won't mean a thing either, because now it's popping up all over the place, like the swastika in Germany." Rubino rubbed his five-o'clock shadow. "No, you say, you're very sorry but you've got to go along with the cops on Onderdonk."

I stared at him as if he'd lost his marbles. "Let's be sure I've got this straight, Angelo. You want me to make him believe that I think Walter Onderdonk killed not only Eunice Sloat but the other three as well. Right?"

He nodded.

"But I've already told him—The Executioner—that I accepted *him* as the killer. I *had* to, goddamn it. The first time he called, he told me explicitly how he'd sexually mutilated Jennifer Hartwick and Diane Summers. *Explicitly,* Angelo. No paper had printed that. I do a flip-flop now and he's sure to be suspicious. You said it before—he's slick."

Rubino gazed reflectively at his desk. "Okay. Then do it this way. You say you believe him, but the cops don't and neither do your bosses on the paper. They think he's just some crank. With them, it's Onderdonk all the way. You've got no choice. Much as you hate to, you've got to line up with them."

I thought a minute, then grudgingly conceded that he might— just possibly might—buy that.

Rubino gave me a limpid look. "It's even better this way, Maury. It brings you and The Executioner closer together—the two of you against the unbelievers. He'll be more ready to agree with what you suggest."

At last, I thought, here it comes. "Which is?"

"You say you've got to have something *concrete* to prove he's the real killer. Say the knife he carved up Jennifer Hartwick with and that he probably used on Eunice Sloat. We could maybe match it to some of the wounds, you say. Or a recording of his voice— saying 'Walter'—for the roomer who heard him on the steps to listen to and identify. Or a drawing of the sex symbol, so we could prove it was the same style, maybe the same kind of grease pencil that was used. Any of these things, you say, would expose Onder- donk as a fake, a scapegoat, and would show up the police as a bunch of dopes. And the real Executioner would be back on the front pages."

I lit another cigarette. "I've got to get used to this, Angelo. It's pretty wild. My God, the police demanding that a fugitive prove himself guilty. Does the chief know about this, or Stein?"

"The chief, no. Stein, yes."

"With Stein it figures. Anything for a headline." I took a few fast drags. "Okay, let's say this loony falls for it. What then?"

"You ask to meet him someplace. A bar, a pier, an alley. I'm guessing he'll trust you not to double-cross him. Why should you? All you care about is publishing the truth, same as him. You want to stick it to your bosses and the cops, who've begun to think maybe you're a little nuts yourself. You're defending your profes- sional pride. He should understand things like that." He paused. "Then you tip me off where to pick him up."

I stood up, this time determined to stay on my feet. "Jesus, An- gelo, you sure are desperate."

His Italian eyes rolled toward the heavens. "That's the word, Maury—desperate. This job they gave me, this special detail, at least a captain should be in charge, not a lieutenant. They picked me because I got a terrific record, and because I want to make captain so bad I can taste it. I'm on a real hot spot. It's only a few months to election and the D.A., Tom Dewey, is working to be a candidate for governor. I've got pressure on me. And I've got a cluck locked up in the Tombs who could break me to just another flatfoot. Yeah, I'm desperate. That's why I'm hanging on to Onderdonk, hoping for a break."

"But that pawnbroker—he said Onderdonk wasn't the man who bought the gun. How do you explain that to the rest of the press?"

"I don't explain it. I don't even tell them, not yet. No reporter was there." He got up and supplicated me with his eyes. "You'll do it, Maury?"

Wearily I said, "If he calls, Angelo, I'll give it a try."

XVII

IT WAS ALMOST one o'clock when I caught the office bus at Park Row. Only a few people were aboard and I sat in the rear, not wanting to talk to the driver, and stared out at the littered streets and the senile tenements that only rats and roaches should have to live in. Instead of feeling eager and excited at the prospect of what Rubino had asked me to do, I was strangely depressed. I kept thinking of that guy's voice on the phone—Walter—not Onderdonk, but Walter *Something*. There had been such a certainty of righteousness in that cathedral-toned voice, an unquestioning belief that he had been divinely selected to dispense God's ultimate wrath. Considering the ghastly things he had done, I guess I shouldn't have felt sorry for him. But I did.

New York was full of people like Walter, but somehow they'd managed to sublimate their hate or at least express it passively. You saw men hurrying along the streets jabbering a blue streak to themselves ("They're just planning their day," Sam Stein once said). You saw bearded, long-haired men, dressed in burlap and carrying crosses, passing out pamphlets. You saw hopped-up down-and-outers bobbing and weaving in the middle of the sidewalk and throwing punches at some imaginary foe. All of them were relatively harmless. In a world they'd never made, they'd found a peaceful way, however peculiar, to express themselves. Respectable people smiled at them, almost sympathetically; they had their irrational fancies too. Walter might have been just as harmless if somewhere, way back, someone had said the right words. Or if his chromosomes had been only slightly different. Or if it had been possible to reach physically into his brain and give it a tiny turn. But through no fault of his own, he was insane,

murderously insane, and thus had to be destroyed like a rabid animal. Unless he could be persuaded to give himself up. Or unless
somehow he could be brought in peaceably. Then perhaps they'd
simply lock him away in an asylum to live out his days in a
blurred world of fantasy. Not entirely happy, perhaps, but maybe
more so than the sane people who crowded those stinking tenements.

Yet I had agreed to help deny him even that, to set him up for
probable death under a hail of police bullets.

I looked up, sensing eyes staring at me. Sitting on one of the
side seats was the kid who had wandered into my office the day
before. A new copy boy, I had guessed. Eager.

His chin was resting on his hand as he smiled and said, "Hi,
Mr. Ryan. I see they've caught The Executioner."

Without thinking, I said, "Homicide thinks so."

His thick black eyebrows went up. "You mean *you* don't think
so?"

I smiled back at him, in no mood to talk but not wanting to be
brusque. "I only know what I read in the papers," I said.

He said seriously, "I don't think he did it. Onderdonk."

I was mildly startled. My God, even a copy boy without a speck
of knowledge about the case couldn't swallow Walter Onderdonk.
I felt a lot less wise than I'd thought myself when I had said the
same thing to Rubino.

"Why not Onderdonk?" I said. "He's got a rap sheet a yard
long."

His eyes gave the impression of suddenly turning inward, as
though examining his thoughts. An odd sort of duck, I thought.
Withdrawn, but at the same time aware. An intellectual, perhaps,
absorbed in his own ideas. Yet respectful and willing to learn.
There wasn't too much of that around. Without much reason, I
found myself liking him.

"A dope addict," he said, but with no inflection of censure. "A
petty thief, a procurer, a sex exhibitionist. It's all so small-time. I
think The Executioner has to be someone who thinks big, who's
clever and has iron nerves. That's not Onderdonk." His face
twisted in disgust. "Phew, what a name. Maybe he should be pitied, but not locked up."

I said, "Maybe you should tell that to Detective Lieutenant Angelo Rubino."

He laughed quietly. "Not me. But maybe *you* should, Mr. Ryan. He'd listen to you."

"I just came from Rubino's office. He's—" I stopped. That was about enough. "He's in a tough spot," I finished lamely. I shook my head and turned to gaze out the window, ending the conversation.

Arriving at the office, he waved me out ahead of him and we went into the downstairs lobby. Sam Stein was there, waiting for an elevator. He gave me a lupine grin.

"I talked to the lieutenant again right after you left," he said, a small needle in his voice. "So you're all set up to be a hero."

"Lay off it, Sam. The whole thing's ridiculous."

"You said that about the appeal." Sam pulled off his horn-rimmed glasses and rubbed the side of his beaked nose with one of the stems. Unlensed, his eyes were reduced to the gimlets they naturally were—greedy, probing, always distrustful. He was a short man, body squared off like an orange crate, but when those eyes ransacked you, you thought he was ten feet tall.

"This is different," I said, lowering my voice. "If it comes off, the chances are better than even he'll be cashed in."

"My heart bleeds, Maury."

The elevator came and we got in with several other passengers.

"Sam," I said, "I'll try talking him into coming in. But this other plan—call it off."

The elevator stopped on the floor below the city room and I stood aside to let the kid on the bus get off. When the door slammed shut, Sam rubbed his dark jaw and said bluntly into my ear, "You keep thinking like that, Maury, and you'll never get my job. Just park by that phone. When he calls—and I'll bet my left nut, the good one, he does—set it up. Just like you promised Rubino. The mayor'll name a street after you."

In my office I sat and stared out the window at some kids skinny-dipping off one of the piers. Then I did the crossword. Then I read the funnies and Bill Corum and—in the morning *Mirror*—Walter Winchell, Damon Runyon, and Drew Pearson. The phone might as well have been disconnected. At about three o'clock I was yawning through one of old man Hearst's editorials, written from San Simeon, warning Americans against foreign entanglements, when I heard a voice say timidly, "Mr. Ryan?"

I swung around. It was the kid from the bus. He stood in the doorway, half on his toes, as if ready to scoot if I so much as raised an eyebrow to question his presence. I didn't question it. In fact, I was glad to see him. I felt as if I'd been locked in solitary.

"I'm probably disturbing you," he said in a smooth, polite voice that I suddenly thought should be on the radio hawking toothpaste. It had the same timbre as Norman Brokenshire's but none of the oiliness.

"Friend," I said, "you have probably saved me from becoming a gibbering idiot." I glanced at the phone. "But I may get a call. If I do, I'll need privacy."

"I understand." He took a couple of steps into the room. "Mr. Ryan, I'm sure you've thought of this and maybe you'll want to throw me out for kibitzing, but after we talked on the bus, something occurred to me."

I thought back to our conversation. "You mean about The Executioner?"

"Yes. I remembered about the gun that was used to kill—what was the man's name?"

"Cranston," I said. "Edward Cranston." I felt a tingle along my spine.

"Yes. Cranston. Well, as you know, the man who used the gun bought it from a pawnbroker. The pawnbroker described the man to the police. The paper even did an artist's drawing of what the man might look like."

"Yeah, sure," I said quickly, hoping to shut him off. "We've gone over all that with the police."

"I see. Then the police did bring the pawnbroker in to have a look at Onderdonk. Of course. Simple routine."

I didn't answer. Instead, I lit a cigarette.

He said, "I saw Onderdonk's picture in the paper. He looked like a weasel. About as far as you could get from that drawing of The Executioner. I went to the morgue and got the back issue and compared the two."

I tried to speak lightly. "The fallibility of man."

"You mean the pawnbroker identified Onderdonk as the man who bought the gun?"

I was no longer glad to see him. "He wasn't sure." Now why in hell hadn't I simply said that Rubino wasn't talking?

"Funny that wasn't in the paper. It wasn't even mentioned that the pawnbroker had been brought in to identify Onderdonk. Shouldn't that have been reported, Mr. Ryan?"

"Well, yes, I guess it should have been. A fast-breaking story like this and you don't always get everything."

"But this is so important." He smiled mischievously. "I think I'll write my first letter to a newspaper. Maybe I'll tell it to the *News.*"

I made a quick decision. He might just do that. If the *News* or any other sheet knew that the pawnbroker had been Rubino's guest at a lineup, they'd be down to see him personally. And they'd hear him say, as Rubino had, that he was positive—"*absolutely* positive"—that Onderdonk was not the man.

"Look," I said, "you work for this paper. You must have some loyalty to it."

"Damned right I do, Mr. Ryan." He sounded very sincere.

"Then I'm going to tell you something. But only if you promise not to breathe it to a soul."

He nodded gravely and crossed his heart with his forefinger.

"The pawnbroker could not identify Onderdonk as the man who bought the gun."

"You mean he wasn't sure. That's what you said before."

Damn this guy. I ground out my cigarette. "I mean what I'm saying now. He simply didn't recognize Onderdonk."

He blinked at me. "Yet he remembered the man who bought the gun so well that he could describe him—at least his profile— with enough accuracy for a drawing to be made. Excuse me, Mr. Ryan, but I think Lieutenant Rubino may be lying to you. I think the pawnbroker said Onderdonk was *not* the man. In that case, he couldn't be the one who was responsible for what happened to Cranston and the Summers girl. That should also clear him of what happened to Jennifer Hartwick and the Sloat woman."

I controlled my exasperation. "Sounds like you've been doing a lot of thinking about the case."

His eyes seemed to glaze over ever so slightly. "I guess everyone in town has. Anyway, it looks to me like Rubino's holding on to Onderdonk just to keep everybody quiet. So he'll have a little more time to catch the real Executioner. But he can't have *much* time. Not if Onderdonk's innocent. Maybe Rubino has a plan."

God save me, I thought, from these smart-ass amateurs. "Look," I said impatiently, "you promised to keep quiet about this—about the pawnbroker. That's all I ask. It could mean a lot to the paper—to *me*. Okay?"

"Sure, okay. Nobody will hear it from me." He shook his head in humility. "Besides, I've probably got it all wrong. I guess I'm just having fun thinking about it."

I began to like him again.

"Thanks for listening to me, Mr. Ryan. And excuse me for busting in." He gave a small farewell flip of his hand and left.

I smoked another cigarette and thought about it. Nothing really to worry about; I was convinced he'd keep his mouth shut. Just an ambitious kid showing off a bit, hoping I'd put in a good word for him with Stein. Maybe I would at that.

Ten minutes later any thought of him was exploded from my mind. The phone blasted, I yanked the receiver to my ear, and that familiar, confident, resonant voice said, "This is The Executioner."

Before I could say more than hello, he cut me off with, "The police are holding a scapegoat, a fall guy. Do you agree?"

His voice was brisk and angry. There was no time for a warm-up.

"Yes," I said. "I told that to Rubino. I told that to my bosses here. They won't listen to me. They've got Onderdonk down for all four killings."

"That pip-squeak. You're lying to me, Ryan. None of them could be so stupid."

"You're wrong. The only thing that will change their minds is concrete proof you did it."

"What if I came in? Isn't that what your paper still wants?"

My God, I thought, was he handing himself to me on a silver platter? Could I skip the deadly runaround proposed by Rubino and approved by Stein?

"I *want* you to come in. We'll give you every protection—legal, medical . . ."

"Forget the medical shit. I'll come in on one condition."

"Name it."

"That Onderdonk is released and you tell me the exact time when that will be."

"I'll have to phone Rubino."

"How long will that take?"

"Ten, fifteen minutes. I don't know if he's in his office."

"I'll give you a break. Half hour. Then I'll call back."

He hung up. I jiggled for the switchboard operator, asked for Rubino, and was connected immediately on the direct line. I told him the deal.

He thought for a moment. "Tell you what, Maury. When he calls again, tell him that the minute he's in your custody we'll spring Onderdonk."

"He won't go for it, Angelo. I know it. He'll insist on Onderdonk being sprung first."

"What's the difference to him?"

"He'll think you want to glaum onto him because you think he's a crank. He'll figure you to throw him into the mental ward but still keep Onderdonk. He's no dumb jerk, Angelo."

I heard Rubino's bronchial breathing. "Try it anyway. If he says no sale, tell him that six o'clock this evening we'll make Onderdonk a free man. Or any time he says. May the Lord help me if he doesn't show."

"Okay. He's calling back in about a half hour."

"Half hour, yeah. He wants that time to get far away, to another phone, in case you're trying to trace him."

When I hung up, I called Sam Stein and told him what was going on.

"We*l-l-l*," he said, very smug, "so my appeal finally got to him. You still think it was a bum idea?"

"How can I?"

"Stick with me, Maury, and you'll be farting through silk. I'll hold the five-star. While you're waiting, start the story. Here's your headline: EXECUTIONER GIVES UP TO JOURNAL! Slug it with a bang. In the subhead you can say it was my idea." He chuckled patronizingly.

I was just finishing as much of the story as I could write when the phone almost made me leap out of my skin.

This time the voice didn't bother with identification. It just said, "Well, Ryan, what time?"

"Rubino says the minute you come in here and I call him, he'll release Onderdonk."

"That proves he knows Onderdonk is a phony. But no deal. Onderdonk goes out first, then I come in. *When,* Ryan?"

"All right. Today. Six o'clock."

"No dice. I need more time."

"Time for what?"

"That's my business. I just need more time—a day."

"Six P.M. tomorrow then."

Short silence.

"Make it nine P.M."

"All right. Nine P.M. tomorrow."

His voice softened abruptly. "I'll see you, Maury." He replaced the receiver, gently from the sound of the click.

XVIII

I'M NOT THE kind of guy who was meant to sleep alone, but it was worse that night. The small bedroom was hot and sultry, dense as a wool blanket, and I lay naked on the dampening sheets trying to get my mind off an abstract character named Walter. I tried the trick of substituting pleasant thoughts, which generally produced sleep. . . .

I stood on a basketball court in my Chicago high school and arched the ball again and again through the hoop, not once permitting myself to miss. I listened to my city editor on the Chicago *Herald-Examiner* saying, "Tomorrow, no more copy boy. Maury Ryan—reporter." (School news, lodge meetings, social notes; but I started carrying a folded newspaper in my jacket pocket, just like the pros.) I stepped off the Twentieth Century Limited in New York wide-eyed with wonder at being summoned to work for the *Journal.* I stood in The Rain House, drinking and playing the match game with a couple of veteran by-liners; then went up-town to Bleek's and miraculously was invited to do the same thing with the *Trib*'s Lucius Beebe and their great city editor, Stanley Walker. I sat in a booth drinking beer and philosophizing with Tim Costello. I stood at a circular bar and traded insults with Toots Shor. I gloried in my first beat, when Vincent "Mad Dog" Coll was mowed down by gangsters in that drugstore phone booth on Twenty-third Street (we hit the streets half an hour before competition). I dropped in on my mother and father in their white clapboard home in Evanston—my father still an engraver on the *Her-Ex*—and glowed under their beautifully exaggerated pride in their only begotten.

But this night none of these thoughts worked. Always the rumbling voice and faceless apparition of Walter intervened. At 1:00 A.M. I got up, shambled to the kitchen, and poured a glass of milk, adding a dollop of rum. I took it into the living room, the blond Swedish modern furniture (it was a sublet) ghostly in the glow spilling in from the street lamp. I stood at the window and stared down into the empty gloom of East Fifty-fourth Street.

In less than twenty hours the man who was terrorizing the country's largest city would walk into my office—calmly, I thought—sit himself down and pour out his appalling story. I would keep him there incommunicado until the following morning, past the deadlines of the morning papers, assuring the *Journal* a clear field. Rubino had agreed to that as quid pro quo for our part in bringing him in (but also had insisted on having a squad of detectives roaming the corridors and stationed at the exits). God, how the competition would howl. When the story finally broke and they picked it up, they'd *have* to credit the *Journal* by name, not just attribute it to "an evening newspaper." The wire services would shoot it out to every daily and weekly in the country, complete with my picture. For a while, as Sam Stein had said, I'd be a hero.

Then why was I feeling so goddamned despondent?

Part of it, I thought, was because I could see little valid glory in playing confessor to a desperately sick man. But there was a much less virtuous reason than that: I was also gnawed by the suspicion that The Executioner might not show.

And of course there was a solid basis for that. He had said he needed more time—a day, in fact twenty-seven hours from the surrender time first proposed. I kept asking myself the same question I had asked him: time for what? Considering past performance, the answer was, time to kill again. But that seemed to make no sense. If he wanted to kill again simply for the sheer pleasure of killing, he'd go ahead and do it without all that telephone rigmarole. He was impatient to be recognized as the ingenious perpetrator of the crimes blamed on Onderdonk, yet for more than a day he wanted everybody to continue thinking Onderdonk was The Executioner. Why? What difference would it make if he was going to reveal himself anyway? Oh hell, I thought, I'm going round and round. Maybe he simply wanted to wind up his affairs, whatever that meant. I was tired and my mind was no more capable of reasoning than a meatball.

I snapped on a lamp and got from the desk drawer the *Journal* showing the artist's rendering of The Executioner. Leaning back on the sofa, sipping my drink, I studied the profile, drawn with hard black lines. The hair appeared thick, starting high on an almost noble brow, the nose straight and a trifle long, the mouth small and seemingly pursed, the chin clean and definite. I felt an inner stirring. The face was vaguely familiar. I tried to relax and empty my mind in the hope that a face I had seen or known would drop in and recall to me where and when I had seen it. Slowly it came into recognizable focus. The drawing would pass as a prototype of the traditional Shakespearean actor—John Barrymore, perhaps, back when he had been filmed with his wife, Dolores Costello, in *Tempest*. I fingered the thickened cartilage in my nose —broken when I had matched it against a charging tackle's knee— and felt myself smiling wryly. How often when I was a kid, I had wanted a face like that, instead of the tough-ugly one nature had given me. My mother used to say that my face had "character." Long ago I had learned to settle for that. Besides, along with my huge lump of a build (if I was a building, I'd have been razed), it had often been a help in dealing with certain recalcitrant types.

I finished my drink and went back to bed—to a long, tossing night crowded with half-awake dreams of a disembodied voice thrumming ceaselessly against my eardrum.

The next day was something like waiting for a time bomb to go off. Walter Onderdonk was still the lead story, but of course there was no hard news we could print. I wrote a warm-over of the same handout we'd used the day before, picking up a few sidelights from the A.M.s and adding a barrage of platitudes from a number of pols up for reelection. The burden of the story—and God, what a burden—was a reprise of Onderdonk's record, which, put together, made it sound as if juicing him with fifteen thousand volts in Sing Sing's electric chair would be a boon to mankind. It was sickening, but with the lid on the real story, it was the only way we could hang on to our readers. Sam Stein poked his head in a few times, looking like a man expecting to win first money in the Irish Sweepstakes but fearful his horse might be scratched. The third time he edged in, I said ill-temperedly, "Sam, if there's any change, I'll call you." His mouth thinned and he fixed me with those gimlet eyes, saying brusquely, "Do that. We blow this and neither one of us could get a messenger job on the North Moose Droppings *Daily Disappointment*." It was the first time I'd ever seen him without his vast self-assurance.

Rubino called twice to convey the same anxiety. He reaffirmed his pledge to spring Onderdonk on the dot of nine, moaning, "I'm taking a big chance, Maury. Your boy's a no-show and what have I got? An empty bag. The chief will stick me in it and drop me in the river." But Rubino knew it was the only chance he had to come out smelling pretty; the charges against Onderdonk just wouldn't stand up and he'd have to let him go anyway.

I stuck it until about four o'clock, then told the switchboard where I'd be, and took the back freight elevator down and went to The Rain House. There were a few guys at the bar, and I gave them a wave but sat in the corner nursing a beer and talking about the Giants with Jimmy, the bartender. In about fifteen minutes the phone on the bar rang. Jimmy picked it up, listened, and handed it to me. It was Sam Stein.

"You pick a great time to sneak across the street and slop up booze."

"Where else?" I said, annoyed. "You've got signs posted all over the walls up there, and I quote: 'Drinking on the premises is cause for instant dismissal.'"

"Beef to the publisher, not me. Rubino just called me. There's been a leak on the pawnbroker. The competition's got a rumor he refused to finger Onderdonk. They're all over Rubino."

The premonition I'd felt during the night returned. "Jesus, they print that and our man will take a fast powder."

"You think you're telling me something? I told Rubino to play it strictly no comment."

"Not good enough, Sam. They'll speculate. Almost as bad."

"Go ahead, tell me my job. I also told Rubino to make a bargain. They print nothing and he gives them a complete statement in the morning. By then we'll be on the streets with the whole son-of-a-bitching story. Rubino bought it—he had a choice?—but he's whining the other papers will murder him for holding out, giving us the inside. I told him we already *had* the inside and the other sheets will understand that. Christ, didn't we publish the appeal!"

"But the pawnbroker—they'll get to him. Like right about now."

"You underestimate me, Maury. I told Rubino to radio a squad car to get down to that hock shop, pick up the pawnbroker, and hold him for further questioning. Rubino'll do it first cabin, even buy the guy drinks and dinner. That pawnbroker's gonna think Rubino wants him to parade up Broadway with Grover Whalen."

"You've got it all covered, Sam. Why do you need me?"

"I need you to get your ass up here and work into the story what I just told you. To do it so Rubino looks good. To make it sound like the only reason for keeping the pawnbroker under wraps—and for us holding the story—was to make sure that justice triumphed. Now, I don't have to tell you how to do *that,* do I, Maury?"

I had another beer and went back to the office. By five o'clock I had the background typed up so that it could be inserted into the big story when it broke. I glanced through the afternoon papers and saw, as expected, that they had no more than we did; they just didn't shout so loud. I read Broun and Pegler and Tom Stokes and Eleanor Roosevelt's "My Day" in the *World-Telegram.* At six Sam Stein came in to read what I'd written and to brag about how this could be the biggest story since the *News* sneaked a hidden-camera photo of Ruth Snyder frying in the chair, or since the G-Men shot John Dillinger in Chicago four years before. Chicago made him think of Jake Lingle, the great crime reporter for the *Tribune* who was killed by gangsters. I'd be another Lingle, Stein proclaimed with unaccustomed generosity, except that I'd probably live as long as Arthur Brisbane or old man Hearst.

At seven we were eating pastrami sandwiches and drinking cartons of coffee fetched by a copy boy. At seven-thirty I left Stein in my office and went strolling through the half-dark, half-empty city room where the early night shift was sluggishly grinding out and putting together the routine news for the inside pages. Guy Turner, one of the night editors, sat at his desk doing nothing except pick wax from an ear with a paper clip. He'd been told by Stein to hold the front page, all eight columns, and two inside pages for a flash story and pix. I stayed there talking to Guy for about half an hour. A number of rewrite men, copy editors, caption writers, and photographers straggled in. Stein had them on overtime, along with a lot of extras in the composing room. Also, the circulation manager was in and the truck delivery men were downstairs on standby. As I walked back down the corridor, I passed at intervals four jacketed men with unfamiliar faces. Rubino's boys, trying to look ink-stained and nonchalant.

It was shortly after eight when I stepped into my office. Sam Stein stood at the window, square hands gripped tightly behind him, staring out at the lights of Brooklyn across the river. He didn't turn around when I dropped into my chair and began doodling on a sheet of copy paper. At eight-thirty he still hadn't moved and I hadn't stopped doodling. Same thing at eight-forty-five. And eight-fifty.

My watch said two minutes to nine when the phone rang. I picked it up, half-anticipating the hand-wringing voice of Angelo Rubino. My heart did a one-and-a-half with a full twist as I heard, "This is The Executioner."

"Yes," I said, nodding to Stein, who had spun around.

"Has Onderdonk been released?"

"Couple more minutes. Nine o'clock. Just as we said."

"Your watch is slow." His tone had a baiting quality to it. "Call Rubino. Make sure. I don't move until I know Onderdonk's a free man. I'll hold on."

I covered the phone, barked his instruction to Stein, who said, "I'll call Rubino." He scrambled across the corridor to the phone in the opposite office. In less than a minute he was back. "Onderdonk walked out of the Tombs thirty seconds ago."

I repeated that into the phone.

Back came a soft chuckle. "Maury," he said, "you've got that place crawling with cops. I can smell them from here."

"You *are* coming in?"

"Hell, no. But—"

"Goddamn it. You—"

"But I'm not exactly letting you down. You come up here. Take the address. Ready? Two one three East Sixty-sixth. Apartment 10C. You'll be smart to come alone, Maury. Got it?"

"Yes, but hold on a—"

There was a sharp click. I banged the phone a couple of times, then hung up.

I told Stein.

"Son of a bitch," he said quietly and picked up the phone and called a number. He got Harry Bressler at the corner hack stand and told him to pull his cab into the alley across from The Rain House, that I'd be right down, and to keep his big mouth shut. I took the phone from his hand, broke the connection, and jiggled for the switchboard operator.

"Who the hell you calling?" Stein said.

"Rubino."

He wrenched the phone away and slammed it down. "The hell you are." He stepped to the door and closed it silently. "The guy said come alone, Maury. You call Rubino now, you give him that address, and he'll have sirens screaming all over the East Side. He's got to. He's lost Onderdonk. Now he sees himself getting euchred out of the real killer. He'll play it about as subtle as an avalanche."

"So I'll live as long as Brisbane," I said, pulling on my jacket.

"The guy won't touch you. He just wants to talk, give you the story. But without any cops around."

"Come off it, Sam. He wouldn't trust me not to give that address to the cops."

Stein scowled in frustration. He smacked a hand on the desk. His face cleared. "Get to the apartment first. When you leave Bressler, tell him to call Rubino. In three minutes you'll have cops swarming all around like you're queen bee. But you'll be inside."

"With a goddamned maniac," I said, but I opened the door.

"This could be even better," Stein said to himself. *"Journal* reporter captures Executioner!" A smile oozed across his lips. "Call me, Maury. On this phone."

My press card got me past the cop at the freight elevator and the one at the rear exit. Bressler's cab was parked down the alley, lights out, motor running. As I came up, he twisted his lard around in the driver's seat and sprung open the back door. "Big one, Maury?" I nodded briskly but said nothing. He loved playing cops and robbers; one word from me and he'd yak my ear off.

Harry laid down a lot of rubber zigzagging uptown. I sat back on the cracked leather seat and tried to rid my mind of The Executioner. At this point, thinking about him would do nothing except put airplanes in my stomach. I considered what Sam Stein would do if I lived to get the story. The morning and evening papers had an agreement that they wouldn't poach on each other's publication hours. My guess was that Sam Stein wouldn't think twice about breaking it. He'd slug the front page MIDNIGHT EXTRA and have the trucks on the streets while the morning papers were still headlining Onderdonk.

We skidded up in front of 213 East Sixty-sixth at quarter to ten. It was a big heap of a building, maybe twenty stories, granite-faced and with a red awning stretching to the curb. But no doorman. I'd written down Rubino's title, name, and phone number, and the apartment I'd be in, and I passed the slip of paper to Harry Bressler. He held it under the dash light. When his shoulders hunched and his beefy face whirled around, I knew it had all registered.

"Harry, go down to that corner drugstore and call Rubino. Now. Tell him where I am and tell him to get some cops up here ready to shoot. I don't think he'll do it but tell him to kill the sirens."

Harry nodded, threw the shift into gear, and was bucketing away as I slammed the door.

In the vestibule I studied the row of brass mailboxes. I found 10C and looked at the name. Robert Childress. It meant nothing to me. Was it The Executioner's real name? A friend? Was Walter part of a pseudonym? I'd soon know.

The main lobby was empty and the elevator was at the main floor. I rode it to ten, got off, checked a couple of numbers, and went down the corridor to the left. 10C—second from the corner. I pressed the bell and stepped back, just in case a fist with a knife in it should come swiping out. I waited. No answer. I pressed the bell again, holding it for ten seconds. I waited some more. Then I reached forward and tried the knob. The door was unlocked. I gave the knob a full turn and tapped the door open, not moving from where I stood. I looked into a small, carpeted foyer, and beyond it, through an arch, to a living room glowing with dim lamplight. It was so damned silent I thought the place was holding its breath.

I stepped forward and pushed the door all the way back, to pin to the wall anyone who might be lurking behind it. Nobody. I went in, closing the door quietly. I thought of calling out but that seemed foolish after the way I'd rung the bell. The living room was occupied only by furniture—furniture that showed that this Robert Childress must be a man of taste. I stood in the middle of the floor looking around at the beige, puffed sofa, the tapestried chairs, the polished walnut tables—and wondered if Rubino's men were close behind, and if the whole thing was about to become an enormous nothing. Then I thought I heard the murmuring wail of a far-off siren. I turned and went down a short hall to the bedroom.

The first thought I had was of a grounded bird I had seen when I was a kid, lying on its back, claws drawn back stiffly, belly ripped to tatters by the orange tom that lived next door. But this was a woman, stark-white naked, head thrown back causing the slashed throat to gape like a clown's mouth. The arms were flung out, legs spread wide, blood still seeping out on the soaked blue satin bedspread. My knees half-buckling, I crossed to her in two long steps and blinked around for the weapon, expecting, and finding, none. I stared at her left hand, the gold wedding band glinting in the light of the bed lamp. Before I unfolded the fingers and took out the square of paper, I guessed rightly what was on it—the male sex symbol: ♂.

On the floor beside the bed a white, blood-spattered dressing gown was spread out, as if placed that way deliberately. Crouching, I saw that a swatch of silk had been torn from the hem.

The phone on the night table blasted into my ear. I jerked upright. It rang three times before I wrapped my hand in my handkerchief and picked it up.

"Maury Ryan?"

It was The Executioner.

"Yes."

"I just wanted to see if you came alone."

"I did."

"It's not what you expected, but it sure as hell is a story."

"The dressing gown," I said. "You ripped off a piece of it. Why?"

"A souvenir, Maury. And it may come in handy if those stupid cops arrest the wrong man again."

He hung up.

I was suddenly aware of a symphony of sirens, bearing closer. I knew I should wait, but a reflex that had been conditioned for a dozen years was too strong. I telephoned the paper.

Numbly I reported to Sam Stein.

His voice came back with no more emotion than if he were bidding a poker hand.

"Her name, Maury. What's her name?"

"Mrs. Robert Childress," I said. Vaguely I thought: That's a presumption; she might be his fiancée, or mistress. "Hold on a minute, Sam."

The sirens had reached a crescendo as I found her bag on the bureau. I fumbled through it and fetched out a checkbook with the name stamped in gold on the red-leather holder: Mrs. Robert Childress. There was also a gold-plated compact engraved with the initials J.C. And a card with a typewritten name on it and a signature. I stared at the card stupidly as I carried it back to the phone. It was a pass, a bus and building pass. Familiar.

"My God, Sam," I said. "She works for us. She *is* Mrs. Robert Childress. But her name—apparently her maiden name—is also Jean Hooper."

XIX

So, WITH THIS LATEST ATROCITY, it became clear that Walter Onderdonk had been less a scapegoat than a hostage, the revelation
of his innocence having been delayed for an additional twenty-
seven hours to permit the planning and execution of a fifth murder. Again The Executioner had made the police, and particularly
Rubino, appear irresponsible and ridiculous. And that goes for
me, and perhaps Sam Stein, as well.

Of course, deal or no deal—Onderdonk jailed or Onderdonk free
—the result, though perhaps more hurried and thus less contrived,
would almost surely have been the same: Jean Hooper would still
have been murdered. All of us—Rubino, Stein, and myself—were
convinced that she was not simply a victim selected at random.
Without discounting The Executioner's egocentric need to return
to the spotlight, we believed she had been marked for murder before Walter Onderdonk had even been thought of. In some way
she must have offended her killer and therefore had to be "saved,"
"cleansed," placed in the spiritual custody of the mad messiah.

The story stammered out by her husband, Robert Childress,
demonstrated that the murder had been carefully planned. A man
giving the name of George Gibson had telephoned him late that
afternoon at the insurance company where he worked. The man
said he had been referred by a friend (nameless) and expressed interest in taking out a sizable policy. Would Childress be obliging
enough to meet him at eight-thirty at the Yale Club, where they
could discuss it? Childress had gone home and joined his wife for
an early dinner, leaving shortly after eight. Arriving at the Yale
Club, he introduced himself at the desk as a guest of George Gibson (there was such a member, an easy thing for The Executioner

to have learned) and was told that Gibson had not appeared. Childress sat down in the lobby to wait. He waited for more than an hour before giving it up. Entering his apartment at ten o'clock, he found it crawling with police. Childress stated that he and his wife always kept the front door locked and chained, being particularly careful about it since the outbreak of the knife murders; therefore he had to assume that his wife knew the caller and had willingly let him in.

The uproar that broke out in the press the next morning had no parallel even in the memory of Sam Stein. Had Roosevelt declared war on Nazi Germany, the headlines would have been no bigger. From the mayor down to the neighborhood hairdresser a blood-lust cry went up for The Executioner's hide. Appeals went out for the formation of citizens' committees. Vigilante action was threatened. Women in droves vowed to abandon the city.

The morning papers had had hours to gather these subsidiary reactions. For, at eleven-thirty the previous night, Sam Stein had managed to hit the streets with an extra that bellowed, JOURNAL REPORTER FINDS BODY OF FIFTH EXECUTIONER VICTIM!

My picture, taken from the files, was there. And Sam Stein's, smaller to show humility. And later, in a replate (after I'd arrived with two filched portraits), Jean Hooper's and her husband's. But there was no photo of Angelo Rubino, and his name appeared in the story only when he could be spared embarrassment. Sam had told the shattered and beseeching lieutenant that he'd go all the way to get him off the hook. Everything that connected Rubino with the deal was omitted, the story reporting only that The Executioner had phoned me at 9:00 P.M. and arranged for a meeting at the Sixty-sixth Street address and that he, Sam Stein, had then notified the police (a sawbuck would keep Harry Bressler quietly happy). Onderdonk's release—the timing was "purely coincidental" —was explained with a nice regard for the truth: The pawnbroker had stated categorically that he was not the man who had bought the gun that had killed Edward Cranston. (There was no mention that the pawnbroker had been brought in twice, leaving him only to wonder why he had enjoyed Scotch and steak at the city's expense.) Of course, playing down Rubino served to emphasize the alert, inside role played by the *Journal,* a point that could not have been far from Sam Stein's thoughts when agreeing to the whitewash. Still, Angelo could be grateful. While not cheered as the smartest cop alive, he was credited with being an honest one, a man whose sense of justice demanded that he free a suspect who, had The Executioner not struck again, might easily have been railroaded to the chair. For the time being at least, Angelo Rubino had survived.

The *Journal* was in an unprecedented position. Having held conversations with the murderer and broken the story, we were the central source of news; and being the employer of the latest victim, we were the focus of police investigation. By mid-morning two detectives had been assigned offices in the rear of the building for the interrogation of employees who had been most closely associated with Jean Hooper, particularly those few who had also known her socially. As this was getting under way, Sam Stein and I were summoned to the office of the publisher, Guy Fleming.

"A waste," said Sam as we passed through the reception lobby crowded with disgruntled reporters from the other papers. He was silent until we were mounting the stairs to the floor above. "All Fleming wants is to gather some juicy morsel for the Stork Club."

I had dropped into the Stork a couple of times with Guy Fleming, marveling at the alacrity with which the velvet rope was unsnapped, the almost fawning attention of Sherman Billingsley as he personally escorted us to a table in the Cub Room. Guy Fleming was an enjoyable companion, very popular in café society, but he was no newspaperman. He had married the daughter of the former publisher and, after that brilliant old man's death two years before, inherited the job. A graduate of Harvard Business School, he tried to stick to administration, but often could not resist involving himself with the supposed glamor of the news side.

Apparently he heard our footsteps, for he was at the door to greet us. He stood just under six feet, a good-looking man of forty, with light, wavy hair over a high forehead and a smooth, pleasant face that had begun to droop. Speaking softly, he congratulated Sam and me on the story, then, shaking his head, added, "But why oh why did it have to be one of our people."

As he turned toward his desk, I saw Lieutenant Rubino sitting up straight in a big gold lounge chair off to the side. He waved a hand at us but didn't smile. Dark patches shadowed his liquid eyes and his usually sharply creased suit was limp. I guessed he had been up all night.

"God," Sam said, "don't tell me this is going to be a strategy meeting." Not waiting for an answer, he said to Rubino, "Angelo, I trust you approved of the story?"

Rubino glanced quickly at Guy Fleming behind the desk before saying uneasily, "It was a good job, Sam."

Sam dropped into a lemon leather occasional chair in front of the huge, immaculate desk. I sat on his left in a big black leather job that looked as if it belonged in the Union League Club. In fact, the great square room itself, with its thick dark-green carpeting and hand-rubbed paneled walls hung with sporting prints, seemed to have been borrowed from those stately premises. Quite a contrast to the partitions of flaking brown metal and frosted glass that housed the shirt-sleeved workers on the floors below.

Guy Fleming smiled a trifle apologetically at Stein. "Not exactly a strategy meeting, Sam. But under the circumstances—a situation that tragically involves one of our executives—I thought it advisable to pool our thoughts. The lieutenant agrees."

Stein peeled off his glasses and rubbed his eaglelike nose. "We've still got a paper to get out. But I guess McCarthy can handle it. All the spot news is right here in the building anyway."

Guy Fleming said, "Did you know Jean Hooper?" Stein shook his head. "Did you, Maury?"

"No. I think I may have seen her in the elevator or on the bus, but we never met."

Rubino said, "I told Mr. Fleming I'm sure it's no inside job. But we can't settle on that. That's why the interrogations."

"Angelo," Stein said, "are you planning to grill everyone who works for this sheet?"

"No, Sam. That's over eight hundred people, I just learned. The manpower we haven't got. We'll stick to those she hung out with. And not just here. Her husband says they knew a slew of people outside the newspaper business. Very social couple, lots of entertaining. Good for his insurance business, I guess. I've got men working in that area now."

"My bet is," Sam said, "that's where you'll find your man."

"There's something different about Jean Hooper's murder," I said. They all looked at me. I lit a cigarette. "Couple of things. First, the three women killed before last night had one thing in common: They were husbandless. Diane Summers—divorcée. Jennifer Hartwick—widow. Eunice Sloat—widow."

"So?" Sam said.

"Only that Jean Hooper was neither divorced nor widowed."

"So again."

"It's out of the pattern. More important is the reason the murderer gave me for killing the first three. He said they were abusing their husbands, torturing them."

"I remember your story of that conversation," Guy Fleming said, looking thoughtful. "You said to him that their husbands were dead—at least they were in two cases—and asked how the widows could therefore be torturing them."

"Yes, and he answered that no one's soul is dead. 'World without end,' he quoted. I took it to mean that the husbands were in some sort of heavenly eternity but still sensible to what was happening on earth. They were being tortured, he said, by their wives whoring on them. He explained the divorcée, Diane Summers, by saying she was even worse—whoring on a man while he was still mortal. In his own twisted way, he may have had a point.

"Jennifer Hartwick sounded as if she might have bedded around. Diane Summers was sharing a love nest with Ed Cranston. Eunice Sloat—" I stopped and looked at Rubino. "Got anything on her yet, Lieutenant?"

Rubino shook his head. "Far as anything we can find out, she could have made it as a nun. But then, she wasn't exactly a looker. And The Executioner could have known something about her we don't."

I thought a minute, feeling my logic collapsing. "She might have made a prim pass at The Executioner herself," I said lamely, "and he marked her down as a mattressback. It's obvious the guy hallucinates."

"Very convenient," Stein said acidly. He fidgeted in his chair, impatient to leave.

Something like a memory tugged at the back of my mind, but it was unrecognizable. We all sat there for a while staring into space.

"All right, all right," Stein said finally. "Let's say you've got it all down pat. The three dames were either widows or divorcées. They either whored around or he thought they did. What the hell has that to do with Jean Hooper?"

"Jean Hooper had a working marriage. A happy one according to her husband, Childress. If The Executioner's motive for killing is to cleanse, to purify, as he says, what was his reason for singling out her?"

Sam's eyes blinked at me like a toad's. "You've got the floor. You tell me."

"Jean Hooper might have had something on him. He might have killed her to shut her up."

Stein's mouth curled contemptuously. "Or she might have insulted him at a party. He blew it all out of shape and decided to get even. In his own sweet way."

"Just a theory, Sam." I stubbed out my cigarette and looked from Fleming to Rubino. "But think about it."

"She had something on him," Rubino said, "why didn't she tell the police?"

"She might not have thought it important." An idea began to form. I started to feel my way. "Look, from the time he called me and I offered him the deal, he had no intention of turning himself in. From the beginning, he planned to set up Jean Hooper. We've agreed to that. Why then, Lieutenant, was he so concerned about you holding on to Onderdonk?"

"That we agreed to also, Maury. Because he was afraid if he killed Jean Hooper while Onderdonk was still behind bars, I'd keep Onderdonk there. He figured I'd say Jean Hooper's murder was nothing but a copy and that Onderdonk was the real Executioner. Then he wouldn't get credit for any of the previous murders."

"Yes, we convinced ourselves of that. And maybe he *was* uneasy about it. And maybe he got a bang out of making the cops look like jerks. But now I wonder if, most of all, he wanted *one* person—Jean Hooper—to keep on thinking that the police had arrested the right man when they nabbed Onderdonk. He wanted her to think that until he had the chance to kill her."

"Because," said Guy Fleming, leaning forward, "if Walter Onderdonk was officially declared innocent while she was still alive, she would know or deduce who the guilty man was."

I looked at him in surprise. "Exactly," I said. "As long as Walter Onderdonk was in custody, she would have to believe she was mistaken."

"Mistaken about what?" Sam Stein said.

It was his usual difficult way when not at least a collaborator in an idea.

Guy Fleming said, "Let's not obstruct, Sam. Maury has given us a direction." He smiled, but grimly.

So maybe Guy Fleming had some traces of iron in his blood. Sam flushed and rubbed his blue-black jaw.

"Look," Rubino said pacifically, "maybe she had something on him, maybe not. Maybe she once made him sore, maybe not. The thing is, we don't know. The only real evidence we've got right now is that the guy's name is Walter something. Okay. Before I came in here I had one of my men check your personnel list. He found three Walters. Only one of 'em knew Jean Hooper personally and he's in the Classified department. So that made him look like a possible. Walter Higgins, an outside salesman—Real Estate on Long Island. He spent last night and the night before at a hotel in Manhasset. My man called out there. Higgins was seen by the room clerk and the bartender about the same time as the murder. Perfect alibi. Forget him."

Guy Fleming was staring into space. "A Classified salesman," he said wonderingly.

"And Eunice Sloat rented furnished rooms," I said.

Sam Stein frowned but said nothing. Rubino's black eyebrows rose slightly.

The phone rang on Fleming's desk. He picked it up, listened, and handed it to Rubino. The lieutenant stood up and stretched the cord to the window, turning his back on us as he talked in low tones. None of us tried to listen. We were waiting to resume the conversation that had suddenly seemed significant. After about five minutes, Rubino turned, strode back, and cradled the phone. He stood at the corner of the desk, square shoulders back, gambler's face as impassive as ever but seeming to scent something in the air.

"That was Sergeant Sanders in one of your back offices. He just talked to two men on the detail who've been uptown interrogating social friends of Jean Hooper. Five men, so far, all married. Two of 'em admitted to a toss in the hay with Jean Hooper. They couldn't wait to say it. They were scared if they didn't, we'd find out anyway and tear 'em to pieces for trying to cover up. Both guys had alibis for last night. But that I don't exactly care about. The main thing is, this Jean Hooper apparently traveled with a pretty fast crowd and spread herself around." Rubino examined his polished, manicured nails.

Sam Stein hitched himself up in his chair, stretched out his neck, and stared slowly and superciliously at Guy Fleming and then at me. "Well, well, so our happily married Jean Hooper was quite a tootsie. Whoring on her husband with her husband's friends. Just the kind of thing to make her a dish fit for The Executioner's carving knife." Stein snorted in disgust. "Why the hell are we wasting time around here? As I said before, you'll find the murderer in that fancy crowd she ran around with."

"That's the way I see it," Rubino said. "I've got to get moving." He started toward the door, checked himself, and turned around. "Oh yeah. About the furnished rooms, the Classified salesman. Sergeant Sanders told me that the first one in to see him this morning—a guy that hadn't even been asked in—said he'd once gotten a furnished room ad from Eunice Sloat. It was so long ago he'd forgotten the name until it came up again in the story about Jean Hooper's murder. He was a young kid, excited, and he thought he might be helping the police some way or other. The kind of guy who'd be scared of mice, Sanders said. Him, too, we can forget."

"Did you get his name?" I said.

Stein threw me a contemptuous look, knowing I was clutching at a straw.

"Maury, I don't remember," Rubino said gently. "All I know is it wasn't Walter."

Later, sitting in my office, I began to get that hollow feeling in my gut that I mentioned before—suspicion, disbelief. I simply couldn't accept Stein's and Rubino's conviction that the murderer was someone who partied around with Jean Hooper.

The reason finally hit me and I shook my head in dismay that it had taken so long. I sat there adding it all up.

The murderer had answered the *Journal*'s appeal to surrender by telephoning me.

The name he had chosen for himself—The Executioner—had been publicized by me.

His reasons for the slayings had been confided to me.

His tip-off to the intended murder of Eunice Sloat had been given to me.

The deal for Onderdonk's freedom had been arranged through me.

The summons to meet at Jean Hooper's apartment, where she lay dead, had been to me.

Why me, why the *Journal,* if he did not have reason to feel an intense sense of identification?

And Jean Hooper—had she been marked for murder because she *was* a *Journal* employee? Did her death simply represent an enormous irony? Or had she, as I had suggested, held the key to The Executioner's identity? I had no answers.

But I was convinced that his acts were influenced by some association, emotional perhaps, that he had with the *Journal.* And perhaps with me.

Was there a way that I could set a trap, using bait that would at least tempt the murderer out to nibble?

LAMBERT POST

XX

I'D ALMOST AS SOON have castrated myself as tell that stone-faced cop that I, Lambert Post, had once taken a furnished room ad from Eunice Sloat. But Charles Walter had directed me to do it, and considering my dependence on him, that was the same as getting an instruction directly from God. I, who had for so long been conditioned by Judeo-Christian teachings, had sought for a time to dissociate myself from a man who had so violently flouted them. That's why I had temporarily avoided speaking directly to Charles, substituting notes instead. Only when I truly appreciated that his militant acts were not prompted by revenge alone, but in fact were deeds of salvation, did I dare resume our dialogues. But not on the same terms as before. Now I was permitted no protest. Now I could only agree and encourage and obey and join with Charles in despising a world that made a virtue of perverting justice.

Yet fear remained, even though insulated by my belief in Charles's higher morality and superior intellect. Sometimes, listening to him exult over the hazards he had so narrowly grazed, I almost had the impression that he unconsciously craved exposure. But not yet (and perhaps never) as was demonstrated when he ordered me to tell the police that I had handled an ad for Eunice Sloat.

I had accepted the assignment with numb resignation, knowing the police eventually would realize that a rooming house often must advertise, thus leading them inevitably to a classified solicitor with the incriminating name of Walter. It wouldn't matter that Walter was not a first name, as they thought; exposure would have been almost certain. But Lambert Post, that was different. Especially when, wide-eyed and innocent, I seemed so anxious to help, charging in as if I might hold the key to the whole frustrating puzzle. The cop had looked baffled, then thoughtful, then amiably tolerant. Well, he sure appreciated my cooperation but, after all, there must be thousands and thousands of people who placed want ads and some of those people got themselves murdered—he couldn't see any clear connection. What was my name again? Lambert Post. Shaking his head, he wrote it down as though only to humor me. Eager kid, seen too many movies, dying to get into the act so he could brag to his friends. I had been coached well.

Even Charles Walter, who had anticipated a more searching investigation and was prepared to flee if he saw his name becoming involved, was surprised at how quickly the police finished off their interrogation of *Journal* employees. By late afternoon of the same day, the office grapevine reported that they had gone.

"Stupid bastards," Charles said that night in the apartment. "They didn't even talk to the guys in the office that Jean Hooper played around with in the back of taxis. Why not? I'll make an educated guess. They found out she was spreading her legs for some of her uptown friends. So that's where they think they'll find their man." The more he thought about it the more appealing the idea became. "A dirty whore," he said with grim satisfaction. "I think that's really why I went after her. I'd have done it even if she didn't have a thing on me. I was saving *her,* not me."

For the next few days Charles remained on the sidelines, absorbed by the attention his exploits were getting in the press. It delighted him that he was getting as much front-page space as Adolf Hitler, who at that time was heating up the crisis over annexation of the Sudeten Germans in Czechoslovakia. Charles was vehement in his admiration of the Führer, seeing him as a like-minded man who understood clearly that certain human problems could be solved only by the ruthless use of force. "Neville Chamberlain," he said, "is the soul of the herd—ignorant, confused, and passive. Hitler is the soul of the elite—enlightened, shrewd, aggressive." Hitler, he said, far from being the monster depicted in the democratic press, was actually a courageous healer. He had not hesitated to purge the poisonous elements from his own party despite the cost in blood. He had cured the sickness of his nation by isolating the parasitical Jews. He had sterilized the unfit, axed the unregenerate, and brought purity to the Nordic race. His was the wave of the future, and Charles was proud to be riding with him, the two joined together by headlines almost identical in size. As Charles's awed disciple, I was swept relentlessly along with him.

So far as could be determined, there was only one cause for uneasiness. Henrietta Boardman. From the morning after the news broke about Jean Hooper, Charles sensed in Henrietta an abnormal curiosity about him. The impression grew that she was studying his profile as if to revive some dormant memory. Finally, one day, he swung abruptly toward her and found her staring at him through her thick-lensed glasses as if he were a bug under a microscope. She was so preoccupied with her own thoughts that it took a few seconds for her to realize that her look was being challenged. She gave a flustered smile, blushed, and quickly returned to making phone calls.

How much did she know? Certainly nothing about the calls to the widows and divorcées; Charles had been very secretive about those. And nothing about the calls to Maury Ryan; she had been away from her desk when they were made. Eunice Sloat? Among the hundreds of people Charles Walter had phoned, it was unlikely that her name would stand out. But Henrietta *did* know that the address of Eunice Sloat's rooming house was in his territory. And she would know from reading the papers after Walter Onderdonk was arrested that the name the roomer had overheard was Walter. Yet she, like the others, must think it was the first name. Jean Hooper? That she and Charles had shared a mutual dislike, even hatred, was understood by Henrietta more than by anyone else.

So Henrietta Boardman had to be considered a bad risk. In Charles's view, the most damning thing against her was an omission: Never once had she asked him if he had known Eunice Sloat or of her rooming house. "The others," Charles said, "wouldn't bother to think about it. But not Henrietta. And thinking about it, she'd be sure to tie in the name Walter. That's got to be why she keeps looking at me. That and her knowing I despised Jean Hooper. I can't take the chance that she's not suspicious."

It was a conclusion arrived at reluctantly. Henrietta had be-
friended him, helped him, and though sometimes critical, more
often had encouraged his self-esteem. Unlike the other women, she
appeared to combine virtue with loyalty. It seemed unlikely that
she would ever utter a word of suspicion unless driven to it by in-
controvertible evidence. Still . . .

"I think, Lambert, you'd better find out just how much Henrietta knows or suspects."

"How?"

"Ask her out. Talk to her. After what happened to Jean Hooper,
it won't be hard to get her on the subject."

"Where would I take her?"

"Take her to dinner. Try Ticino's on Thompson Street, below
Washington Square. For a buck and a half you can both eat like
the king and queen of Italy. See if she can make it for tomorrow
night. It's Friday and Saturday's a half day. Then see if you can
get her to the apartment for some drinks. You'll be alone with her,
Lambert, entirely on your own. She may talk her head off."

"She'd never go out with me."

"I think she likes you. Ask her."

I asked her the next morning, at the drinking fountain just outside the telephone room. I tried to speak casually but instead
blurted out, "Henrietta, would you turn me down if I invited you
out to dinner?"

Her mouth dropped open but there was a curve at the corner
and her brown eyes twinkled. "No, I wouldn't turn you down."

"Tonight, right after work? I know a great spaghetti place in
the Village."

Her face turned grave and she looked at me curiously. Perhaps
she guessed that I wanted to see how much she knew about Charles
Walter. But she said, "Tonight will be fine, Lambert."

Ticino's was seven stone steps below street level and you pushed
through a white, paint-flaking door, the top half inset with frosted
glass. Inside on the left was a long, scarred mahogany bar occupied mostly by old, weathered men in crushed felt hats drinking
wine. Just opposite the bar stood a full-sized billiard table, in
use when we entered by two white-haired men in purple-striped

shirts whose carved faces looked like they belonged on ancient coins. The restaurant was in the rear—small tables with checkered cloths lit by candles stuck in wine bottles encrusted with multicolored wax. The smell of garlic and cheese and exotic herbs hung in the air. You felt relaxed and hungry the minute you walked in.

We were early and only two other tables were taken when we sat down next to the wall. Henrietta was wearing her tight pink sweater and I couldn't help noticing how her breasts swelled as I helped her into the wooden round-backed chair. Sitting down across from her, I stared for a moment at the candlelight dancing in her glasses. Quickly she took them off and put them in her purse. I knew that without them she could see me only as a blur and I felt a sudden pang. But I told myself that she had removed them only to look more attractive, and the pang faded.

We ordered a large bottle of dago red, and spaghetti, and eggplant with meat sauce. The wine came first, and as we drank we exchanged small talk about the office. Either because it was our first date or because we were both on guard, we couldn't seem to get beyond the trivial. By the time we reached the spumoni and coffee, my insides were sweating. I had hoped to find out everything I needed to know and then maybe take her to a movie. Now I would have to ask her to the apartment and hear her refuse.

"We're not far from my place," I said. "I thought we could stop by for a couple of drinks, then go to the movies."

"That sounds fine, Lambert."

It was as easy as that. We walked up Thompson Street to Washington Square and cut through the park, joining the young twilight strollers and passing the old men who sat on the benches patiently waiting for death. Then up Fifth Avenue, past the outdoor diners at the Brevoort, to Twelfth Street and west for three blocks. All the while we barely spoke. But there was no discomfort in the silence. It was as though we were sharing the city and the late-summer evening, withholding speech only to permit the other's keener enjoyment. It was the first time I had ever known a feeling of companionship with a woman. No, maybe not the first. I had a fleeting notion that once, as a very small child, I had experienced that feeling with my mother. But perhaps I had only dreamed it.

When we entered the apartment, she acted as if she were charmed. As I stood in the kitchenette making a pitcher of Orange Blossoms (the orange juice and sugar would mask the gin), I felt flushed with pride at her pleased exclamations over the pictures on the walls. They were no more than the cheap van Gogh prints you saw almost everywhere, as popular as *Baby Stuart* and *The Blue Boy* were when I was a kid. But I had framed them impressively, I thought, and they gave the room a rich, warm look.

We sat back against the cushions on the couch, Henrietta on my left, I next to the only lit lamp. I snapped on the radio and Bing Crosby's deep baritone came out singing "Where the blue of the night meets the gold of the day, someone waits for you." That meant it was just seven o'clock. Inadvertently, my hand touched Henrietta's. I caught my breath as I felt her fingers close gently over mine.

"You're a strange man, Lambert," she said quietly.

I felt myself stiffen and started to withdraw my hand, but she clung to it.

"Strange?" I said coolly. "In what way?"

She sipped her drink and set her glass on the coffee table. As she did so, I cast a furtive glance at the taut line of her breasts straining the pink sweater. She sat back and I could feel her enormous eyes on me.

"You're really so understanding and—and *human*. But you seem afraid to let anyone know you."

I tried a short laugh. "You mean I'm not at all like Charles Walter."

She smiled in amusement. "Not in the least. Charles Walter is really just a great big fake."

"I thought girls liked a man like that."

"Well, *like,* yes. But—"

"I remember what a kick you got when Charles Walter fixed Sol Pincus with that sport coat. And when he gave Molly Hegeman that phony ad for The Park East Hotel, I thought you'd die laughing."

"Only because they both deserved it."

I was close now to where I wanted to be. I filled her half-empty glass from the pitcher and added some to mine. I took a big breath.

"I got the idea you thought Charles Walter was pretty clever from the day he sold his first ad on the phone."

"I remember that," she said. She reached for her glass and took a big swallow. Her hand left mine. She was silent for a moment before saying, "The woman who bought that ad was Mrs. Sloat—Eunice Sloat, the one who was murdered."

Now it was I looking at her. She stared at the glass cupped in her hands.

"I know," I said. "The police were told that."

She flashed me an anxious glance. I smiled at her.

"Did you think anyone with the name Charles *Walter* wouldn't worry about that?"

"I wondered about it. After all, Eunice Sloat, then Jean Hooper, and the name Walter, even though that's a last name. It seemed such a strange coincidence."

"That's what the police thought—just a strange coincidence." She breathed out in relief. "But I didn't really think . . . oh, Lambert, how ridiculous!" She smiled over the rim of her glass. "Let's not talk about it any more. It gives me the creeps."

It was plain that any question she might have had about Charles Walter's innocence had disappeared. I felt a surge of affection for her.

"What *shall* we talk about?" I said.

Her hand came back to mine. "Lambert Post is a good subject."

And soon I was pouring it all out. My loneliness as a kid growing up. The fearful accidents that kept plaguing me. How I hated my stepfather and how my mother always thought he was so right. My solitary days in school and my lone wanderings when I first came to the Village. The absorption in books and movies. I even told her about the redhead and how I'd burned a hole in her dress. But I never said a word about Charles Walter and how he had changed everything. I was afraid that would bring up what she didn't want to talk about; and, besides, Charles didn't seem to belong to whatever was happening between Henrietta and me. I was only glad that she wasn't really interested in Charles Walter, as I had thought, but in me, Lambert Post.

When I finally ran out of talk, her hand was gripping mine tightly and for a long while she didn't say anything. We sipped our drinks in silence, and I was aware that the street outside had grown dark and I wondered if it was too late for a movie.

"Then you've never had a girl?" Henrietta said softly.

I was startled. For years it had not occurred to me that I *could* have a girl, not one who wanted me to have her.

"No," I said and felt a churning inside.

Suddenly Henrietta's head was on my chest and I was breathing in the fragrance of her hair.

"Don't you think you've gone much too long?" she said in a small voice.

Before I could answer, she reached across me and snapped off the lamp. And then, as I clutched my drink, she unfastened my tie and unbuttoned the top buttons of my shirt. I was stunned, deliriously stunned, but not so severely that I couldn't continue where she had left off. We stood up and, in the glow of the street lamp through the drawn drapes, undressed ourselves and each other.

The softness of her! The rounded, curving, dizzying, scented softness of her!

We lay on the couch and her hand gripped the burgeoning part of me that I had feared would never, in love, penetrate a woman. I looked down at her, conscious that my face was bathed in light, thinking that to her unlensed eyes I was a featureless blur, but not really caring because I believed that for once I had found a woman who saw beyond flesh to the person within.

XXI

SHE STAYED ALL NIGHT, a night of dreamless sleeping and of waking and finding each other in the dark and making love and feeling suspended somewhere out beyond the stars.

I wakened to the smell of coffee and saw Henrietta in the kitchenette wrapped ludicrously in my brown robe. Slipping on my shorts, I watched fascinated as she fried bacon and eggs, which she served on the coffee table. She was all smiles and bubbling tenderness, like a bride on her honeymoon. Gaily she talked about herself and her loving Jewish parents, with whom she and a younger brother lived in a small apartment on University Avenue in the Bronx. She was twenty-three, a year older than I, and had thought herself in love only once before, when she was eighteen —"with a *shegetz* like you," she smiled—but the guy had beaten her up and that had been the end of it. She had gone to Hunter College at night, working part time during the day in a Loft's candy store to help support the family. Whatever happiness she had enjoyed had been found with her parents. She pulled on her glasses, glared, and said, "At school, ever since kindergarten, I was Four-Eyes. Sometimes it was The Little Martian. Oh, the kids I wanted to murder!" She looked squarely into my face and lifted her lips and brushed a warm-breathed kiss on the corner of my mouth. I felt my eyes grow moist and my insides dissolve. She smiled understandingly but said nothing.

We did the dishes together, and then she dropped out of the overflowing robe and went into the bathroom, leaving the door open. I followed and we both stood in the tub and showered. Soaping her, I marvelled at how small she was and how perfectly formed. We dried each other with flimsy towels and that produced a warmth and a friction that galvanized us back to the couch and a wide-awake union that left us breathless but somehow strengthened. We took another shower.

Before she left at quarter to eight (she thought it best that we not go to the office together) she called her mother and said that she had stayed over with a girl friend.

"You should have called last night," I said, thinking how her parents must dote on her.

She gave me an impish smile. "I called yesterday from the office and said I might not be home."

I had to laugh. "You mean you anticipated last night?"

"I thought it was a very good possibility."

She kissed me good-bye. When the door closed on her, I suddenly felt shatteringly alone, wondering if I had dreamed it all. Then, as if all the time he had been waiting discreetly outside, Charles Walter was there. Until that moment I had been blissfully oblivious to his presence in my life.

"She doesn't suspect you, Charles. She's convinced it was all just a coincidence." I thought back to her look of relief, to the smile that had ridiculed her wonderings. "Absolutely convinced."

"Great. But we'll have to keep an eye on her."

"That's almost funny. I don't want to take my eyes *off* her."

"So you think you're in love."

"I *know* I am."

"And that she loves you."

"She stayed all night. Nothing seemed to bother her at all. She was wonderful."

"You're a goddamned fool, Lambert."

"No, Charles, *no!* I tell you she loves me and I love her."

"She'll cheat on you the first chance she gets. Women are all the same. They get you to love them so they can abuse you."

"Not Henrietta. She's suffered herself and she knows I have. She'd never try to hurt me."

"Your mother suffered, too. But that didn't stop her from hurting you."

"What's my mother got to do with this! Leave her out of it!"

"She left you for another guy. She cheated you. And together they made you miserable."

"Stop it! Right now! Stop it!"

I was terrified. If Charles Walter kept thinking that way about Henrietta, I knew the day might come when he would feel compelled to liberate her from sin. And not only that. If somehow her suspicions were revived, the result would have to be the same. It was one thing to feel as Charles did about the other women—to celebrate them as rehabilitated and heavenly wives. But Henrietta must remain for me a flesh-and-blood reality, a smiling, tender, loving creature I could see and touch.

I must therefore protect Henrietta from herself—from the temptations of other men, from renewed suspicions about Charles Walter.

Failure on either count would mean the end of her.

And the end of Charles Walter. For then, I knew, I would have to expose him.

XXII

WATCHING HENRIETTA GLIDE down the aisle that Saturday morning, seeing her turn her glowing face to reward me with a sly, intimate wink, I felt my apprehensions about her disappear. She was mine alone. I trusted her completely, just as I knew she now trusted Charles Walter. There was no longer the fear that she might do anything that would prove self-destructive.

The morning papers were also reassuring. The security of Charles Walter's position was summed up by the headline in the *Daily News:* HOOPER MURDER BAFFLES POLICE. The police commissioner, "with a grim-faced Lieutenant Angelo Rubino standing at his elbow," was forced to admit frankly to an office full of reporters, "At this moment we have no definite clues. We are almost back where we started." He also issued a plea: "I appeal to every citizen to be on the alert. If anyone is aware of suspicious circumstances that could possibly relate to this crime or those that preceded it—no matter how remote such circumstances may seem—I urge you to contact police headquarters." He was deliberately asking neighbor to turn against neighbor and inviting a deluge of response from crackpots. That's how desperate they were. For the time being at least, I could rest assured about the safety of Charles Walter.

Later in the morning, as I passed Henrietta, she pressed a note into my hand. I read it on my way to the men's room:

Darling, will you come up to my house for dinner tonight? Mom and Dad are all in favor. You can stay overnight if you like. Please like.

My cup was running over. I pushed into the men's room and found Sol Pincus standing at one of the three urinals, aiming himself with one hand and holding the first edition of the *Journal* with the other. He swung his flat, doughy face around as the door closed, looked suddenly disconcerted, then gave me a smirk. "If it isn't Jack Armstrong," he said, "all-American boy," and slid his oily eyes back to the paper.

I glanced over his shoulder as I passed, and damned near wet my pants. The headline shouted at the top of its lungs: JOURNAL REPORTER HAS NAME OF KILLER!

I unzipped my fly and bore down hard to get it over with fast. I took the front freight elevator down to the street, hustled to where the trucks were lined up outside the loading dock, and begged a paper from one of the drivers. I took it to Friedman's on the corner, got a cup of coffee, and sat down at an empty rear table, spreading out the front page. The story was written by Maury Ryan:

> The identity of The Executioner, the allegedly mad murderer of one man and four women, the latest being Jean Hooper of the *Journal,* was given to this reporter in a telephone tip received at 8:30 A.M. today.
>
> The name, which cannot yet be revealed, appears to be substantiated by evidence previously in the possession of the police but considered of no significance until now.
>
> The informer refused self-identification but mentioned certain credentials that seemed to establish credibility.
>
> Detective Lieutenant Angelo Rubino, heading the special detail assigned exclusively to the mutilation murders that have terrorized the city, was immediately informed of this latest development and is taking all necessary steps.

The rest was a recap of everything that had been printed before.

I folded the paper under my arm and beat it up to the office. In the hall I ran into Henrietta and managed, I think, to affect a surface calm. I told her I'd love to come to dinner but was not sure I could break a theater date. I'd call her at home later in the afternoon.

It was not yet noon, quitting time, but I decided to walk out anyway. All I wanted to do was sit down in some private place and talk over this latest bombshell with Charles Walter.

No one seemed to pay any attention as I yanked my coat from the back of my chair, slipped into it, and strode up the aisle. Even Molly Hegeman, sitting at Jean Hooper's desk as a temporary substitute, didn't raise her eyes as I swung past and out the door.

On the waterfront three blocks north there was a small, narrow saloon frequented by sailors and skid-row types; an old-fashioned place with big frosted windows, brass-pronged chandeliers, sawdust on the floor, and the sound of a leaking toilet. Only two men were there, at the bar, both unshaven, red-eyed, and wearing seamen's blue shirts and black caps. I got two gins over ice and took them to a fly-specked table in a far corner. I spread out the front page of the *Journal* and practically held my breath until I got Charles Walter's reaction.

"Lambert, the whole goddamned thing's a trick. Maury Ryan's just trying to flush me out. He can't forgive me for standing him up in Jean Hooper's apartment."

"But what if it isn't a trick? You've got to think of that. Who could have phoned in the name?"

A trembling silence.

"Lambert, that story's very cleverly written. It doesn't say whether the informer was a man or a woman. That was left out on purpose. If it was anyone, my guess it was a woman. And how about those 'certain credentials' Ryan mentions? That could mean she said she worked in Classified. I think she probably gave her name but Ryan's trying to protect her. You've got to face it—it might be Henrietta."

"No, no, *no!*"

"What time did she leave the apartment this morning?"

"About a quarter to eight."

"She'd have arrived in the office before eight-thirty, the time Ryan says he got the word. She could have called him from her desk."

"But last night—she believed me when I said that Charles Walter's connection with Eunice Sloat and Jean Hooper was only a strange coincidence. She *must* have believed me or she wouldn't have stayed."

"A cover-up, maybe. Or, later, she might have found something we never thought of."

"Oh no. My God, she even asked me to her house tonight for dinner."

"It could be another trick. Maybe Maury Ryan asked her to invite you, thinking she can pump enough out of you to give them the evidence they haven't got."

"Stop thinking this way."

"I've *got* to think this way. You said so yourself."

"All right. But think of something else. Ryan says in the story" —I bent over and read it verbatim—" 'The name . . . appears to be substantiated by evidence previously in the possession of the police but considered of no significance until now.' "

Another silence.

"Oh my God! The name Ryan got wasn't Charles Walter! It was *my* name—Lambert Post. I gave it to that cop when I covered for you about the Sloat ad. When he didn't hear the name Walter, he practically yawned me out of the room."

"That could be it. Wouldn't that kill you! The name of the guy they're looking for is Lambert Post!"

"That must be the evidence that wasn't considered significant until now. Then someone called Ryan this morning and gave him the same name, and maybe some other evidence along with it. He and the cops put it together and realized I was just trying to head them off by busting in with the story about the Sloat ad."

"Then why didn't they make an arrest before the story broke? Wait, Lambert, I think I know the answer. They haven't really got any solid evidence; it's all circumstantial. So they're trying a scare tactic, hoping The Executioner will panic and make some terrible mistake. I've got to admire that Maury Ryan. He's a cute one. But there's one thing he missed—he doesn't yet know about Charles Walter. He couldn't if the name he got this morning matched the one the cops already had—Lambert Post."

"Then that eliminates Henrietta. She'd have named Charles Walter."

"*And* Lambert Post. After all, we're in this together."

"I can't believe she did it," I said stubbornly. "It had to be somebody else."

"Name one other person."

"I don't know. Maybe . . . maybe Molly Hegeman. To her, I'm poison. Remember when she accused me of stealing an ad from her? That's when you got even for me by fobbing off that fake hotel ad on her. She . . . *wait a minute!*"

"What?"

"Sol Pincus! When I went into the can this morning he was standing there reading the first edition. And he looked at me kind of funny. He was staring at *this* headline. Why was Sol so eager to read the first edition, the ink still wet? Because he wanted to see how Maury Ryan handled the story he'd planted?"

"You may have something, Lambert."

"And God, wouldn't Sol Pincus love to shove it to me! Ever since he insulted me and you had the tailor dye his white cashmere coat black. He might have given my name to Ryan just out of pure spite, not really knowing a damned thing. He couldn't have known I'd already talked to the cops. He probably damned near fainted when he read the paper and found out my name was supported by other evidence."

"It makes sense, Lambert. But you'd still better steer clear of Henrietta Boardman."

"I'll think about it. All I'm sure of now is that I've got to make myself scarce until I see what develops. If they catch me, they'll beat it out of me. I'll have to tell them everything about you, Charles. I know it. I'm getting out of the apartment. *Now*. I haven't got much time."

I'd gotten paid that morning and I blew fifty-five cents on a cab. The driver waited outside the apartment, motor running, and in five minutes I'd heaped some clothes in a suitcase and was back in the cab.

We drove uptown and I dropped off at Forty-second and Fifth, then walked over behind the Public Library to Bryant Park. I sat on a bench under a shade tree and agonized over Henrietta. Was it really possible that she had called Maury Ryan? I blocked Charles's words out of my mind and went over every detail of the night before. Her look of utter trust when I explained about the

Sloat ad. Her sincere interest in the story of my stinking life. The way she snapped off the lamp, unbuttoned my shirt, eagerly stripped off her clothes . . . my God, would any woman *volunteer* her body to a man she thought was hiding a series of killings? Hell, no. I had been unnerved by Charles's suspicions only because I had to doubt that such a lovely girl could be attracted to anyone like me. I had said I would call her back and now I could. But I was in no mood for the strained formalities involved in meeting her parents. Perhaps . . .

I phoned from a cigar store in Times Square.

"Henrietta, I got out of the theater date."

"Swell."

"But—try to understand—I'm just not ready yet for a family gathering."

"I do understand, darling."

"I wonder . . . look, these people I was going to the theater with—they're a married couple from New Jersey that I've known for a long time. They're staying at my apartment for the weekend. Henrietta, I wonder . . . I thought . . . all right, will you stay at a hotel with me tonight?"

There was only a moment's hesitation before she said, "I'll be happy to, Lambert."

"Oh, my dear." My eyes were watering. "I don't know what hotel yet. I had to ask you first. It won't be any place fancy."

"Darling, who cares."

"Suppose you meet me in the Astor lobby at five. I'll have checked into some place by then."

"That's fine, Lambert. I'll be there."

I could have checked into a hotel and then called her back. What stopped me? As I hung up, I wondered if there still lingered in my heart a remnant of suspicion.

For a few minutes I felt terribly alone and afraid, aware that with Henrietta I was on my own and could expect no help from Charles Walter.

XXIII

I SPENT THE NEXT HOUR and a half elaborately trying to shake anyone who might be following me. Ducking down to the IRT and taking the shuttle to Grand Central. Threading through the crowds on the main level. Up the passage to Madison Avenue that I knew so well. Through the lobby and the mobbed bar of the Roosevelt. Back to Forty-second and Fifth. East by streetcar to Tudor City. West by taxi to Broadway. Into Loew's State and, in twenty minutes, out again and across on foot to Eighth Avenue. At Forty-third Street, the Metro Hotel, cheap, but a few cuts above a fleabag. I gave my name as Charles Thompson. I was exhausted, the suitcase feeling like it was loaded with manhole covers.

The single room, facing out to Eighth Avenue, was the same sterile, sparsely furnished kind you find anywhere, even to the untouched Gideon Bible in the top bureau drawer. I fell on the bed and lay there, not sleeping, for about half an hour. Every minute of that time I thought about what Charles Walter might do to avoid capture. One thing I knew he *wouldn't* do was return to the apartment. Maury Ryan may not have been given his name but that was just a guess. If the informer had been Sol Pincus—and I was more convinced it was he the more I thought about it—he might very well have named both Lambert Post *and* Charles Walter. After all, both had been responsible for infuriating him about that cashmere jacket, even though I was really the one he despised. But what difference did it make—if they got me, I knew they'd make me confess everything about Charles.

Would he plan to eliminate Sol Pincus? It was too late now for that to help. I kept thinking how clever Charles was, how bold and cool under pressure. Every one of his acts had proved that.

Wouldn't he be even more daringly ingenious now that the police were ready to pounce? I kept thinking about it through a hot shower.

As soon as I was dressed, I got out of there. The walls had begun to close in on me and I had this driving urge to move.

It was after five when I crushed my way through the Astor Hotel lobby. It seemed as though everyone who came to midtown Manhattan chose the Astor as the place to meet, and Saturday was the worst day of all. A milling throng shoved me from right to left and in circles, and as I made almost a complete circuit, I all but tripped over Henrietta squeezed up against a fake-marble pillar. She was wearing a pale-blue organdy dress and a matching blue picture hat with a ribbon. She looked beautiful and helpless. I was surging with a tremendous feeling of exhilaration and all I could do was grin at her, oblivious of how idiotic I must look. She smiled back, her big brown eyes behind the thick glasses warm and inviting.

Taking her arm and pushing ahead of her through the crowd, I apologized for not finding her sooner. "All these people. It's a wonder you weren't suffocated."

"I was afraid I would be. But I'm breathing very easy now that you're here, darling."

So right away we were back where we had left off in the apartment that morning.

We walked east on Forty-sixth Street and stopped in at a Longchamps on Fifth Avenue to relax and let the air conditioning cool us off. Sitting on red-topped stools at the bar, we sipped long Tom Collinses and I told her about the hotel.

"I hope you won't hate it," I said.

"You mean, will I feel cheap? Not with you, Lambert."

Inevitably she brought up Maury Ryan's story about getting the name of The Executioner. I told her I had seen it in the first edition but hadn't looked at a paper since.

"I read a late edition coming down here," she said. "I left it on the subway. But there wasn't anything different—just that the police expected to make a speedy arrest. Isn't that what they always say?" She sighed and shook her head, jiggling her big picture hat. "I keep saying to myself, poor Jean, poor Jean, but honestly, Lambert, I don't feel it. I know I shouldn't say it—and what happened to her is horrible—but she was a mean woman."

"Don't hate yourself. The ones in the office who pretend to mourn her, they're hypocrites. Be glad you're honest."

I stopped in a liquor store and bought a pint of gin and a bottle of Tom Collins mix. Walking out, I began to worry about getting Henrietta into the hotel. This was my first experience and I'd heard tales about unwed couples being thrown out, even threatened with arrest. I told Henrietta about my qualms.

She thought a minute. "Idea," she said. "You give me the room key. Then you go into the lobby first and talk to the man at the desk. You know, ask if there are any messages. When he turns to look in the box, I'll sneak past and into the elevator." She swung the big white handbag she was carrying. "No one would think this was luggage, even though it contains a nightie and a toothbrush." She grinned. "At least I'll use the toothbrush."

We reached Broadway and again were back in the crush. Henrietta pointed a finger up at the *Times* building where the latest news bulletins were flashed in a circling strip of lights.

" 'Fair Sunday,' " she read aloud. " 'High, eighty-eight degrees.' We could go to the park, Lambert."

"I'd like that," I said.

She continued looking up, her eyes squinting. Suddenly her mouth dropped open and I felt her arm go rigid.

"Lambert, look!"

I looked up to the news strip and saw the running lights blink out: POLICE ARREST EXECUTIONER SUSPECT.

I gasped and said, "Well, I'll be damned!"

We knifed our way to a newsstand at the curb and examined the headlines on all the evening papers, including the *Journal*. None had the story. At Forty-third Street we crossed Broadway. As we stepped to the sidewalk, a *Journal* truck, speeding crosstown, braked for a moment and a bundle of tied papers came sailing out the rear and thudded to the pavement. A squat man ran over, coins jingling in his apron, picked up the bundle and toted it to a nearby stand, where he cut the cord. I fished in my pocket with a sweating hand and found three cents. As I handed them to the man and grabbed a paper, my heart seemed to leap into my

throat. Beside me, Henrietta let out a squeal. POLICE TRAP JOUR-
NAL EMPLOYEE AS SUSPECTED EXECUTIONER blared the headline.

Not speaking, we swung away and read the bold type under
Maury Ryan's by-line:

> The man police believe to be The Executioner—identified
> as an employee of the New York *Journal*—was trapped in
> an apartment on West End Avenue and 79th Street at 4:45
> P.M. today.
>
> A swatch of blood-stained silk, which preliminary examina-
> tion indicated matched the section torn from the hem of the
> dressing gown belonging to the latest victim, Jean Hooper,
> was found in a bureau drawer wrapped in an oilskin tobacco
> pouch. Also found was a notepad which at first appeared to
> be blank, but upon closer examination revealed the faint im-
> print of the male sex symbol, trademark of the multiple
> slayer. The style of drawing—apparently done with a grease
> pencil discovered nearby—was similar to that found clutched
> in the hands of the murderer's last two victims.
>
> At least three dozen newspaper clippings reporting the
> bizarre exploits of The Executioner were contained in a large
> manila envelope, also in the drawer.
>
> Police sped to the apartment after a man believed to be
> The Executioner made a long telephone call to this reporter
> and the call was traced. A tie-in line connecting the *Journal*
> phone with the phone on the desk of Detective Lieutenant
> Angelo Rubino enabled the police to act promptly.
>
> Three detectives, including Lieutenant Rubino, broke into
> the apartment, unoccupied at the time, and were investigating
> it when the alleged killer unsuspectingly walked in. He was
> identified as Sol Pincus, a telephone solicitor in the *Journal*
> Classified Department. . . .

I couldn't help feeling a surge of pride. Charles Walter still had
the touch.

MAURY RYAN

XXIV

WHEN I GOT THE FLASH on the capture of Sol Pincus, I typed the story in short takes, handing them to two copy boys who relayed them between my office and the copy desk.

All the time my fingers clattered the keys, that hollow feeling inside me kept growing. How in hell, I wondered, could I have been so gut-sure the murderer had been identified earlier and then be proved so goddamned wrong? I thought back to the guy who had called me at eight-thirty that Saturday morning. He hadn't sounded like a crank; and when he said he worked in Classified and explained exactly what he did and rattled off the names of sub-executives to prove it, I believed him.

With sober conviction he had said, "The name of the man you want—The Executioner—is Lambert Post. He works here in Classified. *Lambert Post*. Got it?"

He refused to give his name and quickly rang off.

I hadn't been very reactive. Ever since the afternoon before, when the commissioner had appealed for public aid, hundreds of people, most of them apparently reputable, had been jamming police switchboards to report the names of suspicious persons. Nevertheless, I called Rubino's office and talked to Sergeant Sanders, one of the detectives who had been down at the *Journal* questioning employees. Something like an electric charge went through me when he stated that Lambert Post was the name of the young man in Classified who had barreled in to report having once taken an ad from Eunice Sloat. I told him I was just making a routine check.

Sam Stein had been unimpressed when I stood at his desk and urged that the lead be investigated. Sourly he accused me of losing my objectivity: "Ever since we met with Fleming, you've had this mania about the murderer being tied in with the paper. Maury, you'll do anything to prove you're right. This guy who called you —he's a mischief-maker. The kind who loves to turn in false fire alarms."

"But dammit, Sam, this is the same Lambert Post who couldn't wait to make what looked like an innocent confession to Sanders. It's like the old saying—the best defense is an offense. All that eagerness to cooperate with the police. What better way to get himself off the hook? And now this phone call from someone who works right alongside him, a guy in a position to know something."

"If he knows something, why didn't he spill it to you?"

"Do I have to tell you how people hate to get involved? He probably thinks that if Post is brought in, he'll crack wide open."

Sam pulled reflectively at his lower lip. "Well, I guess you could go down to Classified and nose around."

That's when I had the big idea. I had been probing my mind for some kind of bait that might induce The Executioner to reveal himself. Wasn't this it?

"Sam, that wouldn't buy us anything more than an internal up-roar. Remember, we don't really have a damned thing on this Lambert Post except that he said he'd done business with the Sloat woman. But try this. Suppose, in the first edition, we blast that we've got the killer's name. Wouldn't that jolt the hell out of him? Chances are good he'd do something stupid."

"Suppose we're wrong? The odds say we are. Remember Onderdonk."

"Suppose we're wrong. Then we admit it. What's so terrible about us acting on what sounded like a legitimate tip?" I looked away. "Meanwhile we'd have sold one helluva lot of papers."

"Maury, you sure know how to get a guy right in the left chest." He whipped off his glasses and meditated into space. "We'd have to tell Rubino." He shrugged. "But *after* we hit the street. Tell him now and he'd probably give me eighty-seven reasons not to do it. Then if I went ahead with it, he'd say I double-crossed him."

The first edition was riding the trucks when Sam gave Rubino the word. Sam disparaged the lead but said the *Journal* had to play it for circulation reasons. Nevertheless, Rubino might want to put a tail on Lambert Post. All very low-key. Rubino made some disgruntled noises but cheered up when told that the name itself had not been published. "Besides, Angelo, if there's anything to this, we might start a little action." When Sam gave him Lambert Post's home address, gotten from Personnel, Rubino seemed almost appreciative. Sam was very pleased with himself—he had his headline and had not alienated the police.

I heard about that conversation later. As soon as I'd knocked out the story (omitting the sex of the informer so that he'd feel doubly protected if he thought of calling again) I got to work investigating Lambert Post. His employment record listed not only his Village address but also the address and names of his parents: Thomas and Vivian Blackwell—indicating that his mother had remarried. They lived in East Orange, New Jersey. I got the phone number, called, and spoke to Vivian Blackwell. Her speech was slightly slurred, as if she'd just wakened, and she seemed somewhat dismayed when I told her I was a friend of her son's and worked with him on the *Journal*. She said she hadn't even spoken to Lambert in more than a year; then, as if regretting the admission, declared she was most interested in how he was doing. That gave me the opening to lie that I was in East Orange visiting friends and that Lambert had asked me to drop by and see her. In about an hour? I suggested. Well, yes, she guessed that would be all right. A confused woman, I decided. I didn't hesitate to give her my name, sure it would mean nothing to her. If she read any paper, it would most likely be the Newark *News*.

I borrowed a car from our ship news reporter and drove through the Holland Tunnel and across the Jersey Meadows to East Orange. In less than an hour I was parked on a blighted street in front of a white-shingled frame house with a scrubby lawn and parched vines growing over a narrow porch. I sat in the car for a while and leafed through the *Daily News,* brought from the office. It was ten-thirty when I rang the bell next to the door that was half wood and half curtained glass. The curtain moved, a pair of eyes peeked out, and then the door was opened by a woman who looked like nobody's mother in the world.

She wore a white, scooped-collar, see-through blouse, a red dirndl skirt, and white wedgies. Her hair was dyed-blond and about as silky as Brillo. Too much purplish lipstick enlarged her thin-lipped mouth and her drooping eyelids were heavily shaded. She was probably in her mid-forties and looked like a chorus girl who refuses ever to admit that it's all over.

She sat down in the small living room on a lounge chair slip-covered in a gaudy floral pattern and asked if she could get me a drink. The way she said it implied booze, but I asked for a cup of coffee. She wiggled through the rust-colored dining room and, as she pushed open the swinging door to the kitchen, I caught a glimpse of a burly, white-skinned man in an undershirt swigging from a water glass. On the table in front of him sat a bottle of gin.

"Well, now," Vivian Blackwell said in a little-girl's voice, still slurred, as she finally brought the coffee, "tell me about Lambert."

She sat opposite me on a mustard-colored sofa, bringing her knees up to her chest and hugging them with her arms, the way children sometimes do. I looked at her too bright eyes and decided she'd had several hairs of the dog.

"He's doing fine on the paper, Mrs. Blackwell. He wanted me to tell you that."

"I wonder why he never calls." Hastily she added, "But I guess he's very busy."

I said that he was. On the way over I had wondered about the reason for their estrangement. Now I took a chance. "Lambert talks about you often. He wishes that . . . that circumstances were different, so that you could see each other."

She gave me an appraising look, then tossed her head and said resignedly, "Yes, it's too bad. But he and Tom—my husband— they just never hit it off." She smiled sadly and rested her chin on her knees. "Just one of those things."

So Lambert Post—now twenty-two according to his employment record—had perhaps spent a good deal of his life under the thumb of an antagonistic stepfather. I read no particular significance into it, but it brought me a step closer to my objective.

I took a gulp of coffee and lowered my voice. "Mrs. Blackwell, Lambert spoke of some pictures—snapshots, he probably meant —that he thought you might still have around. He hoped he could borrow them." I managed an indulgent smile. "I guess we're all sentimental."

"Sentimental," she said, frowning. "Yes, Lambert was certainly sentimental." Her thumb and forefinger darted to the twin vertical lines between her eyebrows and separated them. She smiled and a reminiscent gleam came into her eyes. "Yes, I'm sure I have some pictures. They must be in the hall closet upstairs. I'll look."

She came back with a grocery carton heaped with letters and documents and keepsakes. And pictures. I watched from across the room as she scooped up a handful and thumbed through them. She removed a few, placing them face down in her lap, discarding the others. She repeated the procedure several times until all the pictures had been reviewed. Half a dozen were in her lap and she handed them to me as I came over to the sofa.

All of them were snapshots. I sat down and looked at them slowly, one by one. Lambert with his mother; with someone who was probably his father, perhaps his real father; alone playing in the snow; sitting on a playground swing. . . . In none of them was Lambert Post more than three or four years old.

A hoarse voice shouted peremptorily from the kitchen: *"Vivvie!"*

She sprang from the sofa and, without excusing herself, hurried into the kitchen. A rumble of voices ensued, punctuated by curses from Tom Blackwell and his clearly heard exclamation, "That goddam whelp!" If he was referring to his stepson, it seemed clear why Lambert Post had not called home in more than a year, as his mother had told me on the phone. The voices continued, rising in pitch. Out of idle curiosity I reached into the grocery carton and sifted through the discarded pictures. Most of them were of family outings, Christmas scenes, friends hoisting beer mugs, and a few backyard shots, the surroundings looking much more attractive than the setting I was in now. Beneath the snapshots I came across four glossy portrait proofs, the kind photographers submit for approval. Originally red, they were now faded to a pale pink.

I drew in a breath and sat up straight. The subject was a boy of about seventeen, wearing what I guessed was a navy-blue suit. Each picture was a slight variation of the same pose. I stared at them fascinated, then dropped my eyes to the carton and noticed a large book heavily bound in simulated leather. I picked it up and saw that it was a high school yearbook for 1933. I flipped to the section featuring individual portraits of the graduating class and found the one captioned Lambert Post. It was similar to the proofs

I held in my hand, except that it had obviously been heavily re-touched. I slipped one of the proofs into my side jacket pocket and returned the others. The invective vibrating through the kitchen door had abruptly ceased.

I stood up as Vivian Blackwell came out, her face pinched and forlorn. She forced a trembling smile and said apologetically, "I'm terribly sorry, Mr. Ryan, but Tom—well, he just hasn't been himself lately. This awful recession—he's been temporarily laid off and . . ." She didn't finish but gazed vaguely around the room. "We're only living here until things . . ."

"I understand, Mrs. Blackwell. Anyway, I've got to be going." I held up the snapshots. "I'll bring these to Lambert."

"Oh, yes. And tell him that I wish . . . that I wish a lot of things could have been different. He'll understand."

I had a sudden hunch. "I'll tell him. He's always saying how grateful he is for the way you always stood by him."

Vivian Blackwell's face turned a fiery red and her eyes narrowed in suspicion. "Lambert said that?"

"Yes, quite often."

She gave her head a shake and recovered her poise. "Lambert was always one to . . ." She stopped. "I suppose he was talking about those calamities he was always having. I guess he told you about those?"

"He mentioned them. But there's no need to worry about him now. He's just fine."

I felt like a Judas when, standing at the door, she said almost wistfully, "You sound like a very good friend, Mr. Ryan."

Back in the car I studied the picture of Lambert Post and thought about what Vivian Blackwell had said, how she had looked, and about her husband's tirade in the kitchen. Apparently Lambert Post had been a very troublesome child to his parents. Had he also, while growing up, been troublesome to the police?

It was just past eleven when I reached a drugstore and tele-phoned a friend of mine who was a police reporter on the Newark *News*. Old police records? No problem. My credentials would be sufficient but he'd call the chief and grease the way.

I grabbed a quick sandwich and at noon was standing in the musty basement of the county courthouse in Newark thumbing through the files. I started with the name Post, going back ten years to when Lambert was twelve. Nothing. Possibly he had used the name Blackwell until he left home. I checked Blackwell for the same period. There were two, but neither were named Lambert or Tom, his stepfather. Standing back from the huge green file cabinet, I closed the drawer on the last folder. I strolled past the bank of cabinets, about to give up, when my eye caught one labeled 1915–1920. On impulse, I pulled open a drawer, found the section that included P, and ran through the folders. Again nothing. Next B—Blackwell. I had reached the year 1919, and was cursing myself for being a damned fool, when I found rap sheets on two Blackwells—Thomas R. and Vivian B. I yanked them from the file and placed them, hand trembling, on the table behind me. I checked 1920. Two more sheets, again one on each of them. Like some frantic comedian in a speeded-up film, I sprang to another cabinet and flipped through the folders from 1921 to 1925. No Blackwells, no Posts.

I sat down at the table and stared at what I had. The mug shots of Vivian Blackwell showed a palely pretty woman with long hair done up in a bun and large tragic eyes. Tom Blackwell was a hawk-faced, glowering man with a shock of black hair. I read the charges and the results, making notes. It was not until I finished that I realized I was feeling slightly sick. Jesus. In 1920 Lambert Post was only four years old.

I called Sam Stein from a courthouse phone at two-forty-five.

"For sweet Christ's sake," he said, "where the hell have you been?"

"Where I told you I'd be. In Jersey, checking with Lambert Post's family."

"I thought maybe you'd moved in. Anyway, that headline I ordered this morning seems to have done the job. But Rubino didn't do his."

"Give it to me in English, Sam."

"Okay. This Lambert Post character begins to look like the man. He skipped out of the office before noon, probably right after seeing the story. Rubino's tail latched on to him at his apartment in the Village. Post whizzed up in a cab, ducked into the apartment, and a few minutes later was back in the cab with a *suitcase.* He was dropped opposite the Public Library. Then—and by God you won't believe this, Maury—that blind flatfoot of Rubino's lost him somewhere in Grand Central. Christ Almighty, he should have grabbed him as soon as he saw him with that suitcase! But the stupid bastard said he had orders just to follow, not arrest!"

And he'd gotten those orders, I thought, because Stein had so casually downgraded the story to Rubino.

"It looks now, Maury, like we've got a maniac running around Manhattan about to go berserk. That wouldn't be so bad from my standpoint if I could print it. But Rubino says if I do, he won't give us so much as an item on a run-over dog. If it was just to protect that dumb cop, I'd say screw it. But Rubino's afraid if Post sees his name in the paper or realizes the extent of the manhunt, he'll blow up and start slaughtering every dame in sight."

"I think he'd be right."

"Could be. So anyway, did you get anything over there?"

"Enough to know that Lambert Post's got a couple of beauts for parents."

"You want rewrite?"

"It's nothing we can print now, Sam."

"Okay, tell me about it later. Right now I've got a paper to get out."

It was four o'clock when I got back to the office and inspected my desk for messages. There were none. Four-thirty was quitting time for me and I started back to the city room to check out with Sam Stein. As I stepped outside the door, my phone rang and I ambled back and picked it up. That was the call from The Executioner. The moment I was sure it was he, I pressed the button that flashed a signal to the phone on Lieutenant Rubino's desk.

It was a crazy conversation, and one-sided. The guy had lost his former coolness and sounded like the madman I knew he was as he raved on and on about the women he had "saved" and boasted that he'd never be caught because he was under the protection of God. He was on the phone for almost fifteen minutes. If he hadn't been so obviously nuts, I'd have thought he *wanted* the call to be traced. All the while, I assumed I was listening to Lambert Post, a sorrowful creature who'd probably been kicked around since before he could even remember.

Then, for God's sake, doesn't The Executioner turn out to be somebody named Sol Pincus—caught with the bloody swatch, the marked pad and the grease pencil, the press clippings, the works.

Sam Stein was jubilant that Rubino, grateful for our cooperation, gave us first crack at the story.

Apparently Lambert Post had left the office early and gone to Grand Central merely to catch a train and enjoy a weekend in the country.

XXV

As SOON AS I FINISHED the story on Sol Pincus for the five-star extra, I went down to The Rain House and sat alone at the empty bar and glared at a beer. I felt as hollow inside as if I'd been eviscerated.

Something about the whole business seemed cockeyed. I tried putting it all together again. A guy from Classified, name unknown, calls me and puts the finger on Lambert Post. Okay, that could have been Pincus, diverting attention from himself and maybe at the same time settling an old score. Then Lambert Post gets lost. What time was that? Probably between one and two. Say two o'clock, or even a little later. That left a minimum of perhaps two hours before The Executioner called me at four and ran off at the mouth. Could he somehow have learned that Sol Pincus was the informer and . . . *hey!* I left half my beer on the bar.

"What's the latest on Pincus?" I asked Sam Stein as I bellied up to his desk.

"They just booked him. He's now in Interrogation. He's hollering he's innocent and demanding a lawyer. A *lawyer*—imagine that!" (In those days some people didn't worry too much about a defendant's rights.) "I've got Hollister and two photographers up there waiting outside. It's Saturday, Maury. So go get drunk. We'll handle it from here."

"Sam, I want to talk to this Sol Pincus."

"Are you nuts? Already Rubino's neck's stretched out to here because he gave us the inside on the arrest. I can't push him any further. And why the hell should I? Right now we're heroes."

I told him what I now knew about Lambert Post and what I theorized, showing Stein the picture I'd swiped. That had him

whipping off his glasses and rubbing them against his eaglelike
nose, but still looking negative. The convincer came when I said,
"But all right. Suppose I'm dead wrong. Suppose Sol Pincus *is*
The Executioner. Can you think of a better story than a confron-
tation between him and the man he chose as his confidant—me,
Maury Ryan? That, Mr. Stein, would be called enterprising jour-
nalism."

He gave me a pained look but said, "I'll call Rubino. But
Maury, you better be right."

Rubino wailed and moaned, but when Stein warned him that he
might be risking his badge and reminded him of the Onderdonk
fiasco, he agreed to sneak me in. But I'd better have something
important to contribute or he swore on his mother's grave he'd
book us both for obstructing justice.

At police headquarters I was met by a sergeant who escorted
me up in a back elevator to Rubino's office. While the sergeant
went to summon Rubino from Interrogation, I stood in front of
his bulletin board and stared at the flyer showing the drawing of
the man described by the pawnbroker. I slipped out the faded
pink portrait of Lambert Post and held it next to the drawing. The
photo had been taken five years before and was a full-face shot;
the drawing showed the left profile. I stretched my imagination,
trying to turn the photo around in my mind, but was unable to see
a resemblance.

Rubino came in, nodded, and sat down stiffly behind his fumed-
oak desk.

"Alone I left him," he said wearily. "Alone with a dummied-up
cop. Maybe he'll do some heavy thinking and decide to come clean.
All right, Maury, what've you got?"

I repeated what I had told Sam Stein and showed him the photo
of Lambert Post. His only reaction was a slight flicker in his liquid
eyes.

"The theory's not bad," he said. "And after Walter Onderdonk,
I'm not for turning my back on anything. I had an APB out on
Post but canceled it when we collared Pincus. I'll renew it. Question him is the least I can do. But I'm betting Pincus cracks before
we lay a hand on Post."

He phoned the order for the all-points bulletin, keeping his eyes on Lambert Post's photo as he gave the description.

"How far did you get with Pincus?" I asked.

"No place. He's been framed, he says, and keeps yelling lawyer, lawyer, lawyer. Says he wasn't in his apartment when that call was made to you. But he's got no alibi. Yesterday he bought a car, second-hand job, and he was just out cruising around, he says. I say malarkey. Come on and talk to him. Could be he's got you down for a soul mate and will open up a little."

The Interrogation room was a narrow enclosure with two barred windows set high in the flaking gray wall and furnished with only a metal table surrounded by four metal folding chairs. A heavy-shouldered cop stood erectly against the wall near the door gazing into space. Sol Pincus, shirt-sleeved, tie unfastened, collar open, sat on the far side of the table staring down at his clenched hands. He glanced up, and his bright, hooded eyes dilated slightly as he looked at me. He had a stocky build, sleek black hair combed straight back, and a broad nose shoved into a flat, tallow face. I caught a glimpse of his profile. It didn't in the least resemble the police drawing.

"Maury Ryan," he said in a husky, whispering voice that contained, I thought, a note of hope. His thin lips scarcely moved when he spoke.

"Have we met before?" I said.

"No. I work on the *Journal*. Classified. I've seen you around. I know who you are."

Without speaking, Rubino left us. I sat down in a chair facing Sol Pincus and lit a cigarette. He stared greedily at the pack and I offered it to him. He plucked out a cigarette, hand shaking.

He took a few nervous puffs before saying fraternally, "This is a dirty frame-up, Maury."

"Why would anyone want to frame you, Sol?"

"Because"—he hesitated, taking another puff—"I didn't admit this to Rubino, but now the hell with it. I was the guy who phoned you this morning and accused Lambert Post."

"Why? Do you have evidence against him?"

"No. But I hate the bastard. He screwed me once and I figured this was his turn. Everyone knows he thought Jean Hooper was a bitch, so he'd look like a damned good suspect. I just wanted him to sweat a little. Okay, I'll take my licking for that, but not for those murders. Me, The Executioner! Jesus Christ, it's ridiculous!"

"Could someone have overheard you when you called me?"

"I don't see how. Molly Hegeman—she's pinch-hitting for Jean Hooper—she was at the front desk but she wasn't plugged in. Maybe somebody'd tapped into my phone. Or maybe somebody read your story and took a wild guess it was me."

"Lambert Post?"

"He was there. But I'm not accusing him. Not anymore. But somebody must have found out I called you. Whoever it was planted all that stuff in my apartment. Sometime this afternoon. I was driving around. I got home and walked into a mess of cops."

"Could it have been someone outside the office—an acquaintance, someone you do business with?"

"I don't have those kind of acquaintances. As for business contacts, hell, they don't even know my name's Sol Pincus. On the phone I'm Blake—Jack Blake. It goes with the territory." He looked at me suspiciously and his voice rose. "Why are you here? Rubino think you'll get me to talk because we work on the same paper? I'm innocent, so there's nothing to talk about. Except, damn it to hell, get me a lawyer! I've got my *rights!*"

"You'll get a lawyer, Sol. First tell me what you know about Lambert Post."

"He's a schmuck. Hardly anybody'd have anything to do with him. Henrietta Boardman maybe. She works in the Classified phone room too. But I don't know a damned thing about him, except once he really shafted me." Pincus told me a long, cruelly comic story about his white cashmere jacket that someone had told the tailor to dye black. "I can't prove it but I know damned well it was Lambert Post, calling the tailor and making believe he was me." He puffed furiously on the cigarette and ground it out.

"Why should you think it was Post?"

"Because, well, only the day before I'd run into him right outside the tailor shop, when I was bringing in the jacket. I said something sort of nasty to him. I can't remember what."

"You mentioned someone—Henrietta . . ."

"Henrietta Boardman. I think maybe she likes Post, Christ knows why. I used to see her looking at him, you know? A couple times I saw them whispering together. And this morning I think I saw her hand him a note."

"How would you describe her?"

"A softie. The kind who brings home stray cats. And a bookworm, I think. Small and dark and a body that could drive you nuts. But that's all. Wears huge glasses and has big lips."

"Do you know where she lives?"

"The Bronx, I think. But what's she—"

"Is there anything else you want to tell me, Sol? About the evidence found in your apartment."

"What's to tell? It was a plant. I want a lawyer. I want to make bail. At least fix it so I can make a phone call."

"I'll try, Sol."

"Try schmy. You've got the muscle."

Rubino was not in his office when I got back. I stood at the window watching the sun drop behind the darkening buildings and added what Sol Pincus had told me to what I already knew or surmised. He had dropped the names of two women who might provide further insight into Lambert Post's activities, at least so far as they concerned Eunice Sloat and Jean Hooper: Molly Hegeman, his temporary supervisor; Henrietta Boardman, his friend and possible confidant.

I got a Bronx directory from the side table and found a number of listings for Boardman. On the third try I got the right one, Henrietta's mother answering to say that her daughter was out for the evening.

"When will she be home, Mrs. Boardman? I'd like to call back."

"Please, who's calling?"

"I work on the paper with your daughter. My name is Maury Ryan."

"Maury Ryan yet! My daughter knows *Maury Ryan?*"

"I just wanted to ask her a few questions about Jean Hooper."

"Oh God, that poor woman! Won't they ever catch that crazy schlemiel! My daughter stays downtown all night tonight with a girl friend and I sit here and lose my mind."

"I'm sure she'll be safe. Could I call her at her girl friend's?"

"You can't. They were going somewhere first to a party. Henrietta was meeting some young man—he works on the paper too —at five o'clock at the Astor. Then they were going to the party. Where I don't know."

"You say he works on the paper? Maybe I know him."

"Let's see. He was coming to dinner, then couldn't. His name is Lambert Post."

Hanging up, I felt a racing urgency. Where the hell was Rubino? It was now past six o'clock. Lambert Post had been with Henrietta Boardman for more than an hour. I fumbled through a couple of phone directories looking for a listing on Molly Hegeman. After two wrong numbers, I gave up and called the *Journal* switchboard. Sylvia Rhodes answered and said she'd get the number from the personnel list. Hold on a moment, please.

As I waited, my mind drifted back to Sol Pincus and his protesting righteousness. Suddenly something rose inside me and seemed to burst in my brain. I stood there frozen as the voice from the receiver said, "I have that number, Mr. Ryan, but . . ."

"Yes, go ahead."

"But Molly's still in the office. She just called home. I think she's working late to straighten things out after—well, you know."

"I know. Please ring her."

I hadn't been sure of what I would say to Molly Hegeman when I had thought of calling her. But as she came on the wire, I knew exactly the question to ask. Her answer, though hopefully anticipated, had me sagging against the desk, my mind driven back to a dark scene at a rooming house on Twenty-third Street. With two words—one would have been enough—Molly Hegeman unknowingly broke the case wide open.

When Rubino strode in I was staring again at the drawing of the suspect on the police flyer. Memory had at last made me see the resemblance.

"Angelo," I said, "you'd better concentrate your men in the midtown area. Lambert Post had a suitcase, so that could mean a hotel."

Rubino stared at me warily. "So you talk to Pincus and he sells you a bill of goods."

"He did but he doesn't know it. Anyway, he's clean. The guy

you've been looking for is named Charles Walter. And the way to get Charles Walter is to find Lambert Post."

I found I was staring down at Lambert Post's bleached graduation portrait, a shadowed, punished face that so clearly explained his passionate surrender to a monster he had conceived as a god.

XXVI

I TOLD RUBINO ABOUT Henrietta Boardman meeting Lambert Post in the Astor lobby, which got him on the phone to order the search intensified in the Times Square area, with particular emphasis on the cheaper hotels.

As he hung up, the phone rang under his hand. A voice snarled from the receiver and with a resigned roll of his eyes Rubino handed it to me. It was Sam Stein.

"For chrissakes, Maury, what gives? I've got a headline standing in the composing room reading EXECUTIONER CONFESSES. Do I use it or do we toss it in the hell box?"

"I was about to call you, Sam. Get a stenographer on the tie line in my office and you listen in too. I'll dictate everything I know. We'll need it when this thing finally breaks, which could be tonight."

"Pincus hasn't cracked?"

"No. And he won't because he's innocent." Rubino's black eyebrows shot up, corrugating his smooth forehead.

"Okay. Give me a couple of minutes."

I switched to the phone connecting with mine, sat down, and waited. I had almost finished a cigarette before a light finally flashed on and a voice said, "Sorry to hold you up, Maury. Harry Talbott here. Sam's on, too." Harry Talbott was a former legal stenographer, now a reporter assigned to the criminal courts.

"I can't even try to construct this in the form of a news story," I said. "Parts of it aren't completely clear in my mind. You'll have to give the transcript to rewrite. Also, Sam, you and Angelo have already heard some of it."

"Stop wasting time," Sam said. "Just blat it out."

I took a deep drag on the cigarette, noticing Rubino plant his elbows on the desk and rest his chin on tightly folded hands.

I spoke slowly, trying to put events into proper sequence. "Let's review a couple of items. After the first two killings—Diane Summers and Ed Cranston—we got the first clue to the murderer's identity: the description from the pawnbroker of the man who bought the gun. The police drawing based on that was probably fairly accurate but no one came forward to say he recognized it. I'll get back to that. The second clue seemed more understandable. It was given to the police by a ground-floor tenant of the rooming house on Twenty-third Street owned by Eunice Sloat. He heard a man outside the front door announce himself several times to Mrs. Sloat as Walter. Everyone assumed this was a first name. Instead, it was the *last* name. The first name was Charles. Charles Walter."

"How'd you get it?" Sam said.

"I'll come to that. Charles Walter, of course, was the same man who'd murdered the others and also Jennifer Hartwick; later, Jean Hooper, although in her case it was probably for a different reason. I think Jean Hooper had evidence that could expose him as The Executioner and he had to silence her. But why were the other three women killed? The motive can't be fully appreciated until we understand something about the man closest to Charles Walter— Lambert Post."

Sam Stein broke in again, almost shouting: "Sweet Jesus Christ, Maury, you leave here on one track and now you're off on another. I've got a paper to publish! Give me something for a headline! All this can come later!"

I held the phone away from my ear as he ranted on. Rubino listened impassively to the crackling noise for a moment, then silently reached over and took the receiver from my hand.

"Indulge me, Sam," he said quietly.

"How?"

"Shut up."

Rubino handed back the phone.

"Sam," I said, "you can't print a headline, not yet."

"Okay," he said sulkily, "keep talking."

"Now, you know about this but I want Harry to get it down on paper. I visited Lambert Post's mother today in East Orange, New

Jersey. I also caught a glimpse of his stepfather. I don't know what happened to the real father but his mother must have married this guy—his name is Tom Blackwell—when Lambert was about three years old, or even younger. The mother, Vivian Blackwell, let slip that when her son was a small child he had suffered numerous accidents. I had already swiped a picture of him—a photographer's proof of a portrait for the high school yearbook. He was seventeen. You and Angelo saw that picture, Sam."

"Yeah, yeah. That and what you told me made me think he *could* be homicidal. But now the murderer isn't Post, it's some pal of his. Jee-*sus!*"

"Harry," I said to Talbott, "that picture was carefully lighted to drop a strong shadow on the right side of Lambert Post's face. Nevertheless, in the proof, what existed there was still plainly visible. That side of the mouth is twisted into a grotesque grimace, fixed there by a layer of drawn scar tissue. I'd say the nerves are paralyzed."

I heard Talbott suck in a breath.

"That picture plus the accidents started me wondering. So I went to the Newark courthouse and looked up the records. Sure enough, in 1919—when Lambert Post was three years old—his mother and stepfather were twice hauled in on charges of child abuse. In both instances Lambert Post had been beaten unmercifully, the second time sustaining a broken arm. God knows how many beatings he suffered that went unreported. In the first case, the Blackwells got off after claiming their son was attacked by hoodlums while playing in the backyard. In the second case, a judge gave them each six months, but suspended it and granted probation after a plea from Vivian Blackwell. He made the child a ward of the court for the length of the probation, one year. Then comes late 1920, when Lambert was four. Neighbors were aroused one evening by screams, and when the cops arrived, they found Lambert writhing on the kitchen floor and clawing at his face—out of his mind with pain. It seems that Tom Blackwell had grabbed up his stepson and partially dunked his face in a pot of water boiling on the stove. This time there was a jury trial. Vivian Blackwell passionately defended her husband, insisting it was an accident. The Blackwells somehow got a not guilty. The judge was infuriated and bitterly reprimanded the jury. But back went Lambert Post into that brutal household. I don't know anything about his life after that but it must have been miserable. Perhaps the worst blow of all was the rejection by his mother. As an infant, when his real father was around, he may have worshipped her. Then she married Blackwell and sided with him as Lambert's tormentor. Probably Blackwell, who I suspect is a drunk, was jealous of the child and probably his mother was scared to death of losing Blackwell. From what I saw of her, I'd guess she lives in a dream world and may also be an alcoholic."

"Maury," Sam said, "you'd better check this out." Sarcasm crept into his voice. "That is if it has anything at all to do with the murders."

"It has. Here's a kid who's been horribly abused—lacerated, fractured, facially deformed. Perhaps consciously he believes, as he was taught to believe, that he was simply the victim of a series of accidents. But wouldn't the truth be buried in his *unconscious,* ordering him about without his knowing it?"

"Thank *you,* Dr. Ryan," said Stein.

"It's nothing, Sam. All right, the kid grows up—rejected, let's say, at every turn—and he suddenly meets up with a character named Charles Walter. This Charles Walter is a silver-tongued smoothie—clever, confident, dominating—and he's completely sympathetic to the needs of Lambert Post. Post at first admires him, then worships him, finally is enslaved by him. You could say that Lambert Post became hopelessly submerged in the Walter syndrome. Something deep inside him ordered him to look upon Charles Walter as some sort of superman, superior to all moral and civil law and responsible only to the God existing in his imagination. When Charles Walter killed a woman, Lambert Post saw it as the obliteration of his own pitiless and, to him, adulterous mother. He could escape any feeling of guilt by telling himself that the deed had been accomplished by an acolyte of God, that the woman had actually been purified, saved, that she had been elevated to the status of a heavenly bride—the bride that Lambert had secretly yearned to find in his mother, who had cuckolded him with Blackwell. Charles Walter was the perverted sublimation of all the hate and resentment that had burned in Lambert Post since childhood."

Stein said impatiently, "I like the rhetoric. I like the theory. But what does it buy you?"

"We're almost there, Sam." I lit another cigarette, enjoying his suspense. "I've seen this Charles Walter."

"What!" This time it was Rubino who broke in.

"I saw him on the bus and he stopped in my office a couple of times. He questioned me about The Executioner and fed me some ideas of his own. Once, Sam, he was in the elevator with us. I thought he was an ambitious copy boy. Only a few minutes ago I realized he was the same guy depicted in the police drawing. If the pawnbroker had been able to describe more than his handsome profile, I'd have recognized him long before this."

"But son of a bitch, Maury," Sam said, "if you knew this kid's name was Charles *Walter,* how come you didn't suspect him?"

"I never asked his name. I got it only a little while ago by calling a woman in Classified. Molly Hegeman—she's replacing Jean Hooper. Hold on a minute."

The sergeant who had ushered me in stood in the doorway. "Lieutenant," he said, "we think we've located Lambert Post. Metro Hotel, Forty-third and Eighth. The clerk remembers him as the guy with the mouth and scars. He's registered as Charles Thompson."

Rubino leaped to his feet. "I'm on my way."

"What's going on?" Sam said.

Rubino froze at the door as I raised my voice and said quickly into the phone, "No wonder Charles Walter wasn't listed as a *Journal* employee. Molly Hegeman told me that Lambert Post and Charles Walter are one and the same man. The name that Post uses as a classified solicitor is Charles Walter. It goes with the territory."

LAMBERT POST

XXVII

I LAY BACK IN THE BED and watched Henrietta as she stood naked in front of the bureau mirror combing her dark hair. I was at a slight angle and could see her round breasts rise tautly, then flex as she drew down on the comb. She had just come, perfumed and lovely, from the shower, and the small of her back was still faintly speckled with moisture.

I slowly sipped the gin she had poured and listened to the soft music of Guy Lombardo piping in through the speaker on the wall. I felt warm and relaxed, as if cradled in a womb.

Henrietta turned and smiled at me. "It's your turn," she said.

I had been too lazy, too spent, to join her in the shower. Now I got up, snatching my brown robe from the open suitcase on the floor, and went into the bathroom, closing the door. It was past six-thirty and we planned to go to an early movie, eat afterwards, and then come back to bed.

The copy of the *Journal* that had so startled and then upset Henrietta lay in the trash basket next to the bathroom sink. We had said all we wanted to say about Sol Pincus on the way to the hotel. Once in the room, we had much better things to do.

I turned the bathtub shower on hard and hot and stepped under it, sighing with pleasure as I became encased in the warm fluid. I was just washing off the soap when I thought I heard a phone ring. Probably it came from another room, I decided. As I shut off the shower, the pipes giving a loud metallic bang, I thought I heard Henrietta's voice cry out to me. Quickly I skimmed water from my body with the towel, slipped on my robe, and opened the door.

Henrietta, fully dressed, sat stiffly on the edge of the bed staring as though stunned at the telephone on the night table. Her head jerked toward me and her magnified eyes through the glasses seemed to regard me with a strange puzzlement. I felt a surge of apprehension.

"Did the phone ring?" I said.

"Phone? No, of course not. Who would ever call you here?"

She said it nervously, without conviction, forcing a small, brittle smile. Rising to her feet—warily, I thought—she stepped to the bureau and gingerly picked up her big handbag.

"I'm starving, Lambert . . ."

("Lambert"? Not "darling"? After the way we'd been in bed?)

". . . I thought while you're dressing I'd go down to the deli and bring back a sandwich. We can split it. After the movie, we can eat more."

She started for the door, leaving her picture hat on the bureau, as if as a hostage to her return. I crossed the room swiftly and stood in front of her.

"Someone telephoned," I said. "I heard the ring."

"No. *No.* Lambert, *please . . .*"

It was more than she wanted to say. She closed her full lips into a pursed line and the color drained from her face. Oh God, I thought, she's like all the rest. She had been so wonderful, such an idyllic reprieve from all my harrowing fears. And now she was going to turn me in, destroy me. I was engulfed by a terrible sense of loss.

"Who was it, Henrietta?"

She stared at me mutely. I saw her throat twitch as she gulped.

"Was it the house detective?"

She seized on that. "Yes, yes, it was the house detective. I . . . I picked up the phone without thinking. I didn't want you to feel embarrassed, so I was just going to go on home and call you from there. I . . ." She stopped, her anguished expression showing that she appreciated how pathetic the explanation was.

"And leave your beautiful hat? Henrietta, you're a liar."

She bit at her lower lip, veering slowly around me. Suddenly she bolted for the door. She was reaching for the knob when I grabbed her by both elbows, pinioned them behind her in an arm

lock, and clapped my left hand over her mouth. I swung her strug-
gling back into the room. Her glasses were flung to the floor and I
felt my heel shatter one of the thick lenses. The grinding sound
seemed to convince her of how helpless she was and her body
went limp. I turned her around, my hand still muting her lips, and
looked into her bulging, myopic eyes. She blinked them and nodded, as if to say she wouldn't try to scream. But I was taking no
chance. I dragged her into the bathroom, muffling her with one
hand and unscrewing my safety razor with the other. Delicately I
plucked out the single-edge blade and held it in front of her eyes.

"That's a razor blade," I said, in case she couldn't see it. "Very
sharp."

She nodded again. I guided her out to the bed, pushed her down
on her back, and sat next to her. Slowly I removed my hand from
her mouth and wound my fingers tightly around her thin wrists. I
held the blade pinched in my fingertips and brought the edge up to
her throat. She appeared transfixed, but her breasts heaved up and
down.

"Now tell me," I said. "This time the truth."

Her tongue darted around her lips, those lips that had so hun-
grily tasted my body.

"It *was* a detective," she said in a whisper.

I touched her flesh with the blade.

"Not a house detective—a . . . a policeman." Her heavy lids
closed over her eyes.

"What did he say?"

"My God, Lambert," she said breathlessly, "you've got to get
out of here—run away. Maybe . . . maybe the fire escape."

"The fire escape?" I smiled, beginning to feel that strange exhilaration. "Perhaps that's how someone got into Sol Pincus's apartment." I bent closer to her face. "Tell me what the detective said."

She opened her eyes and looked at me pleadingly. "He said
that"—she exhaled a long breath—"that you're The Executioner."
Her lips trembled as she turned her head away.

"What else?"

"He told me to get away if I could. That if they broke in, you
might . . . do something to me."

"But what if *I'd* answered the phone? I guess he would have hung up or said it was a mistake."

"Please, please give yourself up. Nobody will hurt you. Oh Lambert, Lambert, you're sick."

"I'm not Lambert," I said. "I'm Charles Walter."

I felt her wrists jerk and saw that her whole body was shaking. I thought of the boy she said she had once loved, the one who had beaten her. *Once* loved? She probably still dreamed of him, wanted him. She would have abandoned me in a minute if he merely crooked his finger. She was a cheat and a whore, just like they all were. But I could save her.

Knuckles rapped lightly on the door. I covered Henrietta's mouth with the heel of the hand holding the blade.

A woman's muffled voice said, "This is the maid. I've brought fresh towels."

How unclever they were. No wonder they were incapable of governing. I looked down at Henrietta. Her eyes were wide open and they no longer held terror. Some strange emotion shimmered there. Strange, yet familiar. I had seen that look in the eyes of a mother consoling a crying child. I gazed at her breasts and had a sudden impulse—sudden, but seemingly dredged up from a million years ago—to part the chiffon covering and bring my mouth down to suckle. Some shapeless but agonizing memory compelled me to withdraw my hand and rise slowly to my feet. Silently I turned away and went into the bathroom.

I closed the door and quietly turned the lock. For a moment— as I reached for the wet soap in the bathtub dish—no sound came from the bedroom. Then—as I drew the soap across the mirror— I heard her footsteps running across the carpet. I heard a babble of voices.

"Where is he?" one of them said.

I drew an X through the drawing of the male sex symbol soaped on the mirror.

I heard the doorknob turn.

"Come out with your hands up or we'll shoot through the door."

"No, Angelo, don't. We want him alive!" Maury Ryan's voice.

I dropped the soap in the basin and let my brown bathrobe fall to the floor. I switched the razor blade to my right hand and looked down at my naked body. I stared at my genitals.

Wasn't that the source of it all?

I was on my back on the cold tile when the door smashed open. *"Sergeant, call an ambulance. This guy's bleeding to death."*

Maury Ryan's voice seemed to come from far away: *"My God, Angelo, he's castrated himself!"*

Epilogue

MAURY RYAN

XXVIII

THAT ALL HAPPENED more than thirty years ago.

Often during those years I promised myself to write a novel about it. But I remarried—a wonderful girl, as no-nonsense as her name, Mary O'Brien—and she bore us two lovely girls followed by, hallelujah, a strapping boy, and the joy absorbed me and I made it to managing editor, following after Sam Stein, who died, and there never seemed to be enough time.

It took retirement (ten months ago) and the gentle prodding of Mary to make me at last sit down at the typewriter and keep the promise. I had long ago gathered all the material I needed—photostats of the interminable and often incoherent confession, abstruse psychiatric reports, transcripts of the lengthy hearings before a judge, notes of two melancholy interviews with Henrietta Boardman (she's been married now for almost thirty years to an accountant named Silverman and they have three kids), frequent conversations with Angelo Rubino (he made captain, and later chief of detectives), and of course the information I had from my personal involvement.

Only one thing was lacking to complete the story—an appraisal of Lambert Post as he was now, in the year 1970. From the day in 1938 when he had been legally certified as a hopeless schizophrenic—and therefore immune from prosecution—he had been confined in a state hospital for the insane in upstate New York.

It was a beautiful morning in June when I drove up to the long red-brick building, went inside, and cleared my credentials with the administrator, with whom I'd already talked on the phone.

I found Lambert Post sitting alone on one of the gray benches in the midst of sweeping green lawns patrolled by a few men in crisp white jackets. Lambert was dressed in an ill-fitting dark-brown shirt hanging over loose tan dungarees that all but obscured his sandaled feet. He wore a rabbinical beard, pure white although he was only fifty-four years old, the matted hair not quite masking the drawn scar tissue. His hand gripped a long tree limb that had been stripped to make a walking stick.

He stared straight ahead, a small smile playing on his contorted lips, and seemed not to notice when I stood beside him and announced my name.

"Lambert . . ."

He silenced me with a softly remonstrative glance.

"Lambert isn't here just now," he said. "I'm Charles Walter."

His voice was thin and reedy. I had forgotten the administrator telling me that he insisted on being known as Charles Walter.

"Of course," I said, sitting down a couple of feet away. "Do you remember me—Maury Ryan?"

For an instant his eyes flickered, but he said, "No." He turned his head and fixed me with a messianic stare. "You are dead, you know. Your name was buried with your earthly body." Waving his hand deliberately he indicated a scattering of patients, most of them reading newspapers, clustered on surrounding benches. "They are all dead."

"Are *you* dead?"

His expression became condescending. "Naturally not. Who else would preside over their souls?" He cupped his free hand to his ear. "Listen."

I raised and angled my head, as if listening.

"Do you hear that?" he said, his voice sadly indulgent. "They are complaining again." He smiled reassuringly. "Soon they will stop. They are reading my gospel. When they have finished, they will be comforted."

I felt a shiver wash across my spine. I suddenly had the astonishing notion that this man, who in a wilderness of despair had fantasized a monumental sanctuary named Charles Walter, was different only in degree from many people considered normal.

I said quietly, "When did you last speak to Lambert Post?"

"Lambert? Why, only last night." He frowned slightly. "Something has happened to Lambert. He seems to have become so distant, his voice so hushed."

"Could you call him to you now?"

"Oh yes." He tilted his head and closed his eyes. His lips moved but no sound came out.

Suddenly he jerked erect. His eyes blinked open and dilated. His head darted frantically back and forth.

He called out, "Lambert?"

He looked dismayed and I knew he heard no response.

"*Lambert!*"

Again he cupped his hand to his ear.

"LAMBERT!"

He thrust forward and his features twisted into an expression of anguished disbelief.

I'm sure you know why. . . .

LAMBERT POST

The end.